THE DALHART GIRLS

Other books by Sandra Fox Murphy

<u>Historical Fiction</u>

A Thousand Stars

That Beautiful Season

Let the Little Birds Sing

On a Lark

Mourning of the Dove

<u>Poetry</u>

Aging Without Grace

THE DALHART GIRLS

SANDRA FOX MURPHY

atmosphere press

"And in the sweetness of friendship let there be laughter,
and sharing of pleasures. For in the dew of little things
the heart finds its morning and is refreshed."

Kahlil Gibran

Chapter 1

A small church sits on the south side of Dalhart, a small church with two cathedral windows of glass stained in hues of blues and greens to dress either side of the front door. A large oak door had been constructed in an attempt to make the structure look more grand, to draw in the faithful. The white clapboard building, Victory Church, its paint peeling on the north side, stood humble with two glass windows on each side of the church and a window and small door in the back. It was the third Sunday in December of 1952, and though our church was modest, it was the center of the community.

At 9 a.m. the usual churchgoers sat in place waiting for Pastor Connor to rise and walk to the pulpit when Willie Bob Preston strode in with a new girl on his arm. Though a girl on the cowboy's arm was a common sight, this young woman did not resemble a woman who normally attended Victory Church, much less any small-town Texas church, and the sway of her hips seemed to tilt the chapel askew as a peculiar hush ran through the yawning room. The shapely blonde seemed oblivious to the sudden hush and smiled at everyone whose eyes met hers.

Jane Connor, the pastor's wife and my best friend, sat next to me in the third pew from the front, our usual spot for Sunday service, when the couple walked by and toward Blanche Preston, Willie's mama, in the pew in front of us. Jane nudged me with her elbow as the couple scooted into the pew.

"Who's that?" I whispered to Jane, dressed in a deep purple sweater and her familiar straight, black skirt with her patent pumps.

Jane shook her head. Let me tell you that Willie Bob Preston was a corn-fed Texas fella, tall with a resolute jawline and a cowlick that highlighted his walnut-colored hair, and he was no stranger to church. Though he'd graduated high school seven years before, voted Most Handsome of the class of 1945, he still lived with his mama, who always made sure her son put on his suit and bolo ties for Sunday services, at least when he was not out rodeoing. He often arrived at church with a pretty girl gracing his arm, but this blonde was new in town. A stranger.

Willie Bob stood as the woman—or should I say girl, for she looked no more than eighteen, sat, and as Willie Bob turned to sit, he nodded and smiled toward Jane and me. As he did so, Willie's charmed smile reminded me of the precocious nine-year-old he'd once been, but those were the years of the Dust Bowl when I'd just met my husband, Jim. As I sat next to Jane, I thought that boy should come with a warning for all the girls.

Jane, my very best friend, raised her eyebrows and looked at me.

We sang one of our standard hymns, "Shall We Gather at the River," as if there were any river 'round here. Deacon Tippett made the announcements, we recited the Lord's Prayer, and then, Henry, our pastor, rose and walked to the pulpit. In our plain ol' church, the pulpit was the one extravagance that stood out—an altar of polished cypress old man Tippett's brother had brought back from the Piney woods. It was a fine piece, and Henry gently lay his worn Bible on the pulpit's lectern before opening to a marked page. As if unaware of the mood in the chapel, or one might reckon because of it, he began speaking of acceptance and Jesus' encounter with the woman in Sychar.

I breathed a sigh, audible to Jane, who smiled at hearing it. I always could feel when Henry was about to preach fire and brimstone and the certainty of Hell by the way his Bible fell. If he quietly laid the Lord's book on the lectern, pausing in thought, we were saved, or when it landed with a thud, I knew we were doomed to a roasting. Jane knew my theory and found it amusing and to be a true insight.

As Henry read from the fourth chapter of the book of John and spoke of the woman who'd drawn water for Jesus, he described her as a woman of Samaria and a stranger to the Jews. Immediately, I pondered the stranger sitting in front of me as Henry continued speaking of Jesus' conversation with the woman and the Messiah telling her of the living water as she drew water from the well. The Messiah's words confused the woman, he said, and as Henry spoke, I wondered where the young blonde next to Willie Bob came from and what possessed such a woman to come to a patch in the road like Dalhart.

"Jesus asked the woman to bring her husband, but the woman said she had no husband, and Jesus said she'd been truthful," said Henry, and after those words, he paused and looked at his flock sitting before him, measured their mood. "Jesus said, 'You have had five husbands, and now you live in sin with another.'"

And then, as if called forth, muffled snickering echoed in the pews behind me. It crossed my mind that Henry shoulda been preaching about those who believed they were sinless or something about throwing rocks at glass windows, for there were uncharitable thoughts being tossed through the church by the very people I knew had plenty to hide behind their own closed doors, and let me tell you right here that gossip and judgment were the sport of Dallam County. Not even Jane's husband could stop it, and he'd thrown out much rebuke of his own in sermons about devilry that might could take us each to Hell.

Henry paused a moment. I divined that he'd finally witnessed the rustling in the pews. He hesitated, perhaps revisiting his words, wondering if he'd misspoken. His brown eyes narrowed as he looked out toward the familiar faces, and then he proceeded to speak of how Jesus endowed acceptance of the woman in Samaria, a woman that the Jews would have shunned, the same as Jesus had once received the nameless harlot who'd washed his feet with her tears, the one whose sins he'd forgiven and then he'd blessed her. When Henry concluded the sermon, he turned to the pianist, Hadley Brown and asked him to play the hymn "Count Your Blessings." Hadley looked up, wide-eyed, and lit out shuffling through papers on the piano before pulling out sheet music and proceeding to play the hymn Henry had requested.

When the service ended, the churchgoers in south Dalhart were quick to assemble in the meeting hall at the back of the church, finding fresh-brewed coffee and Mabel Dickens' home-baked brownies. The buzz of chatter filled the room and echoed from the walls. I searched the crowd to find Willie Bob introducing his new lady friend to old Joe Tippett and his wife Beulah before the couple walked in our direction.

"Well, Shelby, here comes the new couple," warned Jane, nodding in their direction as we both stood by the wall, sipping our hot coffee. Like a couple of schoolgirls, wallflowers to be exact, we enjoyed blending into the scenery and watching the room. People-watching and remarking on the discourse and mischief in the church.

"I'd like y'all to meet my girlfriend, Curtye Lee Logan." Willie Bob's voice had a gentle drawl that made one lean in to listen. "Curtye Lee's come down from Colorado and is looking for a job here in Dalhart. Curtye Lee, this is Mrs. Connor. She's our pastor's wife. And this here is Mrs. Hauser. The Hausers live on a fine ranch south of town, out near Lake Rita Blanca."

Jane extended her hand to Curtye Lee.

"Pleased, ma'am," said the young woman, all smile from ear to ear, her mouth curved in a shade of rosy red. As she leaned closer to take Jane's hand, the cleavage at the low cut of her bodice moved with her. I didn't recall ever seeing a girl fill out a cotton dress like she did, and I realized this young woman wasn't even trying to tease the men all staring from behind their wives' shoulders. Sex just oozed out of her.

I took the girl's hand when it was offered and found Curtye Lee's handshake warm and confident. Genuine, and I instantly liked her.

Peggy Brown from the women's Bible Study group walked up after Willie Bob had escorted Curtye Lee on to meet other church members, and Jane excused herself and walked across the room to assume her greeting duties with her husband.

"Shelby, you are looking nice this Sunday morning with your hair in that French twist. Can you believe that woman Willie Bob's brought into our church?" Peggy whispered, all uppity with her emphasis on the word woman. "That girl should've at least pulled a sweater over that flimsy dress." She shook her head and asked, "Where do ya reckon she's come from?"

"Willie Bob said she's from Colorado." I paused a moment. "And I loved the blue floral print of Curtye Lee's dress. Peggy, I reckon you'll like her once you get to knowin' her."

"Well, all that, and she's a Yankee," said Peggy.

I excused myself and went to find Henry and thank him for the morning's sermon and I hugged Jane. "I'll see you on Tuesday."

After my farewells, I walked from the church to my car, finding the skies had turned dark, boding winter's first storm coming later than usual. I rarely left church alone. The kids, Billy and Lorene, were usually with me, and most of the time, Jim was with us. My husband Jim was a church deacon, and on some occasions, he'd drive his own pick-up since he'd have duties or visitations after church, but on this Sunday, he'd taken the children to visit his elderly uncle in Amarillo. I was hoping they'd be home before supper was ready, and I prayed the storm didn't hinder their trip home.

My thoughts returned to Curtye Lee. Dang, that boy Willie Bob. The boy goes through girlfriends at the speed of the moon going new each month. That poor girl had come all this way from home for such a gamble, but I reckon she'll have the offer of a job before the day ends.

I looked toward the horizon and saw heavy skies. Dark clouds in the daytime fretted me. Made me edgy. Like echoes of the black blizzards. Back when I was a girl, a farmer's daughter, the high plains were crushed by the depression and dirt falling from the heavens onto droughted fields endless and void as if the end of the world had come. One can't know the end of the high plains, that beauty of the tall grasses in the breeze, unless you've been drowned in the dirt that took it all away. The sound of cattle lowing in the distance fell upon my ears, and though I lived on a ranch and milked our dairy cow, the cries of cattle often unsettled me. I hurried toward the car. The clouds hung heavy and still as if snow might come before morning, and I started the Chevy, hoping it was a good sign that the winds weren't wailing.

Chapter 2

Blanche Preston had decorated her home for Christmas, every little detail in light of her son bringing his newest girlfriend to supper on Christmas Eve. She didn't always decorate for the holidays since losing her husband in 1936, but she'd done all she could to give her son the best life. He'd begged her to host this supper to impress Curtye Lee, and the table was set with the best dishes and slim tapers in the crystal candlestick holders. Like a bull, Willie Bob charged in the front door full of loud laughter, his new girl in tow.

"Oh, Mrs. Preston," said Curtye Lee. "Thank you for inviting me to supper. *Merci*, as my mama would say. My nana was half Osage. She'd often speak French to Mama." She smiled at her hostess. "I hope I'm not intrudin' on your holiday. Your house looks so pretty, all fixed up for Christmas."

"What's an Osage?" asked Blanche Preston as the three stood in the hallway.

"An Indian tribe, mostly from Missouri. They got moved west by the government. They're known for huntin' with French fur trappers—back in Missouri."

Blanche looked at her son and back at Curtye Lee. "Well, I had no idea you were an Indian." Suddenly, Curtye Lee knew she should have kept this to herself.

"Oh, just a bit of me, Mrs. Preston. My papa's family is four generations, counting me, come to America from Wales, and my mama's father was Irish. I'm just a mongrel." Curtye Lee knew that word, *mongrel*, would not sit well with Mrs. Preston, but she was intent on speaking truth. "And I can't wait to learn more about Willie Bob's family. As I'm sure you well know, he's always talking about horses and riding wild bulls. 'Spect he came from a long line of cowboys."

"Yes." Blanche looked around the room as if, for a moment, she was lost. "I'm about to put food on the table, Willie, if you'd like to pour Curtye Lee some sweet tea or perhaps a glass of wine."

"Sweet tea for me," said Curtye Lee to her beau, and she followed him into the kitchen.

"Can I help you with anything, Mrs. Preston?"

"Oh, no. You and Willie go make yourselves comfortable at the table," said Blanche.

Mrs. Preston didn't talk much during her meal of roasted chicken, sweet potatoes, and a bean casserole, but Willie Bob talked endlessly about his last two rodeos.

"We'll have dessert later, with some coffee, after Willie Bob's friends come over," said Mrs. Preston.

"I didn't know your friends were comin'," said Curtye Lee, turning to Willie Bob.

"Yep. I'm gonna go get 'em right now," and he stood up.

"The dinner was delicious, Mrs. Preston. I'll help you clean up in the kitchen since Willie's leaving."

"No need, Curtye Lee."

"I insist. No point in my sitting here twiddlin' my thumbs," and she smiled at her host.

The kitchen cleaned, Curtye Lee sat in the living room with Blanche Preston as they waited for Willie Bob's return. Lights twinkled in the glass of a large window, both streetlights and the reflection of the Christmas lights on the tree in the living room. Curtye Lee rose and walked to the tree, looked at the ornaments, and carefully touched some of them.

"These are exquisite, Mrs. Preston. Such a beautiful tree."

"Yes, I've collected those ornaments over the years. We didn't have much through the hard years before Willie's father died, but no one had much during the horrid years of the thirties. Not only did dust fall everywhere, no rain, but the dying crops caused many to lose their farms. The banks had to close for a spell. But one by one, year by year, I've collected trimmings and decorated a beautiful tree for Christmas. For Willie Bob."

"Oh dear. I was young back then, but I do remember hearing talk of the storms. We weren't affected in the mesas and the mountains. Sometimes, in summers or winter holidays, I'd go out trappin' or huntin' with my papa. Into the White Mountains. But most time, for schooling, I lived with my aunt. Aunt Mabel in Grand Junction. She's Papa's older sister."

"Was she an Indian?"

"No, ma'am. Aunt Mabel is from the Welsh. Strict, but she took care of me. She's a widow with no children of her own. In summers, I'd sometimes stay at Papa's cabin."

Curtye Lee was coming to see just how smallminded Willie Bob's mother was, and she'd seen a bit of that in the church on Sunday. How friendly everyone was to her as she was introduced around, but she'd not missed the slanted eyes on her. The judgment in them. She was no fool but knew honey worked better than piss. Some of her best friends back in Colorado had once badmouthed her before they got to know her.

"Would you like another glass of tea, Curtye Lee? Or some wine?"

"No, thank you, ma'am."

Blanche walked over to a console and poured an amber liquid from a bottle into a fancy glass. With tongs, she pulled an ice cube from a canister and dropped it into her drink before walking back and taking a seat. An awkward silence filled the room as Curtye Lee wondered why Willie Bob hadn't returned. She couldn't help but wonder how Mrs. Preston had purchased such a lovely home after her family had lost their farm. How she supported herself.

"Do you go to the rodeos, Mrs. Preston? To watch Willie Bob?"

"I used to," she said. "Back when he ...."

A ruckus at the front door interrupted her as Willie Bob barged in with two fellas following him, all of them laughing about something.

"Hey, Mama," said Willie Bob. "Sorry I took so long."

"Hi, Mrs. Preston," said the taller fella with wavy brown hair and smiling eyes.

"Good to see you again, Theo," she said and turned toward Curtye Lee. "Boys, this is Curtye Sue. I'm sorry, what was your last name?"

"It's Curtye Lee. Curtye Lee Logan," she responded, without a look to Blanche Preston and reaching for Theo's hand to shake it. "And your name?" She reached to shake hands with the shorter blonde fella.

"I'm Colt. Pleased to meet ya, ma'am." He shook Curtye Lee's hand heartily. "Where you been hiding her, Willie?"

Willie Bob put his arm over Curtye Lee's shoulders. "She's been here, in Texas, only a week, fellas, and she's all mine. So, keep your hands to yourself."

Willie Bob and his friends talked mostly rodeo and horses as dessert, a carrot cake, was served with coffee before the fellas opened a few bottles of beer.

"Hey, we gotta get that wheel fixed on the trailer," said Theo. "That black mare needs to be in Lubbock in two weeks."

"Yeah, I hear ya," said Willie Bob. "We'll get on it this week."

"Hey, Curtye Sue, ya need to get Willie to show you our barn. Our horses. You ride?" asked Colt.

"It's Curtye Lee. I do ride. At least I used to up in the mountains with Papa. When we'd go huntin'."

"You hunt?" said Theo, his eyes wide with wonder. "We don't know no girls that hunt, do we, Colt?"

"Nope. Just the ones huntin' for us," said Colt, and he looked at Willie Bob. "How'd you find this girl, Willie?"

Blanche Preston turned away and walked back to the console. Refilled her glass.

Curtye Lee saw the smirk on Willie Bob's face, and she started to wonder who'd be sober enough to drive her home, but finally, past ten on the clock, she and his friends piled into his truck. He dropped her at the boarding house and said he and the boys were headed out to the barn.

"I'll have to see it one day," she said as she closed the truck door and waved. "Night, boys. Merry Christmas," and she heard their laughter fade as the truck drove away.

Chapter 3

Christmas morning rose chilled and lit by a distant winter sun. Outside, the fields lay beige and fallow as I stood at the kitchen window, the coffee percolating in the early quiet. I watched Jim walk from the barn to the house. My mother, who'd come from town for the holiday, would smell the coffee and likely wake the children. I always relished the morning silence before the flurry of activity and voices came to a day.

"Mornin'," said Jim as he entered the room and took off his jacket. "Feels like winter. I think it might snow."

"Well, that'll make the kids happy."

I gathered the makings for pancakes and started browning bacon on the griddle, and Jim disappeared.

"Good morning, Dear," said Lizbeth, walking into the kitchen with her graying hair a bit mussed.

"Oh, Mom. You're up. Of course, I'm sure the smell of coffee lured you down here. Did you wake the kids?"

"Yes. Billy sprang out of bed like a feral cat, but it took me a few tries to get Lorene raised from the dead."

I handed Mom a cup of steaming coffee, and she sat down at the table and spooned some sugar into her cup.

Breakfast went effortlessly, and I left the dirty dishes for later so the kids could dive into their gifts. Mostly Billy, for Lorene had reached that age of disinterest, at least on the outside.

"Billy, what's that behind the drape?" said Jim as Lorene and Mom opened presents. Gift wrap began to litter the floor like every Christmas morning since the kids had arrived.

"A bike!" yelled Billy. "For me." His eyes searched the room for verification it was his.

"Well, I don't think Santa brought that for me," said Jim, "and it's not a girls' bike."

Laughter ensued as we all watched Billy touch every part of the bicycle, a shiny blue.

"Can I ride it? Now?"

"Billy, let's finish opening our gifts," I said. "There's something from Grandma over there for you, and then you can bundle up and take it outside. Okay?"

"Alright."

As I gathered the ribbon and crushed wrapping paper strewn about the living room, Mom walked in with two cups of coffee. Billy was outside with his new bike, and Lorene had returned upstairs with her bounty.

"Honey, I need to run into town," said Jim. "For just a bit."

"On Christmas?"

"Promised old man Wilkins I'd help him with some chores needed doin'."

"Well, the old man shouldn't be doin' chores on Christmas. I'll be expectin' ya home by supper. By three." I watched out the window as his truck stirred up dirt out the driveway toward the gate.

"Sit with me a bit," said Mom, and I set the box of Christmas remains near the kitchen door and chose the comfort of the old chintz chair I always favored and where Mom had set my coffee on the side table.

"I heard over at the Baptist Church that the Preston boy brought a new girl to church on Sunday. Sure was a lot of talk about her. She musta been somethin'. Not from round here, I take it." It didn't surprise me one little bit that the gossip from my church had spilled over to hers. There were no secrets in Dalhart, Texas.

"Well, she was a surprise, Mom, but I liked her right off,

and I reckon Jane will come around once she knows her better. You know darn well, though, that nothing lasts with Willie Bob Preston, so I feel sorry for her. She came all the way here from Grand Junction. Up in Colorado. I reckon I'll invite her out to the ranch next week or so, but her entrance on Sunday did stir up things at the church. She was a bit of sunshine on an ordinary Sunday morning."

"Well, now I want ta meet her, but you're right. There'll be no future with the Preston boy. How's Lorene doing? I see she's hit that not-talking phase you and your sister went through." Mom sipped her coffee. "Well, not you so much in those hard times when you were that age."

I gulped down the rest of my coffee before it turned cold.

"Her grades are just mediocre. Not as good as they could be. She does seem to enjoy singing with the choir. You should come with me next time. When they have a concert."

I picked up my Viceroys on the side table, pulled one out and lit it. I drew in the spell of the smoke's magic, and my back relaxed into the chair. Snowflakes drifted outside, and I thought of my young brother, Paul, who loved the snow so much. A sense of guilt filled me as I thought of the life I've lived and how he never got his own life.

"Mom, we shoulda visited Paul's grave before the holidays. Taken a Christmas wreath." I propped my cigarette in the ashtray.

"I wish you wouldn't do that, Shelby. Smoke," she said as if I didn't know what she was speaking of.

"Mom, it relaxes me. Sometimes I just need that."

"I went to the cemetery. Left a wreath last week when the sun was out," said Mom. Inside, I cringed. Was hurt that she had not invited me to go with her. We always went together, but then I wondered if that was true. Paul was her son, her only son, and she likely did go alone at times.

I took another drag of my cigarette and placed it back in the ashtray.

"I hated seein' him struggle, Mom. Such agony for him to breathe. How he faded to such frailty, in spite of Grandma always dotin' on him until she, too, went ill. How unfair it all was while I thrived." I picked up my coffee cup, putting my hands around it as if an empty cup would warm my hands. "At least until the government came and shot the cattle, one by one, and I thought I'd lose my mind. The horrible cries drove me mad." I paused as the memory brought back the eerie sounds. "Do you remember?"

"Oh, Dear, yes, I do. And even the rabbits. All the rabbits who ate every last bit of green in the fields and how the men clubbed them to death, and you would cry. I was horrified. But those cries of the injured cattle—the ones dying slow and the young calves left with no mama. That horrible wailin' sent you to a spin. We knew President Roosevelt tried to help by letting the government buy up the stock still fit for slaughter, keeping the farms from bankruptcy, but no farmer wanted to let their cattle go. God knows that drilled-in persistence kept them thinking it would all turn around. But it didn't, and it was all I could do to comfort you—try to explain what happened. Why it had to be done when all of God's wrath made no sense at all to me."

I sat silent in the memory of it all. That any of us survived, but those of us who'd stayed in Dalhart moved on with life. Had rebuilt what we could and with the help of the Conservation Corps President Roosevelt had sent. The horrible days had driven my older sister away, into marriage and off to California.

"Child, I reckon if I hadn't been so busy tryin' to calm you, those awful cries from the fields would have made me mad as well. And those Miller moths. Everywhere. I just couldn't keep 'em out of the house."

"I still get a chill when Tex Owens sings 'Cattle Call' on the radio." I shivered at the memory of his yodel. "Do you ever wonder what Paul's life would be if he'd lived?"

"Once or twice. But it's all make-believe, Shelby, and at times, I suppose Mama might have stayed with us a bit longer if she hadn't been so intent on helping Paul. If he hadn't died only to have her follow him."

My cigarette had gone out, so I lit another one and inhaled. Drew in a deep breath full of smoke, akin to the skies full of dirt when I was just sixteen. I remembered little Paul's endless cough and, near the end, his gasps in search of fresh air, any air at all, and I crushed the long cigarette in the dish.

"We can't outrun our past, Shelby. It just is, and we move on. Keeping this ranch after your pa died was the right decision, and I'm glad you and Jim make good use of it. Jim made it look decent again after the Depression and before he went off to the war. Maybe one day it'll be Billy's."

"Yes. I'm glad we stayed here." I looked across the room and saw the snow falling. "And glad Jane came back to Dalhart and stayed."

I walked over to the side door and yelled at Billy. "Put your bike up and come in." The boy, his nose red and snow freezing on his hat, waved in response, and I returned to the chair in the living room.

"Well, Shelby, tell me about this new girl the ladies at dominoes are talking about. The one all curvy and blonde and turning heads at the church."

I laughed. Gossip in Dallam County never takes a holiday.

"Well, Mom, she does look like a pin-up girl. But she's the sweetest and most real person I've met in some time."

"She'll be running home to her mama and papa in no time."

"I don't know, Mom. I don't know much about her family, but the girl seems to have spirit. And a good heart. Lots of determination. We'll see."

As Lorene set the table in the dining room, Jim walked into the house just in time to wash up for supper.

"Got a little something for ya, Shelby. Santa left it in my truck," he said as he grinned.

"Did ya get Charlie Wilkins taken care of?" I asked as Jim placed a foil-wrapped box in my hand. Jim paused at my question and, for a moment, I thought his visit to old Wilkins' home might have been a ruse to run out to buy my gift, but I knew nothing would have been opened on Christmas.

"Yep. He's good. Gonna' wash up for supper."

"Wait. Let me open the gift," and I proceeded to untie the ribbon and pull loose the foil. It was a small box, so I suspected jewelry.

"Oh, Jim," I said as I opened the box.

"They're diamonds," he said as I touched the earrings and then showed them to Mom.

"Well, well, Jim. Those earrings are special. Hope ya haven't been up to no-good." Mom chuckled as I clipped the diamonds to my ears and modeled them.

"Well, ain't those lightin' up your face, Shelby," said Mom. "Nice choice, Jim."

"Merry Christmas," said Jim, and he kissed me on the cheek and scooted off to wash up.

Chapter 4

The dawn of Christmas Day crept through the window of Curtye Lee's upstairs bedroom at Sue Jones' boarding house. Sue Jones was a widow and a gracious landlord, and Curtye Lee knew she'd been lucky to find such a place. She expected Willie Bob might stop by, so she dressed in her green wool skirt and a sweater the color of butter pecan ice cream. Before going downstairs to breakfast, she added a bit of her favorite rosy lipstick.

There were two other women boarding at the house, both closer to Sue Jones' age than Curtye Lee's, and they all greeted her with a "Merry Christmas" and easy smiles.

"Merry Christmas," said Curtye Lee. "Look at this spread. Waffles and eggs and bacon. Thank you, Mrs. Jones. After this and supper last night at the Preston house, I believe I'll need to take a walk around the block this afternoon."

"How was Blanche Preston?" asked Sue as she placed a pitcher of fresh orange juice on the table.

"She's fine. A good cook, I discovered firsthand," said Curtye Lee, intent on avoiding gossip. "And I met some of Willie Bob's friends."

"You be careful 'round those boys," said one of Sue's boarders. "I've heard a couple of them are ruffians. Not unusual for the rodeo men."

"Yes, ma'am," said Curtye Lee.

"I've heard Blanche Preston is a great cook," said Sue, "but she has a tight rein on that boy of hers."

"I'm beginning to see that," said Curtye Lee.

There was a knock at the front door, and Sue rose and left the room.

"Well," she said as she walked back into the dining room with Willie Bob following her. "Look who's here."

"I'll put my plate in the kitchen," said Curtye Lee. "Just give me a minute, Willie."

Settled into the living room, Willie Bob, in unfamiliar surroundings, fidgeted on the chintz settee. Curtye Lee settled into the tufted blue chair near him.

"I wanted to come by to wish you Merry Christmas. Got your gift, uh, and wanted you to have it before I head out to the barn." He handed her a box covered in silver foil with a perfectly tied blue bow, something his mother had clearly wrapped.

Curtye Lee smiled at him and opened the gift as Willie Bob stood and looked out the window and then sat down again.

"Oh, Willie, this is lovely," said Curtye Lee as she pulled a golden chain with a dangled heart from the box. She tried to fasten it behind her neck and then asked her beau to fasten it for her as she stood up, turned, and lifted her hair from the back of her neck.

Her hand touched the pendant at her collarbone, and she stood on her toes and kissed Willie Bob on the cheek. "Merry Christmas to you."

"The guys are waiting for me. We're headed to the barn. To feed the horses and doin' some riding." Curtye Lee peeked out the window to see his friends waiting in his truck. "Ya wanna go?"

Curtye Lee paused, stuffing her disappointment inside. "Not today. You guys have fun. I'll go another time. When just you and I can ride a trail."

She knew they'd be downing beer, likely more than they could hold, their horses neglected, and she'd remembered the advice given at breakfast.

"Next time," said Willie Bob before a quick kiss on her lips and he was gone. In a flash, having fulfilled his Christmas Day duty. Curtye Lee sighed, gathered the wrappings to discard, and returned to the dining room, where the ladies admired her new necklace.

After all the women had gone their ways, Curtye Lee put on her coat, having decided to take a winter walk through nearby streets and check out the neighborhood. The trees sat leafless and quiet as families hibernated behind walls and celebrated their holiday rituals. A preteen cruised down the street on his shiny new bicycle, and Curtye Lee felt the need for family, yet hers was so far away. She'd call Jane when she returned to the house, and when she did, Jane told her to come over.

"Jane, I'll come by after supper. Perhaps for a bit of dessert and coffee. See you then."

"We look forward to seeing you, Curtye Lee."

"I have nothing to bring you," said Curtye Lee.

"Don't be silly," said Jane. "We expect nothing but the joy of your company." Curtye Lee thanked her friend.

"Wait," said Jane. "Do you need me to come pick you up?"

"Oh, no, Jane. I'll walk. Your address is in the phone book, but can you give me directions?"

Jane told her the way to their home, only four blocks away from Sue's boarding house.

An early dusk was slipping through the winter sky when Curtye Lee knocked on the Connors' front door. The house was small and well-kempt, with black shutters on white shingles and neatly hedged around the house. Curtye Lee wondered who did the yardwork, Jane or Henry. The door opened.

"Curtye Lee! We're so glad you're here," exclaimed Jane as Henry stood, smiling, behind his wife, with a tall glass of what looked like tea. "I wouldn't let Henry have any dessert until you came, and he's just itching for his sweets."

Curtye Lee laughed as she entered a dark hallway and followed the couple into a living room. The room was cozy, with a large window framing barren trees in the backyard, and the streetlights layered the depths beyond, making the room seem larger. There were shelves full of books, and Curtye Lee noticed a wall of black and white sketchings of buildings, all framed in black and each sized the same, like a gallery.

"Sit down," said Henry.

"Would you like tea or coffee, Curtye Lee? We're having pecan pie for dessert."

"Oh. Then coffee would be nice."

"I'm sure it's lonesome on this holiday with your family so far away," said Henry as Jane walked away into another room.

"Sometimes." Curtye Lee fidgeted a bit in her seat, a straight-back caned chair with a green velvet seat cushion. "I do miss my papa. Especially."

"Does he live in Colorado?" asked Henry.

"Yes, he used to keep the engines repaired for the railroad. The Denver & Rio Grande Western Railroad in Grand Junction, but now he leads the team doing that work. They call it the D&RGW, but Papa's a bit of a mountain man like his own papa, a grandpa I never knew. Papa spends time huntin' and camping in the White Mountains when he's away from work. He used to take me with him. In summers. When I was young. And he'd talk about his days in the woods with his papa."

"That's interesting. I find there are so many cultural differences through this country. Even here, where these people struggled, relentlessly growing wheat through such terrible times. Such grit. Is your mother there too—in Grand Junction?"

"Mama, she died when I was young. Typhus, they told me. Then, I spent a lot of time with Nana, who spoke French and English. Nana, Mama's mother, was half Osage. They'd come from Missouri. I learned some French from Nana, and when she died, I lived with Aunt Mabel, who'd take me to the cathedral sometimes. Aunt Mabel believed in the spirits. And saints."

"What an interesting childhood, Curtye Lee, showered with too much loss for a young girl. We don't believe in the spirits. Or saints in our church. Someday, you'll have to tell me more about your forays into the mountains with your pa. I can't imagine growing up as you did. Me, I just worked, beside my siblings and Pa, on the farm, chores day in and day out."

"Where're you from, Pastor Connor?" Curtye Lee asked as she heard dishes being set on a table in the next room.

"Grew up in Georgia. A little town called Aaron where my family farmed, but I did well in school, so my folks sent me off to Southern University in Statesboro to study agriculture. But I took a philosophy class and was mesmerized. After I'd finished about two years at college, my church in Statesboro called me to be a deacon. When our pastor died, I went to preaching sermons, and it went from there to me being here." Henry picked up a pipe from the table next to him and started pressing the bowl. "Sorry, Curtye Lee. That's way more than you asked me."

Curtye Lee didn't know the pastor smoked, but she never saw him light the pipe.

"Oh no, Mr. Connor. It's interestin'. I've never been to the East. Or to the ocean," said Curtye Lee as Jane walked in.

"I've put dessert on the dining table. Fresh coffee. Let's enjoy," said Henry as he rose from his chair. Curtye Lee followed them into the room where Jane had walked earlier. She saw the bright light through the kitchen door adjoining the dining room. Curtye Lee found the room to be cozy, with a soft green color on the walls and a large mirror that reflected the chandelier over the table, giving the room a glow.

"Here, Curtye Lee, sit here," said Jane, pulling a chair out.

"Jane, this is a beautiful room. Pastor Connor told me how he came to be here all the way from Georgia," said Curtye Lee as she scooted closer to the table. "Oh, this looks so good. Thank you, Jane, for inviting me over. Oh, and Mr. Crawford hired me to work at his department store. So, I'm a working girl," and she giggled.

"That's wonderful, Curtye Lee. I knew someone at the church would lend a hand. By the way, it's quite by chance, at the church, that Henry and I came together," said Jane as she passed the cream and sugar around the table. Curtye Lee added a bit of cream to her coffee, Henry added sugar, and Curtye Lee saw that Jane took her coffee straight up. It made her smile.

"Henry arrived here, in Dalhart," said Jane, "shortly before I came back to Dalhart from college to start teaching. I went to the North Texas State College in Denton. Studied to teach English and history. Henry was building this church, and my parents joined the endeavor, dragging me along. All of us, the early members, organized and painted and were filled with excitement about the new church, and then this handsome man asked me to dinner one day. From there, it didn't take long for him to woo me into wedded bliss."

Curtye Lee loved how the two laughed together.

"Yes," said Henry. "She's the Flemings' daughter. They'd escaped the storms in the thirties. Moved to Santa Fe, where they now live. But God smiled on me when Jane's parents decided, for a while, to return to Dalhart. Just when I moved here to build the church. I'd have never met her otherwise."

"That's true. Mother and Daddy loved New Mexico but decided to move back here. After the bad storms," said Jane as she placed a slice of pie on a plate for her friend and then one for Henry. "Curtye Lee, I thought you were spending Christmas with the Prestons."

"Well, turned out we spent Christmas Eve ... had supper at his mother's house. I'm not sure his mother likes me, but I met Willie's bull-riding friends. Willie came by the boarding house this mornin' and gave me a gift." Curtye Lee flashed her new necklace for Jane's admiration. "He went with his friends out to their barn today. Where they keep their horses. Asked me to come, but I thought it best not to go." She decided not to mention that she was certain the boys would be drinking.

"That was the right choice," said Henry, his face set stern.

"Yes," said Jane. "You be careful of those boys. They're bull riders, which kinda says it all. A risky way to live."

"Or die," said Henry.

"Yes," said Jane. "We lost a young fella from Dalhart at a rodeo last year. And be careful around Mrs. Preston. No one is good enough for her son, so it's not only you she's been judging. She's judged them all. You might just be too good for that boy of hers."

Curtye Lee winced and finished her pie as she saw Henry taking a second piece. Her pastor had a sweet tooth.

"I'm sorry, Curtye Lee," said Jane. "I shouldn't have said all that about Willie. You came all the way to Texas because you saw something in him. I should mind my own business."

"Well," said Henry. "You're a member of our church, so don't think we won't be lookin' out for you. And you call me Henry. No last names here in this house."

"I'm so grateful to have met you," said Curtye Lee. "I can't have my papa here—but I have you two. And Shelby."

"Well, Curtye Lee," said Henry, "you have certainly brought some sunshine into our somewhat stagnant church."

"Awww," said Curtye Lee, feeling full of Christmas.

Chapter 5

It was a sunny Tuesday morning in January when I marched into Crawford's Department Store and told old Gene Crawford that I was kidnapping his employee, Curtye Lee. He looked at me, puzzled.

"We're fixin' to go riding today. Can someone cover for her?"

"Shelby, you always catch me off guard, but nothing ya do ever surprises me. You've been telling me what to do since you were a sprite of a girl always gettin' your way."

He looked around the store with hands on his hips as if he were in charge.

"Well, we're not busy. I'll cover it till she gets back. She's coming back, right?"

"We'll see," I said as I turned and walked to the back of the store where I'd seen my friend.

"Hey, Curtye Lee, get your stuff. We're going to the ranch," I said.

"But I can't ...."

"Yes, you can. It's cleared with Crawford. Let's go."

After we'd gone by Curtye Lee's room to get her boots and pants and a proper jacket, we headed south. The winter day was warm enough to crack a window, and I turned on the radio; "Jambalaya" was playing.

"You know how to ride, right?" I asked. "I'll give you the mare, Lucy."

"It's been so long. Was workin' so much back home—at the

hospital. I can't wait to get back on a horse. Papa and I used to ride all the time when I was young."

"It's like riding a bike. Come back to you like it was yesterday. I packed some sandwiches and canteens, and we'll head out toward the creek. Maybe find some of the cattle on the way."

"Oh, I love this song," said Curtye Lee as the song changed on the radio to "Half as Much" by Hank Williams.

"I didn't know you liked honky tonk," I said.

"Well, I think we just called it country up in Grand Junction, but yes, I listened to it."

I smiled and felt the cool breeze on my face. Curtye Lee started singing along with Hank Williams, and I joined in. Suddenly, I felt like the young girl I was before Jim and I married.

After Curtye Lee ran into the house and changed and I'd grabbed the lunch satchel, we saddled the horses. Curtye Lee had already mounted Lucy as I tightened the last buckle.

"I can see you still know your way around horses."

"Yes, it's in the blood once you learn to ride. I think Willie and I are going riding on Friday, my day off. Papa had about four horses at his place, but I only lived with him in summers after Mama died. He said I needed a woman's touch. Better schoolin', so I lived with Nana and then my aunt."

"Oh, Curtye Lee. That sounds hard. Losing your mama and Nana. But I well know it's the trials that make us who we are. And look how you turned out." I smiled at Curtye Lee, dismounted and unlocked the gate to the road, took the horses through, and locked it. We rode in silence a bit down the back road.

"See the trees up there. That's the creek," I said, and in no time, we were there.

"Does Jane ride too?" asked Curtye Lee.

"No. She had an accident right after she came back to teach. A horse threw her."

"Oh, that's sad. I love the horses."

"On some days, you'll see her walk with a bit of a limp," I said.

"Oh, look. There's some cattle." Curtye Lee pointed toward the pasture. "Are they yours?"

"Indeed. There's a new one. That's a brand-new calf. Let's ride over so I can check it and tell Jim. Then we'll eat."

I dismounted near the calf and walked up slowly, its momma eyeing me. Looked it over and walked through the small herd until I saw the calf move around.

"He looks good. It's a bull," and I mounted my horse. We chose the best spot near the creek, which was almost dried up.

"Here. Let's land here. Watch out for that devil's claw there. It'll spike ya." I pulled the satchel from my horse and spread an old blanket, and I led the horses down to the water.

"How's ham, tomato, and lettuce with a bit of mustard? Or there's a chicken salad."

"I'll take the ham if that's okay," said Curtye Lee.

"Of course. And I'll pour you a cup of iced tea," and I pulled the thermos from the bag. I looked at Curtye Lee, her hair loose, looking cute in her cotton shirt and jeans. This girl had no idea how cute she was, and I'm not sure she'd even care. She was the real thing wrapped in a stunning package. Some people were still gossiping about the new girl, but they had no idea.

"How are you and Willie Bob doing?" I asked cautiously. I was certain this bond with a bad boy would end one day, and we'd lose our friend to Colorado.

"We're okay. I look forward to seeing the barn where they keep their horses. It's out of town on the ranch of one of his friends. Or rather, the fella's parents. Willie Bob asked me to go out of town with them to a rodeo, but I'm not so sure about that. I wanna see him ride—at the rodeo. Ya know, that's how

I met him. At a rodeo in Grand Junction, but he wasn't with his friends then. He'd traveled to Colorado alone. We rode the Ferris wheel together, and he said it was too long a drive with his trailer and won't do that again."

"There's plenty of rodeo fellas around here, what with the XIT Ranch. They were a bit of a godsend back in the day. Back when we needed the help during the storms and depression. Cattle were the bounty of the plains before the farmers came. But some of those fellas that still rodeo are a bit rowdy, Curtye Lee. No place for a lady."

"Well, I'm not sure I'd call me a lady. The daughter of a mountain man. But I know the women of my family always stood up for themselves, and Papa'd have it no other way. He pounded it into me. Independence and a bit of mulishness."

"We call that sass."

The two of us laughed, and I told my new friend about the town and some of the people she'd run into. She told me about the scenery of Colorado. Nothing like the flat plains I lived in.

"Oh," I said as I looked at my watch. "We need to pack up. I want to get back before the school bus comes."

In no time, we'd packed up and eased the horses back toward the ranch. I'd report the new calf to Jim when he got home. Curtye Lee and I sat on the porch when the bus stopped out at the gate. Billy climbed over the fence before Lorene could unlock the gate.

"Billy, Lorene, this is my friend Curtye Lee. You were both in Amarillo the first Sunday she came to church."

Billy ran up and gave Curtye Lee a big hug, but I noticed Lorene looking my friend up and down in judgment before she walked on into the house. I'd taught her better than that and knew I'd have to say something to her later, and she'd ignore me. I pulled a cigarette out of my pack of Viceroys and lit it.

"I didn't know you smoked," said Curtye Lee.

"Well, I catch enough hell for it from my mom and from

Jane, so don't you start." I winked.

"Just didn't know. I'm used to it but got no taste for it myself."

"Well, that's good. You're too pretty to get those wrinkles, and the sun here ain't good for your skin either. I'm certain you're used to longer winters than we are, but we'll get some snows off and on well into March."

I saw Curtye Lee watching the smoke from my cigarette hover in the air.

"Do you ever wonder about ghosts? The past and our ancestors?" asked Curtye Lee.

"Heavens, no," I answered. "Do you believe in 'em?"

"I just wonder. About the unknown."

"Well, don't mention that to Henry. Or Jane."

"I suppose I shouldn't. It's all those Catholic saints and my Osage heritage coming out. But, really, would you and Jane want to have a group to discuss such things? Mystical things, like spirits and reincarnation and that thing they call *déjà vu?*"

"Wow. That would be quite an ask of Jane, her being married to the pastor. But she went to college and is a curious one, I think I'd find it interesting, but we'd have to be like shadows, keeping our talk secret." I sat for a moment. "I'm game. I'll have to talk to Jane though."

"Okay, but I should be getting home. I hope Mr. Crawford didn't expect me back at work today."

"Don't you worry about him. Let me finish this cigarette, and I'll drive you home, but you're welcome to stay for supper. We'll eat when Jim gets home. About five thirty."

"No. I should get back. I think Sue will expect me for supper at the boarding house, and you've already been so generous. Willie Bob said he'd call me at six. I've enjoyed our visit and the ride out to the creek."

"You're welcome, and we'll do it again. And, next time, I want to hear more about that Indian heritage." I tossed the stub of my cigarette off into the gravel, and after gathering our stuff and telling the kids I'd be right back, I drove Curtye Lee back to the boarding house, and I watched the young woman walk away. Even from the back, she was so full of sparkle, a true courage in her step. I saw a steadfast hope walk with her, but hope, like faith, is a thing that taunts me. There are days that fill me, and then, there are days that strip me of belief in joy and better tomorrows. It's always the barren landscape, an endless horizon full of life so cunningly veiled, even the Miller moths, even the husks of what once was. The skies both terrify and awe me—it's that coupling of what fires made here that has always saved me. Permits me, in a moment, to live in the light. That and riding my horse ground me, yet I craved the mettle I saw in Curtye Lee's nimble step.

On the way home, I picked up a couple of things at the grocery store for supper. Jim and Billy were already sitting at the kitchen table as I set the bowl of beef stew on the table with the biscuits.

"Lorene," I called. "Supper's on."

"We ain't waitin'," said Jim, and he grabbed a biscuit and asked Billy to pass the butter. Lorene came running down the stairs. I took a serving of stew and passed the bowl to Lorene.

"So, Lorene," I asked, "what were those bad manners when I introduced you to Curtye Lee today? You weren't very nice."

She slowly buttered her biscuit, not looking at me.

"Well?"

"I'd heard said she's a tramp, and I was just looking for myself."

"Where'd you hear a thing like that?"

"At school. That's what Melody's parents said, and some of the girls from church were talking about her. And Willie Bob."

"You know better than that. People who don't know her at all are making judgments, and I imagine there's a few jealous women at the church. You don't even know her, and it turns out, regardless of how cute she is, she's a delightful young woman." I took a sip of my sweet tea. "And a good horsewoman I might add."

Lorene rolled her eyes and said nothing.

"By the way, Jim, there's a new calf, a bull, out in the south pasture. He looked healthy."

"Good," he said. "Was expectin' a couple new ones."

I asked Billy about his homework, and after the meal, with little conversation, I started clearing the empty plates.

"I'll go out tomorrow evening and check the cattle. Got work to do in the barn," and before I turned around, Jim was gone.

Chapter 6

Willie Bob showed up early Friday morning in his pickup. Curtye Lee sat on the front porch, dressed in jeans and comfortable boots, the only ones she had but properly worn in. After an early breakfast of oatmeal and orange juice with the boarding house ladies, she'd pulled on her wool-lined jacket and a scarf and waited. The crisp morning sparked her excitement for a day riding with Willie Bob.

About twenty minutes late, he walked up to the porch and sat in the chair beside his girl.

"Whatcha doin'?"

"Just waitin' for you. Look at this beautiful morning. I watched the sun come up yonder."

"Damn, girl. It's frigging cold out here," he countered. "But it'll warm up by the time we get the horses saddled out at the barn. Besides, ya got me to keep ya warm." He smiled and stood up. He reached for Curtye Lee's hand to pull her up and, in the snap of a moment, had her wrapped in his arms and planted a kiss.

"Willie!"

"What?"

"We're on Miss Sue's porch," said Curtye Lee. "Right out here in the open, and there's already 'nough talk round town about me, the outsider from Colorado."

He backed up.

"Let's go. Don't fret about all that talk. They know you're my girl." He opened the door on her side of the truck, letting her scoot in.

They'd only gone two blocks when Willie Bob pulled into the market.

"Gotta get some beer. I'm sure the guys didn't leave any in the ice box at the barn." He ran in and came out with a six-pack he left in the truck bed.

There wasn't much traffic as they left town. Curtye Lee watched the horizons of harvested fields turned beige and the skies of blue-gray with bits of indigo reminding her it was winter. It wasn't cold enough to snow, but just enough of a fickle breeze to hold a chill.

He pulled off onto a dirt road with a rickety gate, stopped the truck and pulled out his keys to unlock the padlock on the chains. After he pulled the truck through, he closed the gate but didn't lock it. For a moment, Curtye Lee felt an uneasiness. He'd told her it would just be the two of them riding.

The barn came into view, an old barn with a large horse trailer sitting beside it. He started talking to the horses in the stalls, checking each one and pulled a gray mare out.

"This is Sweet Pie. She's a good horse for you. Mine is the black gelding over there." He pointed to a stall behind him. "Here's Pie's saddle. Can you do it yourself?"

"Sure, but I don't need no gentle horse." Curtye Lee took the saddle and bridle, ran her hand over Sweet Pie's nose, and gently rubbed her ears.

"Oh, she's got some spirit. She's a good one for ya. I'll get my Rider saddled. His name's really Rough Rider. Jus' call him Rider most time." Willie Bob worked in silence as Curtye Lee whispered to her mare before she buckled and tightened all the straps.

The two started down the pasture along the fence until they came to a gate. Willie Bob unlocked it, and the two horses ambled down the back road.

"Not much traffic out here."

"Well, seems one could see a car coming from about twenty miles out with this flat land all the way to the Earth's horizon," said Curtye Lee.

"Yep. About a mile more, and there's a track on Miller's

property we can use. We'll put 'em through the paces."

As the two rode on, Willie Bob talked about some of his rodeos, how many times he'd broken a bone or a record, and how the ladies loved watching the cowboys ride the bulls. When they reached the track, about half a mile long and back, they put their horses into a gallop. Curtye Lee knew Willie Bob thought she wouldn't be able to keep up with him, but she did, so he took his horse to a full run. Curtye Lee didn't bite. No need to wear out her mare, and she knew Willie Bob's horse was practiced in racing. She caught up to him after he slowed down.

"I like this horse. She follows the lead well and has a spring in her step."

"Well, you can come out any time with me and ride her. Or come on our rodeos with us."

"Willie, you know I have a job," said Curtye Lee. "I'll come watch when you have one near Dalhart."

"Well, there's the XIT in August. Might be a smaller rodeo in June this year, I think."

The sky started to cloud over, and the two headed back toward the barn. Willie Bob locked the gate he'd left open for their return and walked his horse.

"Let's walk back."

Curtye Lee dismounted, stroked Sweet Pie, and walked alongside her beau.

"You know, Ma is headin' out of town in a couple of weeks. You come on over, and I'll cook supper for us. How's that."

"Sounds good," said Curtye Lee. "I didn't know you can cook."

"Good 'nough. Nothing fancy. I'm good at making cornbread."

He stopped walking near the oak tree, a lone tree near the fence.

"Let's sit a bit." He pulled a flask from his saddle bag. Took a swig.

"Want some?"

Curtye Lee took the flask. "What is it? Rye?"

"Close enough." He snuggled over closer to Curtye Lee as they sat under the tree.

Curtye Lee took a sip and found it strong, not smooth like the whiskey her papa drank, and as she handed it back to Willie Bob, he took it with one hand and with the other pulled her face to his lips, kissing her long and greedy.

"Oh, I need some air," said Curtye Lee as she pulled back from the kiss.

"I'll give you mouth-to-mouth," he said and pulled her into his arms, kissing her more urgently. When he stopped, Curtye Lee quickly put her hand to his chest, pushing.

"That's enough," she said as she stood up. "This'll go too far, too fast, and I know you ain't eager to raise a brood of kids. Let's head back and decide where we might find a bite to eat for lunch."

She'd already mounted Sweet Pie before he was back on his feet, his flask put in his back pocket. She could tell he was taken aback at her firm stand, but no matter how much she loved him, she'd be no one's pushover.

Curtye Lee wasted no time stalling her horse and getting to Willie Bob's truck, and when he scooted into the driver's seat, she leaned over and gave him a quick kiss.

Chapter 7

It was the regular Tuesday coffee klatch at Jane's home, and the nation had just inaugurated a new president, Dwight Eisenhower, a general from the war. Curtye Lee was at her new job at the department store downtown, so it was just the two of us. Jane set a cinnamon crumb cake on the table and placed the percolator on a trivet after filling our two mugs. We looked forward to our Tuesday meetings where we'd reminisce about our early years in Dalhart, about activities at church, and girl things such as hairstyles and what new movie was at the local theater. I told Jane all about the day I'd spent with Curtye Lee out at the ranch.

"Jane, Curtye Lee wants to start a group, just the three of us, to talk about mysticism and reincarnation and all those unspoken things the church frowns on. I was game, but I told her you'd likely have a problem with it. I could go down to Amarillo and have my cousin Esther get me some books from their library."

Jane took a sip of coffee and looked at me with a thoughtful expression. She'd always been a good listener, even when we were in high school. Taking things in and pondering before she'd speak.

"I don't know why I'd have a problem, do you?" said Jane, and she grinned and winked at me. I loved Jane. We both knew the church would condemn such a topic, but I also knew Jane was as full of curiosity as Curtye Lee and I, and she'd never been shy about her education. She'd been an excellent teacher in Dalhart schools but had quit when she'd become so involved in the church and helping her husband. I knew she missed teaching.

"That means you'll do it?"

"Sure," said Jane. "But we need to find a place. Curtye Lee's boarding room won't work. Too many other ears and eyes. Why do you think Curtye Lee wants to learn about this?"

"Mostly, I think it's curiosity, but you know, she went to a Catholic church in Colorado with her aunt. I think some of it comes from all their talk of saints. Their idols. Like Virgin Mary."

"Oh, yes," said Jane. "And she mentioned to me and Henry that her grandmother was part Indian, and her papa spent time in nearby mountains. That he befriended the natives there. So, now I see it. And yes, it would be fascinating to learn more. I'm in."

"We'll be discreet," I said. "I think I'll ask old Crawford about his back room. We can meet there."

"Let me know when."

"As soon as I can get some books, I'll tell you and Curtye Lee," I said, wondering just what I was getting myself into. If found out, Jim would be just as miffed as Henry would.

It was another Sunday as Curtye Lee, Jane, and I gathered in the corner of the lobby. Outside of the church's warmth, there was no promise of spring as winter held tight in the Panhandle.

"I'm headed down to Amarillo next week," I said. "To visit my cousin. Get some books."

Curtye Lee looked over her shoulder. Willie Bob would be looking for her, always expecting her to be hanging onto his arm. I saw him on the other side of the room with a rodeo fella, but he was looking around the room.

"Thank you. Y'all are the best friends." She was wearing a green wool skirt and a silky blouse that tied into a bow, accentuating her assets. Still keeping the men at church looking, hankering for what they didn't have, yet she seemed so blind to her lure. She was like a magnet when she walked past the men.

"Jane, you are so lucky to be married to Henry. He's just the sweetest man," said Curtye Lee. "I love the way he looks at you. So devoted." She jumped as Willie Bob tapped her shoulder from behind like a pirate showing up to collect his booty.

"Been lookin' for ya," he said. He looked over at Jane and me. "You ladies are monopolizing my girl."

"Honey, she's God's gift to all of us. Not just yours," I said and looked hard at him, making him look away.

"See ya later, girls." And then she was being eased across the room by our town's handsome bull rider.

"You be safe driving down to Amarillo," said Jane as we watched Curtye Lee leave. "I've got to go find my Henry. And talk to Stella to follow up on our Ladies Group activities. See ya on Tuesday morning."

"I'll be there. Right after I drop the kids at school," I said as I watched Peggy Brown walk over toward us. When Jane turned and saw Peggy coming, she turned back to me and said, "Good luck."

"Howdy, Shelby. How's your sweet Lorene doing? She's such a pretty girl."

"She's just fine, Peggy," I responded. "Keeping her grades right and singing in the choir now."

"That's good. Hadley's girl, Ella, she talks about joining the choir when she gets to high school. Glad to hear it. That girl's such a tomboy. My daughter-in-law has a time getting her to even comb her hair. Did you hear about the Tippett girl? Lord, what are the kids coming to?"

"Which Tippett girl?"

"Oh, Janet, Joe Tippett's granddaughter. Heard whispers she's in a family way. There's talk she might be going down near Fort Worth to stay with her aunt, and we all know what that really means." She shook her head.

"No, Peggy, I haven't heard such."

"Well, Joe's got no business being deacon if he can't keep his family in the Lord's way. Don't know what Henry's gonna do about it."

I looked at Peggy with her lips pursed in judgment. Full of pride in being first to spread news, be it real or imagined.

"I'm sure Henry will do the right thing, and I'm sure Janet Tippett will be just fine. Jim and I are fixin' to leave, so I'll see you next Sunday, Peggy." I walked away, looking for my husband in the mix of people talking.

Chapter 8

The sunrise was magical, and then Willie Bob turned west, and the rising sun was behind them as they drove out to the barn. Curtye Lee had Tuesday morning off work, and Willie Bob had convinced her to go out to the barn for a morning ride. It was a warm, late winter day, and instead of her pants, she'd worn her cotton dress, a pale blue button-up sweater that matched the floral of her dress, and her worn-in cowboy boots.

The barn sat large and quiet in the dewy morning. Willie Bob had promised her that his friends wouldn't be there, and she'd told him she had to be back in town at noon. Old Crawford expected her at the store after lunchtime. Curtye Lee wiped down the saddle as Willie Bob fed all the horses.

"I'll clean the stalls out after we ride," he said. "I brought a thermos of coffee. Still hot. There," and he pointed to where he'd dropped his jacket.

Curtye Lee poured coffee into the cap of the thermos and blew on it before sipping the strong brew as the horses ate. Willie Bob pulled out Sweet Pie for Curtye Lee and his horse, Rider, and then he strapped the saddles and reins onto both horses. He gulped a bit of coffee and stuffed the thermos into his saddle bag.

"Let's go across the pastures toward the ranch house. The fields have been plowed for planting, and we'll edge 'round them."

The two rode in silence for a bit. A breeze chilled the air, and Curtye Lee wished she'd brought a jacket. Had worn pants. The clouds held the sky low and gray.

"When's your next rodeo?" asked Curtye Lee.

"'Bout three weeks. Up in Oklahoma." He slowed the gait of his horse to let her catch up to him. "Wanna come?"

"No, Willie. I'll wait for you to ride around here, near home."

"Hey, there's Rollo," yelled Willie Bob, reining his horse to a stop, dismounting.

"Who?"

"That's the bull. Rollo. He's a frisky one." With those words, Willie Bob had jumped the fence and was hooting at the bull. Of a sudden, the bull spied him and came running, and Willie Bob started running back and forth along the fence, taunting the bull that came upon him fast.

"Willie," screamed Curtye Lee, and just in the nick of time, Willie Bob popped back over the fence and stood behind a shrub. Now, the bull was snorting and taunting Willie Bob.

"You're not doin' that again," Curtye Lee shouted as Willie Bob started climbing the fence rails. He turned and looked at her. "And you've ripped your Levi's."

"Guess I shouldn't. You'd have a hard time dragging my body back to the barn."

"I'd toss it over your horse and smack its rump." With those words, Willie Bob was back on his horse and riding beside her.

He laughed. "S'pose you would. The next local rodeo should be in June. Weather'll be good then."

"I'll be there. If you're still alive. I'm certain Crawford will give me some time off."

"He better." Willie Bob urged his horse to speed up and went ahead to where the ranch house was in the distance. "That's where Theo's family lives. Ya wanna race back?"

Before the words had left his mouth, he'd kneed his mount and was flying back the way they'd come. Curtye Lee followed. Hurried because she knew if she lost sight of him, she might not find her way back.

In a full run, excitement flowed through Curtye Lee she'd

not felt since riding near Grand Junction. The pure thrill and power of the air rushing at you and breaking through it like you're the wind itself. Like a storm. She reined her horse slower as she saw Willie Bob waiting at the barn. They were alive with the flurry of a race.

Willie Bob, full of gusto from the romp with Rollo and the race, tied the reins of the two horses to a rail at the barn, and before Curtye Lee had barely caught her breath, Willie Bob took it away with a piercing kiss. In no time, they were wrapped together on his cot in the back of the barn, half undressed before they'd gotten there. It wasn't long before Curtye Lee laid back, breathless and exhausted, like the horses idling outside.

"Damn, girl. That's the best horse ride I've ever had." He smiled, looking down into her face. As she reached for her dress, he fell onto her, kissing her again.

"No," she said, pushing him away. "No more. I shouldn't have let that happen." Her regret was mixed with the fire of it all. He stood up, naked as the day he was born, still aroused.

"Awww. C'mon, Curtye Lee." She saw his face, so like a puppy pleading. It was too soon for all this, she thought. Too risky. Yet she was close to being drawn back into the muss of blankets on the bed.

"Get dressed," she said as she pulled her dress over her head. "It's cold. And we need to brush down the horses."

"I'll take care of it." He reluctantly pulled on his pants, pulled his red and white pack of Lucky Strikes from his jacket and lit one. Inhaled as he walked away.

Curtye Lee turned to a mirror on the wall and pulled herself back together, pinned up her mussed hair and then sat to pull on her boots. She stood to see herself in the mirror again and saw a woman living on the brink, a woman unlike who she was, and she wondered what had brought her here. *Where was the clear-headed girl from Colorado?* She'd rebelled against expectations before, but always with reason. Papa'd always taught her to respect herself first and expect it from others. This day had been folly, an abandon both thrilling and unfamiliar to her, and she began to doubt her decision to follow this charming cowboy so far from home.

She found Willie Bob swearing under his breath as he cleaned out horse stalls.

"I'm ready."

"For what?" asked Willie Bob, his voice turning hopeful.

"To go home. I have to go to work this afternoon."

"Let me finish up." He tossed fresh hay into a stall and began cleaning another. Curtye Lee walked to the truck and waited. She looked up at the sky that had turned gray and realized how foolish she'd been to come out here with Willie Bob. She'd been properly warned by the pastor on Christmas Day, and now she was standing here hoping Willie Bob would take her home. He could be so sweet, so charming, but he always wanted his way. The passions of the moments, earlier, the animal desire of it all, had carried her away from her usual caution. She'd slipped, and shifting course would not be easy.

It was ten days before Curtye Lee woke to a stain in her bed that gave her a sigh of relief. She'd fretted and lost sleep through those days waiting, fearful she might just have ruined her reputation. Would disappoint her family. That she'd end up being just who all those tittering ladies in Dalhart had said she was. She'd also prayed a lot and was certain, on that morning, that God had heard her prayers. Had looked kindly on her.

It had also been ten days of a stand-offish period between Willie Bob and her, days where he'd been miffed and, when he did call, she was always engaged otherwise. That afternoon, she agreed to go bowling with him.

"Thought you'd kicked me to the curb," said Willie Bob as she climbed into the cab of his truck.

"I considered it a time or two," and she winked at him.

"But you're too cute to turn loose."

He chuckled as he pulled away from the curb. Curtye Lee knew well that the test would come later. When he made his move on her.

Though Curtye Lee bowled her best games, Willie Bob won the bet, and she was thankful she'd bet no more than a root beer float at the soda fountain. Willie Bob called out to friends as they walked into Bowers and took seats at the counter.

"Ya shoulda seen me ride the bull up in Boise City last week." He put his thumb inside his belt and pulled up the buckle. "Look at this. Pretty fancy, huh? Earned it." He pulled loose the back of his shirt to show her the bruise on his back. "This could use some tender lovin'."

Curtye Lee sipped the root beer at the bottom of her mug, saving the ice cream for last.

"Glad you're not hurt worse," she said. "Seems crazy to be riding those bulls."

"Well, Mama'll probably have this buckle on display by the Fourth of July. But I'm wearin' it for now." He leaned over and kissed Curtye Lee on the cheek.

The sun was setting when they got in Willie Bob's pick-up, and, the truck idling, it didn't take long for Willie Bob to pull Curtye Lee into his arms and kiss her, a long yearning kiss. She put her hand on his chest and pushed him back.

"Willie, I can't do that again." She looked him straight in the eyes. "I don't mean kissin', but you know what I mean. I've been sick and fearful the past days that I might be pregnant. I know you don't want that, and I shouldn't have let things go that far out at the barn. I wasn't teasin' you. Everything just went too fast. I'm a proper girl and expect you to treat me that way."

He sat quietly for a few minutes. Clearly reckoning his next move.

"Well, Mama's going out of town next week. Since you're a proper woman, let me make you that supper at the house.

Show you I can cook somethin'. That I can do more than fall off a bull."

He grinned at her, and Curtye Lee paused. She'd already made a mistake going alone with him out to the barn.

"Do I need to bring a chaperone?" she asked.

"Ha." He turned on the ignition. "No. I'm just gonna fix us supper. Light some candles."

Curtye Lee told him she'd come.

"You'll have to pick me up," she said, and then she leaned over and gave her beau a lingering but less-than-passionate kiss.

Chapter 9

In February, frost still covered the pastures and the fields, and friends and family chatted and enjoyed fresh coffee in the hum of the lobby after the Sunday sermon. Just as the sermon wrapped up, I'd snuck out to pour fresh-brewed coffee into the thermal coffee urns in the lobby. Filling my own cup, I joined Jane and Curtye Lee who were talking to Peggy Brown.

"Well, I'd be sorry to see Joe Tippett step down as deacon," Jane said.

"Why would Joe step down?" I asked.

"Oh, Shelby, didn't you hear? It's going around his grand-daughter's being sent away. Like I'd told ya. Remember? I heard at the salon that another student at the high school got her in the family way." As always, Mrs. Brown always seemed to delight in someone's misfortune, while feigning to be aghast. "Such a shame. You saw that Joe Jr. and his family weren't here today. I reckon we'll need to replace old Joe."

"Peggy, I've not heard this," I said, my voice firm, and I looked over at Curtye Lee and Jane, who was holding back her grin in anticipation of my response.

"I hope you're not spreading about an untruth. The Tippetts are a wonderful family, Peggy, and I'm certain they'll do right by the girl if what you say is true. They're church family, and we're here for them." And with those words, I strutted away and back to the pots to check on the supply of cream and sugar. I could never abide Peggy Brown's constant gossip, yet I strove to be kind because she was the mother of our piano player, and Hadley was nothing like his mother.

Winter fields of frost lined the road on Tuesday as I drove south toward Amarillo on a mission to get some books and a long-overdue visit with my cousin, Esther. The kids were in school, and Jim had promised to be home before the school bus came in the afternoon, though Lorene was certainly old enough to watch her brother. There was a catch in my chest as I thought of just how fast these children were growing up. How it hadn't been all that long ago that Jim and I had frolicked in the hay, how we'd work side by side in the field, just the two of us, talking about our dreams, and fixing up the ranch house, adding a gas stove and an indoor toilet. Then, there was a baby girl before the government called Jim off to fight in a war. How such things changed our lives.

I saw some hope for spring around me as I followed the highway, a few fields plowed and ready for planting in March and April. Farmers waited to be sure there would be no more frosts. The edges of Amarillo were upon me before I knew it.

I found my way to Esther's house, a small clapboard on Wayne Street that looked in need of a paint job. Esther and her husband Hank were getting up in years, Esther being the oldest child of Mom's older brother. They'd had a son who'd moved out to California during the Dust Bowl and seldom visited, from what Mom told me. I pulled to the curb and parked, noticing how quiet the street was on a Tuesday morning.

Esther opened the door and came down the stoop. Waited for me. She was a short woman with curly brown hair cut short and grayed like it had been sprinkled with salt. She squinted as I walked up and hugged her.

"Good Lord, child, how long's it been?"

"I know. I know, Esther. Far too long. Two years, I think, and here I am alone, not even bringing the family," I said.

"Well, come on in. I got fresh coffee." Esther filled two mugs and carried over a small pitcher of cream as the women settled at the small drop-leaf table. A dog barked in the backyard, and a radio played softly in another room.

"That's Hank. Listening to his radio when he's not talking to his buddies on that new ham radio. You probably saw that tall antenna he put out back, towering like a windmill."

"No, I didn't notice it. I'll have to tell Jim about that. Sounds like something he might be interested in."

"Well, be careful. That pricey equipment is like boy toys they can't get enough of. Hank got interested during the war, but once he retired from the Post Office, he's on that damn radio all the time."

Esther rose and put the banana bread I'd brought on a plate and set it on the table, cutting us each a piece and serving it on a napkin. Esther loved feeding people.

"I'll give Hank a piece later. Why don't y'all come down at Easter? I haven't seen your little ones for so long. I'll bet that Lorene has grown."

"Esther, she turns sixteen next month. I'll talk to Jim about Easter. We can visit both y'all and his uncle Joe over near Bell Avenue."

"Lordy, sixteen. And what's this about us going to the library? Sounds like you're up to some kinda mischief, and ya know I love that."

"Well, yes. Some friends and I want to learn about mysticism. All those things some people believe in, but we can't see. And ya know the church frowns on it, so we've got a little secret group."

"I love it. Wish I could come, but I ain't drivin' to Dalhart."

I told Esther how Jane was doing and how, at Christmas, this sweet girl called Curtye Lee showed up in town following young Willie Bob back from Colorado, stirring all kinds of gossip and turning heads.

"Well, well. That'll stir up all those stodgy old men. I can't believe you got the pastor's wife in on this scheme of yours," said Esther.

"It's not a scheme. We're just curious and want to know what it's all about. Or if it's just make-believe."

"Well, I'm not sure Amarillo will be a fan of these books you're looking for, but we'll go and see if they got anything."

Before we left for the library, I walked into the spare room where Hank was listening to some big band music on the radio. I saw all his new equipment and gave him a peck on the cheek.

"Don't turn it down," I said, shaking my head. "We're on our way out, but I reckon we might be down at Easter."

At the library, I went to the drawers of cards and searched for "Mysticism," finding nothing but the name Evelyn Underhill. I had trouble finding the book, so Esther asked the librarian, who took us right to it. There were two books by this English woman, and after Esther and I paged through them for a bit, I chose the smaller one called *Practical Mysticism*. The librarian also showed us a couple of novels written by Miss Underhill, and I chose to check out one called *The Grey World*.

"We hadn't decided to read a novel, but this one looks interesting and is written by this woman who studied mysticism," I said to Esther. "That's enough for now. Enough to get us into some trouble, I reckon."

It was still early when we returned to Esther's house, and the two of us visited a bit longer over sandwiches and sweet tea.

"I was going to stop by and visit a bit with Jim's uncle Joe at his farm over near Bell Road. Brought him sweet bread, banana bread like I brought you. I should go." I hugged my cousin. "Thanks, Esther, for the help at the library, and I'll let ya know if we need an extension on the books, which'll be most likely."

"Well, I might just read 'em when you bring 'em back. You be careful goin' home, love."

I enjoyed the solitary drive home, my bounty in a cotton bag on the back seat. Gene Crawford said he'd give me a key to the store so we could come and go for our meeting. Tuesdays, he'd said. Only Tuesday, because he had card games on other nights. I wasn't sure what I was getting myself into. Old Crawford, whom I'd known since I was just a girl, was a member at Victory Church, and I wondered at all the secrets of a small town, how some were well kept, others suspected and overlooked, and the whispered ones that could destroy a man or woman's reputation. Gossip was a fluid and mysterious thing, like mysticism.

Chapter 10

Willie Bob picked up Curtye Lee precisely at six on Monday evening, greeting her with a single pink rose. She wore her wool plaid skirt and a green sweater and pinned her hair up with a tortoiseshell barrette. The drive across town to the Preston house held high hopes for both Curtye Lee and Willie Bob, each picturing the night ending differently.

"What are you fixin' for supper?" asked Curtye Lee, suspicious of her fella's cooking skills.

"Well, Mama left frozen suppers for me, and I set one out for tonight. A chicken and cheese casserole I'm gonna' heat up in the oven. And some cornbread. I can mix up some cornbread, and I got us a fine bottle of wine." He parked in the driveway, and Curtye Lee sat in the truck, waiting for him to come open her door. She remembered the days up in Colorado when she first met him, how he couldn't run around fast enough to help her out of a truck or open a door for her. Now, she was an afterthought.

She stood at the kitchen counter and watched Willie Bob unwrap the dish his mother had made, turn on the oven, and get out a bowl and canister of cornmeal. She'd seen he'd already set the dining room table and added a couple of candlesticks.

"Ain't ya gonna' help?," he asked Curtye Lee.

"Oh, no. I'm just gonna' watch. You said you'd fix me a fine supper. But I'll take a glass of that wine."

Willie Bob struggled to get the cork out of the bottle. Said nothing as he looked at her cautiously, poured the wine to near the top of the glass, and handed it to her.

"Madame."

"It's *mademoiselle*." She grinned playfully. "*Madame* is a married lady."

"Ah." He grinned at her. "Ma'am'selle."

"Close e'nuff. I know your mother's a good cook. I guess I'll only get to check out your cornbread skills." She sipped her wine, hoping to make the full glass last at least halfway through the meal. "But there's a lot to be said for good cornbread."

When everything was ready, and they sat across from each other at the table, Willie Bob took out his lighter and lit the two candles. Stood and turned off the light switch.

"Look at how you glow in that candlelight, Curtye," he said as Curtye Lee spooned the casserole onto her plate.

"Don't you sweet talk me, Willie Preston. It'll get you nowhere."

His face twisted into a grimace, and then, in the next moment, he said, "Ain't gonna stop trying."

The two chatted about rodeos through supper—Willie Bob bragging and Curtye Lee asking questions. She managed to make that first glass of wine last long, for she knew too much of a good thing would only bring trouble. Willie Bob wanted to leave the dishes, but Curtye Lee insisted they clean the kitchen.

"You didn't make dessert," said Curtye Lee as she washed the last glass.

"Nope. I'm your dessert." He winked at her. "Well, I did get some chocolate ice cream 'cause I know it's your favorite."

"Let's visit a bit, in the living room, before ice cream. Maybe listen to some music. What's your favorite?"

"Hank Williams. And Eddie Arnold." He spun around as if he was holding someone in his arms. "We should go dancin'."

"Your church frowns on dancin'."

"Don't stop me." They both laughed.

"I want a sweet tea if there is some. Pour me one while I

wash down these counters."

Willie Bob poured a tea with ice and opened a bottle of beer, and he blew out the two candles at the dining table as they passed before going into the living room and settling on the sofa. Curtye Lee kicked off her shoes and pulled her feet up beneath her while Willie Bob slouched on the embroidered pillows Mrs. Preston had placed so precisely.

"So, Willie Bob, tell me about yourself. You always talk about the rodeo. What was your childhood like? Bet'cha were a cute little boy."

"Oh, no. Don't wanna talk about that. But you can tell me about living in the mountains. Those Indians you always talk about."

"Alright, but then you'll tell me about the little boy you used to be. How ya came to be a bull rider." She put the glass tumbler on the coffee table. "My ma died before I had many memories of her, and Pa didn't feel able to raise a girl, so he left me with my nana and then my aunt. But Pa always showed up. He took me into the mountains in the summers. Taught me how to start a campfire and make a pot a coffee before he even allowed me to drink it. He worked at the railyard, but he loved the mountains. Riding his horse. Knew the other hunters and the Indians that lived on the edges of town, and I got to meet them. Woods wisdom. I watched and listened, breathed it all in."

"Woods wisdom," repeated Willie Bob. "That's interesting. I wish I knew your Pa."

"My aunt taught me to be proper, and Pa taught me to be curious. I know you'd love him. I miss him so." And with those words, Willie Bob scooted over close to Curtye Lee. Moved in for a lingering kiss. Curtye Lee moved away from him when the second kiss turned more passionate.

"Hey, you promised." She glared at him. "It's your turn. Who were you as a kid? Your family?"

He stood up and grabbed the empty beer bottle.

"Need another one."

When he returned, sipping on a bottle of Lone Star, he sat down next to Curtye Lee and snuggled close.

"Well, let me hear where you came from," said Curtye Lee.

"I don't like talking about it. From the farm. From Dalhart. I helped my pa harvest the wheat or sorghum, even when I was a little boy, but the storms came, and nothing would grow. All the topsoil blew into the skies."

"Oh, that's what Shelby said happened to her family. And she told me about the jackrabbits."

"Oh, yeah, those jackrabbits. The men went out clubbing 'em. They was everywhere eating the last of anything growing. I was just a boy, but all that struggle and Mama and my pa were bickering all the time. By the end of it, we'd lost the farm, and Ma was working as a seamstress where she could find the work."

"That's sad, Willie."

"Well, I do remember when I was little, learnin' to ride my bike. How Pa helped to show me, brushed me off when I fell, and finally, when I could do it, I broke that leash to the farm. Went to town. Go see my friends. That's a glad memory."

"Yes. You seemed close to your pa."

Willie Bob was quiet. Curtye Lee saw a tear at the corner of his eye.

"I'm sorry. I didn't mean to make you sad, Willie. I guess you miss your pa."

"He killed hisself. Just like that. And he was gone."

His stark words surprised Curtye Lee, and then Willie was crying. He bent over into Curtye's lap, sobbing. His body jerked with his cries.

"Oh, Willie. I didn't know. I'm sorry I pushed for you to talk about it. I'm sorry." She ran her hand over his shoulders and stroked his head. "I'd no idea."

"No one does." He sat up. "No one knows 'cause Mama hid it. Don't know how she hid the truth, but I found the death certificate at the bottom of a drawer one night. In January. Saw what really happened written in black and white, and I remembered that night like it was yesterday."

He had to catch his breath, and his body lurched with spasms.

"Pa knew he was losing the farm. Ma called him a loser. Kept repeatin' it. 'Loser' in the most hateful voice. He went to the bedroom and came back to say he'd be in the barn. Ma was still yellin' at him as he left. He never came back. I just remember the wind blowin', and he never came back."

Tears fell from Curtye Lee's eyes. She held him tight until his body calmed down, and then, of a sudden, he snapped back to his self. He'd realized he'd allowed himself to be seen as weak and slugged down some beer. Leaned back on the sofa.

"Don't know what got into me," he said.

"I'm sorry, Willie. Really." She pulled him close, and he kissed her with a passion like that day at the barn. Needy.

"Not feeling that sorry for you, Willie. Let's have that dessert."

"I want you for dessert."

Curtye Lee stood up and took his hand.

"Let's go. That's not gonna work." She pulled him up and toward the kitchen, wondering if the tears and story had been a way to get her into bed, but she knew his pain had been real and knew Mrs. Preston well enough to believe that scene might have just happened as he described it.

They ate ice cream in the kitchen, talked of Willie Bob's favorite horse and his next rodeo, and laughed awkwardly. Willie Bob had given up wooing Curtye Lee into the bedroom.

"You gotta take me home, Willie. I don't want there to be any more talk about me and my wily ways than there already is in this town." She set her bowl in the sink. "Thank you for supper, Willie. I love ya for doing it for me. And for sharing with me tonight."

Willie Bob finished his ice cream. "It's nothin'."

At the curb in front of Sue's boarding house, Willie Bob gave Curtye Lee a peck on the cheek and said goodnight. As she readied herself for bed, she wondered just how far Willie Bob would go to get her back in bed. *Had she made a mistake coming to Dalhart ... or was this cowboy she'd followed to Texas so broken he couldn't be the man she hoped for?*

Chapter 11

The door at Crawford's was unlocked when I arrived on a bitterly cold day, and I found Curtye Lee sitting inside. She'd stayed after her work shift had ended and was tidying up the back room.

"Hey, Curtye Lee, thanks for straightening up the room. I'm afraid what we might find on these messy shelves, but we'll only be here once a month."

"Oh, I saw no need to go home. It's so cold outside. I've got the mysticism book here." She pointed to the table. "Jane's gonna' bring the novel. That was a crazy read."

I'd only seen the room once, briefly, when Gene Crawford showed me where it was. The table was cleared, so I set the thermos of coffee down and unwrapped the cupcakes. There were four straight-back chairs around the oak table, a faded old chintz easy chair, and a couple of odd chairs near the shelves. More than we needed. The floor lamp behind the easy chair was a bit dim.

"Dibs on the soft chair," said Curtye Lee.

"Dear, you can have it. You're a brave girl 'cause that frayed chair's got its share of stains. Want some coffee?"

"I do." Curtye Lee fell into the comfort of the old chair and took the warm cup from Shelby. "I'm so excited about our group. Been a while since I was in school and learnin'."

"Well, you know Jane was a teacher, so I'm sure she's excited about it." I poured hot coffee into my cup and stirred it. I'd added a bit of sugar and cream back at the house, believing none of us drank it black. Well, sometimes Jane did, and I heard her at the front door and walked out to greet her. The gust of a frigid wind came in the door with her, and I locked the storefront, leaving old man Winter outside.

"Well, girls, this was some interesting reading. Miss Underhill must have been a fascinating woman," said Jane as she took hot coffee from me and sat at the table.

"I'm gonna' say right now, after going to the library, I'm not sure how much is out there for us to read and study, but I reckon Esther and I will keep trying to find some books or magazines."

"I've heard there's quite a resurgence of mysticism in the big cities. Going on now. Just not in the Bible Belt," said Jane. "Can we eat these cupcakes?"

"Sure, Jane. It's why I brought 'em." Curtye Lee and Jane both reached over and took one.

"Thank you, Shelby."

"I just finished reading this novel. Had to read when Henry wasn't home," said Jane before taking a bite of her cupcake. "He usually pays no mind to my reading, but once in a while, he'll pick up a book and scan through it with curiosity."

"What did you think of it?" I asked.

"First of all, it's written in current times. Just not our current times. And the perspective of the young boy. Such imagination. How Underhill tied healing to the crafting of art. Overcoming loneliness. Oh, the tragedy of it." Jane looked at me. "Shelby, I can't believe you found this treasure. In Texas. I will rethink this sad story for some time to come."

"Well," said Curtye Lee, "the words were old-timey to me, but I felt the gray right away. Like the little boy, the writer carried me to that unseen place. Being dead, but he keeps looking for connection. Like the writer describes in the other book. It made me sad, though."

"Yes. Me too," I said. "That opening line from a play—those words gripped my heart. Made me think so much of the dust years and all the loss of that. *Death .... Snatches us as a cross nurse might do.* Oh, my. Those words took me right back to the 1930s.

And this little boy searching for his way. I didn't understand, in the beginning, about the mother giving him the bread that killed him."

"Yes, its vagueness makes the reader wonder about the time and place," said Jane. "Maybe she did that on purpose—because of mystery. This story reminds me of Edgar Allen Poe's line from one of his short stories: *The boundaries which divide Life from Death are at best shadowy and vague. Who shall say where the one ends and where the other begins?*"

"Ooh, that's good, Jane. What about *Practical Mysticism?*" asked Curtye Lee. "So different than the other book—the story."

"Well," said Jane. "She ties a lot of this book to her religious beliefs, but that's not surprising since much of mysticism originates in religion. And paganism." She picked up the book and lay it down again. "You know, Henry would never admit this, but some of our own religion mimics pagan rituals."

"Really? Underwood talks about God and the light," I said, "and how they are in us and all around us. And she keeps comparing it to reality, which confuses me a bit."

Curtye Lee picked up the book and flipped through it. "I love this, in Chapter 3: *That invulnerable spark of vivid life, that 'inward light' which these men find at their own centres when they seek for it, is for them an earnest of the Uncreated Light, the ineffable splendour of God, swelling, and energizing within the heart of things.*"

"Yes," said Jane. "That is beautiful—the inward light. Yes. Curtye Lee, that *spark of vivid life* reminds me of you."

"Aww, Jane. That's sweet."

"Give me the book, Curtye Lee. There's a short piece that spoke to me." I thumbed through the pages to it. "Here it is: *At the centre there is a stillness which even you are not able to break. There, the rhythm of your duration is one with the rhythm of the Universal Life.*" I closed the book. "I can't say I understand all the meanings behind her notions, but this did move my heart. Maybe it's from all the years I've lived on the prairie. The stillness and the rhythm. The rhythm of everything. It rings so true. And feels like the mystery we seek here—here in this group and even out in the world we live in."

The room fell silent for a few moments, all the words sinking in.

"I saw it in our darkest days," I continued, "right after the black storms passed. I still feel it out in the pastures on a quiet day and in my precious early hours before the children wake."

"Well," said Curtye Lee, "I think both books will force me to see more. Beyond what I think, I see and feel. To see more from the heart."

"Curtye Lee," said Jane, "I'm so glad you encouraged us to do this. Your curiosity and big heart inspire me."

"To change the subject," I said, "I'm crushed that Joe Tippett felt he needed to step down as deacon. The gossip's run amok about his granddaughter's being pregnant and that she's been sent to visit family near Fort Worth. Where is our compassion?"

"That's why Mr. Tippett has stepped away?" said Curtye Lee. "I had no idea."

"Yes, our little community can be that way. Perfection required in a world where we all fall short." I said, passing out the remaining cupcakes.

"Well, I pray for the family," said Jane. "For Janet Tippett, so young, and for Joe. I'll keep working on Henry. Really, I don't think Henry wanted him to go, but when Joe stepped down, Henry didn't argue with him."

"Well, all of that's a shame. It's not like teenagers haven't been doing that forever," I said. "Give me the books. I'm making another trip to Amarillo. We're going down to my cousin's for Easter."

The three of us indulged in a bit of our own gossip and talk of events at church and about the town.

"Thanks, Shelby," said Curtye Lee. "I really enjoyed this talk tonight. And reading the books."

"Yes, me too," said Jane, turning out the room lamp. "We'll walk out with you, Shelby."

Bitter cold greeted us as we left the store.

"You be careful getting home, Shelby," said Jane. "I'm certain there's ice on the road. Call me when you're home safe." Curtye Lee jumped into the passenger side of Jane's car as snow fell. Before I opened my car door, I looked down the street to see a winter beauty as the snowflakes fell over a couple of cars parked on Denrock Street, and the whole scene was lit by the eerie glow of dim yellow and red neon lights and the streetlamps. It was a beauty I'd seldom seen, and fleetingly, little Dalhart looked like a wonderland.

I drove slowly on the dark road out of town toward home, watching for slippery spots. It would all be ice in the morning. I thought of all those years in the wrathful skies when I was young. The struggles and loss of Grandma and little Paul. So young and Pa's only son. So many others. And I thought of the young boy in *The Grey World*, how he lived on after death and endured such loneliness. Searched for meaning. *Did my brother struggle so? Craving to be with us?* I might have to read that book again before I take it to Esther. I wished I could meet the woman who wrote it, but she might be in her own gray world now, searching for the connections she wrote about in her graceful old-timey sentences. I was heartened to see the glow of the porch light as I neared the gate to our ranch.

Chapter 12

March always held the promise of spring, but in this drought, green was still scarce on the plains as Jane drove southeast toward Denton on a Wednesday morning, full of guilt for having been less than truthful to her husband. When Henry had insisted that she spend the night and not make that long trip to and back in one day, she'd written to her friend, Amy Goodwin, who now taught history to wannabe teachers and historians at the college.

"I think while I'm there, I'll stop by and check on Janet Tippett," she said to Henry, not sharing that was her purpose for the trip all along.

"That's a good idea, Jane. You are the best pastor's wife I've ever been married to," and he winked at her.

It was about 2:30 in the afternoon when she parked in the lot at The Stone Cottage in Denton. It looked familiar but updated. New shutters painted dark green and shrubs around the foundation had livened up the house. The sign read The Stone Cottage and, in smaller script, A Home for Young Mothers. Jane was amused with how they'd omitted the word *unwed.* On the porch, a young woman full of new life sat reading a book as she rocked in a wooden chair, and Jane stood there for a few moments, her hand on the handle of the door, before she'd breathed in all the confidence she could find and opened the door.

"Can I help you, ma'am?" said a middle-aged, aproned woman who walked in from the kitchen.

"Why, yes, you can. I'd like to visit a bit with Miss Janet Tippett."

"Are you family?" the woman asked.

"No. I'm the pastor's wife. From her church." The woman introduced herself and said she'd get Janet. "Just go find a seat in the living room." She pointed to the large room through the archway, but Jane knew where the living room was. She'd once lived here. "Make yourself comfortable."

Jane sat in the caned straight-back chair, leaving the comfortable chairs for Janet to choose. There was new artwork on the walls, cheerier than she'd remembered back in the late thirties. Janet Tippett's eyes lit up like a lamp when she walked into the room and saw Jane sitting there.

"Oh, Mrs. Connor. I cannot believe you came to visit me. All this way," said Janet as she gave Jane a brief hug and settled into an overstuffed chair.

"Oh, I've been wanting to visit, but it's a long way to get here," said Jane. "I've come down to visit with a friend at the college. I knew you probably felt abandoned here. It's hard being away from home when so young, and everything changes so quickly."

Janet smiled.

"You look wonderful, Janet. Glowing, like they say pregnant women do. You're one of those who glow."

Jane sensed the poor girl felt embarrassed by her condition in the presence of the pastor's wife, and Jane scooted her chair closer to Janet.

"Thank you, Mrs. Connor."

"Just truth. I can't stay long, and I know you're probably on a schedule here. But I want you to know we haven't forgotten you. And I brought you two books to read for your lonely hours. I know the nights are sometimes long, but these books are full of storytelling and wisdom a girl might need at a time like this." She handed the books *The Little Prince* and *A Tree Grows in Brooklyn* to Janet, and then, Jane lowered her voice to a whisper.

"And I want you to know that I've been here before, Janet. Lived here when I was young. About your age—my parents sent me, but I miscarried my child. Or I should say, she just came too early to survive. I ask for your confidence in this because only my parents know. But you—you are a young woman. Your own person, so make your choices carefully. If I can tell you anything, it's that only you can choose your path. Don't be swayed by others or gossip or ridicule. Be swayed only by what's best for you and your child."

"I didn't know," said Janet. "You. You were here."

"Yes, I was," whispered Jane. "And look at me now. Everything turned out alright for me as it will for you."

Jane saw tears in the girl's eyes. She reached for the girl's hand and squeezed it before she stood to leave.

"I can't tell you what to do, but you stand strong. And I'll send you notes when I can, just to remind you that you are still part of our church family. Part of our community. That you are loved no matter what you decide."

Jane stood and gave Janet a long hug, the promise of new life profound between them. She smiled at the girl and walked away, full of memories of the days she spent here before her life moved on to college and an unknown future. The memory of that year when she'd learned the weight of choices.

Jane drove slowly through the campus in Denton, seeing the changes and those places that had stayed the same. She spent the evening visiting with her friend and meeting her family, and the two women compared the joys and dilemmas of their years teaching. Jane knew she might never see her friend again, invited her to visit Dalhart, and promised to stay in touch before she began her drive back to Dalhart early the next morning so as to arrive in the afternoon, just in time to start a meal before Henry arrived home.

"Well, how was your visit with Amy? Did you rehash the

good old days?" asked Henry after he kissed his wife.

"A wonderful visit. But, oh, it's such a long drive, yet it was nice to see the campus again. And my friend."

"Did you stop to check in on Janet Tippett?" asked Henry.

"I did. She looks well. Lonesome, as one would expect."

"I don't understand this ritual of sending the girls away to visit some fictional family member," said Henry. "Seldom does anyone believe such a ruse, and these girls need their mothers in such a time."

Jane looked at her husband in wonder.

"Well, dear, you are clearly more evolved than most men. And women, I should say. I don't understand it either, but I know they believe they are protecting a daughter. Or a son that did wrong. A reputation. It's still a shame." She set plates and flatware on the table. "But ... it's been going on since time began. Too much reproach in our small world."

"You know. That day you walked through the doors of my new church was the luckiest day of my life," said Henry. "How can I help?"

"Pour some tea into those glasses of ice," she said as Henry kissed Jane's cheek.

Chapter 13

It was Easter Sunday as Jim drove the Chevy down the highway toward Amarillo with all four of us in the car, plus a basket of food for supper at Esther's and a small ham and pumpkin pie to drop off at Uncle Joe's home. Joe had been invited to join us at Esther's but had declined, understandably, since he had trouble walking and getting around, always preferring to stay home. As we headed south, the fields looked eager for the sprouts to come, all plowed and seeded, and clouds and gusting winds still lingered, threatening rain. Welcome rain in our perpetual drought.

"Can we see the donkey?" asked Jimmy.

"Yes, after supper at Esther's, we'll go to Uncle Joe's farm for a short visit," I said and turned toward Jim. "I don't know how Joe manages to care for those animals."

"He manages, slowly, because it gives him a reason to get up in the morning," said Jim, and I felt a deep sadness and a bigger love for Uncle Joe.

As Jim explored Hank's new radio equipment and Billy pestered Lorene as she took a walk down the street, thinking she could escape family, Esther and I busied ourselves in the kitchen, pulling together a fine meal. As we worked, we chatted, in our quiet voices, about my meetings in Dalhart with Jane and Curtye Lee. Esther said she'd found a book for us, and I told her I'd brought the other two back. We'd exchange them later.

"Is that Curtye Lee still datin' the rodeo boy? Billie Bob?"

"It's Willie Bob, and she is. Surprised it's lasted this long," I said, pulling a casserole from the oven. "We had a great talk on those two books from your library. Just makes us wanna know more."

"Good. So, tell me more about that young Curtye Lee. Odd name for a girl."

"Well, I told you she's a looker. Pretty girl, but no conceit to go with it. Like she doesn't even know she's a knockout. Curious, which likely explains her courage to follow a boy to Texas. She likes the horses and rides with me at the ranch."

"Well, I can tell ya like her. Hope ta meet her one day," said Esther as she arranged things on the dressed-up table. "You go yell for the kids, and I'll get the boys."

We ate a fine meal with the six of us gathered around Esther's small dining room table as gusting winds rattled the windows.

"Gotta reframe some of them windas," said Hank as he sliced ham. "Darn poor plannin', us getting old at the same time this house starts creakin'."

"Happens to us all like that," said Esther, and she stood up with her plate in hand. "Dessert. Now or later?"

"Well, we're going over to visit Joe," said Jim.

"Yes, we'll have a bit of dessert now," I said. "We can visit a little longer. Let's make some fresh coffee." I took some plates and followed Esther to the kitchen.

"Can I be excused?" I heard Lorene ask Jim, thinking her daddy would give her the answer she wanted.

"No," I called back to her. "We're having dessert."

We talked for almost an hour over dessert. Hank talking about his new high-frequency transceiver and other radio enthusiasts he'd met across the country and a couple overseas. Jim asking questions. Lorene rolling her eyes, and Billy asking for seconds. When we finished, I sent Lorene to the kitchen to start washing dishes, and Esther and I went to her bedroom, where I pulled the two Anne Underhill books out from under the towel at the bottom of the box that had held the deviled eggs.

"Here," I said, handing the books to Esther. "Thank you."

Esther took them and pulled another book from her dressing table. Handed it to me.

"*The Way of Mysticism*," I read from the cover. "Joseph James. That sounds right up our alley."

"Y'all are downright ornery. And I love it," said Esther, full of enthusiasm. "Hank and I don't worry about all those rules anymore. I'm one of them wayward Methodists. We go to church on a whim."

"I sometimes think Jim's that way, but he's a deacon, so he's tied to the church. And, of course, there's Jane and Henry, so I don't think we'd get away with being delinquent. It's the community I love. I already know the Lord loves me."

"You're a stronger woman than me," said Esther, as I buried the new book beneath the dishtowel and carried the box to the kitchen to place the cleaned dishes in it. I took over at the sink and told Lorene to go find Billy and tell him we needed to go.

"I think he's with your pa in Hank's radio room," I said.

We spent almost two hours at Uncle Joe's farm, giving the kids enough time in the barn. Billy took a ride on the mule, and we each had a small piece of pumpkin pie with Joe.

"We'll come down at Thanksgiving. Have supper with ya, Uncle Joe," said Jim. "But I'll be back this summer, if not sooner."

The old man's loneliness was unmistakable. Made me sad in my heart to know he had no family in town and most of his friends had passed. Made me sad to know this was the path for most of us unless we died young.

As we drove home, Jim was quiet, so I turned on the radio, finding one of Lorene's favorite stations. Billy had fallen asleep before the car left Amarillo's city limits, and it would turn dark before we arrived at the ranch. With my stomach full, my mind wandered to thoughts of my mom. To the past. For a farm wife who'd married young, at seventeen, she had a fair share of spunk, which I knew was what had carried her through all her hardships. Kept us on track, and when Pa died five years ago, she was hell-bent on living a good life near friends and family, which is why she stayed at the house in town Pa had bought as an investment in the hard times. I wanted to be more like her. Learn how to embrace her joy in friendship and humor. After all the struggle and grief of those years before, she'd learned to carry no weight of the hardships. She was a gift to me, and I suddenly felt sad that my sister in California had not seen this side of our mother.

When I saw that Lorene had fallen asleep, I switched the radio to a classic station out of Oklahoma.

"That's better," said Jim, his voice slicing the silence and reminding me I was not alone.

Chapter 14

It was our scheduled Tuesday evening in April when I walked into the back room at Crawford's department store to find Curtye Lee with her nose in the book, so immersed she didn't even look up. As I set a plate of brownies on the oak table, I thought I should have first wiped it down with something sanitizing. God knows we were in old Crawford's poker room.

"Some coffee, Curtye Lee?" I asked.

She looked at me and smiled.

"Yep. Thanks, Shelby." She marked her page and laid the book in her lap. "You know, I'm certain Dalhart's put a curse on me."

I handed her a mug full of hot coffee.

"Really?" I said. "Watch it, Curtye Lee. It's hot." I pulled another mug from my basket and filled it from the thermos. "So, why do ya think you've been cursed?"

Curtye Lee took a sip and grimaced.

"Whoa." She blew into her cup. "Well, Willie Bob hasn't called me since we went bowling last week. Hasn't returned my calls. His mama still snubs me at the church. And today ... well, the wind blew my hair into knots and sent those rascally tumbleweeds through town."

"Wow. That's quite a curse. What's that book say about curses?"

"Not a flippin' thing," replied Curtye Lee, and our laughter filled the somber room like music at a honky-tonk. I looked at the shelves along the wall, all the things tossed there, and wondered if it was all watching us, as if the deck of cards, the cigar boxes, the sports magazines had eyes. Ears. How strange the laughter of women must sound to them.

Jane was late, and as she hurried in, her face held a frown.

"I just—just before I left the house—got a call from my father. He said Mother is ill, and I need to come, so I'm leaving tomorrow. For Santa Fe. I wish they hadn't moved back there, but they love New Mexico, its culture and the mountains, so much that one cannot deny that kind of contentment."

"Oh, Jane. I'm sorry about your mama," said Curtye Lee. "I'll pray I get to meet her. One day soon. Every night, I'll send up a prayer till you're back home."

I hugged Jane and remembered how her mother had always been so fastidious, trying so hard to keep her house clean while the skies dropped more dust every day and then they moved away. Jane and I sat at the round table, and Curtye Lee stayed in her favorite overstuffed chair. She seemed not to be bothered as much by its stains and tattered seams as Jane and I were. "It's lived in," she'd once said, but I could only imagine what "lived-in" shenanigans might have happened in the back of Crawford's store.

"Well, we'd planned to talk about shamans at this meeting, and we have a new book that Curtye Lee has absorbed, *The Way of Mysticism*," I said. "Where shall we begin?"

"I'll talk about what I found in the book first," said Curtye Lee. "There's plenty a references to the Bible here, but this book also mentions ancient works. I don't know all the ancient writings or names written about, but there's not much in this book of what we're looking for."

"Well, you looked pretty absorbed in its pages," I said.

"Yeah. There's a bunch of good quotes here. Meaningful sayings. Or, more exactly, quite a few that interest me and, likely, would speak to y'all. It's odd how the writer starts this book off by mentioning the massive bomb we dropped on

Japan. He says how man—meaning humans, I s'pose—has this need to destroy man and his enemies, and he quotes a man he calls Sir Jeans. But who is that, and who is the fella writing this—this Joseph James?"

"I know nothing about the author," said Jane, "but Sir Jeans is an English physicist. He wrote *The Mysterious Universe*. Why don't you read a few quotes you like from the book, Curtye Lee?"

Curtye Lee paused and flipped through the pages as she sat up straight.

"Here's one: *Man sleeps, but the forces of nature rest not either night or day; no one considers how they go on—while all take delight in the beauty of the fields and fruit of the pastures. So is love manifest in the same way; it presupposes that love is present like the germ in the corn,* and there's more by someone called Kierkegaard. I don't know who that is."

"He was a philosopher from Copenhagen. In Demark," said Jane. "And more? Read another one."

"Here's another: *We may know we have had the vision when the soul has suddenly taken light,* by Plotinus, whoever he is. And another by Kierkegaard: *As God dwells in a light from which every ray of light which illumines the world issues, yet by none of these ways can a man enter in order to see God; for the way of light changes to darkness if one faces the light: so love dwells in secret ....* The quote ends with this: *So the life of love is hidden, but its secret life is itself in motion and has eternity in it.* I'm not sure what it all means. Sounds a bit ghostly to me and full of a depth I'd need to ponder to understand. And though all these writings relate to God, I believe spirits and omens are part of God. Some people dream of things that will happen, and then it does."

"Well, I agree," said Jane. "But don't tell Henry I said that."

"This writer calls those who seek to understand and dialogue with God 'mystics.' Isn't that what we're doing in searching for the mysterious?" I asked. "Mr. James calls us 'seekers.' I like that. We are seekers."

"I think we are," said Jane. "You know, there's a line by John Locke—not in this book—that speaks to me. Always has, but probably 'cause of all I learned from children when I was teaching. Something like: *there's frequently more to be learned from the unexpected questions of a child than the discourses of men.*" Jane paused in a reverie. "But I'd like to read that book, Curtye Lee, and believe I'll risk taking it home, or rather on my trip to Santa Fe, if that's okay, Shelby."

"Sure. I don't know when I'll get back to Amarillo, and I'm sure Esther can arrange with her friend at the library for us to keep it longer."

"Well, let's talk about healers," said Curtye Lee. "I remember the Osage and the tribes in Colorado relied on healers, sometimes calling 'em medicine men. At times, the men were women, such as with the Cherokee, as I've heard from Pa's stories. I don't know the Cherokee. I've met some tribal healers in the Colorado mountains—a couple Osage hunters—and Pa was familiar with men and women of the Ute tribes, including the healers some called shamans. When I hunted with Pa, I'd see him take offers of their potions and herbs. And some tribes danced to their spirits for healing, the Bear Dance and the Sun Dance, as if calling to spirits for help, but I've only heard of such from Pa's stories. Never seen 'em dance."

"You know the church would call that pagan. Did it work?" I asked.

"The herbs often eased a complaint. Once, when I was overcome with a rash, Pa took me to an old Ute woman in the valley. She gave Pa a mix of muddled greens in a bag that held a long feather, and the poultice worked. Pa swore by their healing powers. I'm not sure about their calls to spirits, and Pa was doubtful of such, but he'd tell me they knew much about the plants and trees of the mountains."

"I can't say I know much about it. There aren't many greens around here," said Jane, chuckling, "but the tribes around Santa Fe and Taos, I've heard, had natural remedies that were said to be helpful and were used by locals."

The very topic of Santa Fe and healing seemed to distract Jane as I watched her hands begin to grasp and turn the other. Worry crept over her face.

"I think that's enough about shamans and spirits for tonight," I said. "I'm glad to see Joe and Beulah Tippett back at the church. Literally, at the back of the church, but at least they've returned."

Jane sighed a deep sigh.

"Will the family keep the baby?" asked Curtye Lee.

"Not likely," said Jane, "but we'll see. At this point, they can't pretend it's not Janet's, and if she comes home an unwed mother ... well, we'll see. What makes me sad is how much Joe and Beulah would love a grandchild."

With those words, the mood faded dimmer than the naked bulb in the floor lamp behind the old chintz chair.

"Well, shall we choose a topic for our next meeting in May? Do you believe you'll be back by the middle of May, Jane?" I asked.

"I'm not sure. Let's leave it open and just bring our questions for next time," said Jane. "Maybe you can find a novel or story for us, Shelby. Maybe something ghostly." My friend managed a flimsy smile.

"Well, I'll do one better'n that." I pulled a book from my bag. "Here is Edith Wharton's *Ghost Stories*. My cousin mailed it to me, and I think Curtye Lee should read it first. I've already read some of it, and Jane can read it after you, Curtye Lee." I reached to hand the book to Curtye Lee and paused.

"Wait. Jane, do you want to take it to Santa Fe?"

"Oh, no. Let Curtye Lee read it, and I'll pick it up when I get home. I'll just take this blue book by Joseph James and meander through all these quotes," said Jane as she fanned through the pages of the book. "Perhaps I'll find a few inspiring Bible quotes for Henry to build upon for his next sermon," said Jane in a fading voice that seemed addressed to herself more than those of us here in the room.

I gave Edith Wharton's book to Curtye Lee and passed the plate around with the last three brownies, one for each of us. The coffee was gone.

As I drove back to the ranch, I thought of Jane and her mother. Her parents had grown elderly since I'd last seen them. Before she'd gone off to college, Jane had the experience of living in a place so rich in Indian cultures, whereas we, in north Texas, had driven the tribes away decades ago. Jane never talked much about her life in Santa Fe, and now, I wondered why, yet clearly, her parents had loved it enough to return. I'd experienced nothing but the winds and prairies of north Texas. Been to Oklahoma a couple of times and once over to Clovis in New Mexico. As I drove toward our ranch, the night skies were dark with stars that sparkled like jewels, and I thought of the words Curtye Lee had read about God's light and wondered what secrets were held in the darkness. I suddenly felt small and vulnerable and was surprised to find it comforting.

Chapter 15

Henry and Jane left early Wednesday morning on the five-hour drive to Santa Fe. The morning was clear and sprinkled with white clouds, and the pink dawn followed behind them as they drove west. It was decided Henry would spend a couple of nights and drive home on Saturday morning since they only had the one car, a 1946 Packard Clipper Henry had purchased in Amarillo, and though Jane was familiar with the drive, she did not want to leave Henry without the car because, as the pastor, he often had unexpected visitations to make.

"I don't suppose you have any idea how long you'll be gone," said Henry as he drove across the New Mexico state line.

"No, dear. I hope no more than two weeks, but Papa didn't reveal details of Mother's illness. Both Beulah Tippett and Marcy from next door promised to drop off a casserole every few days, so you can just heat them up."

Jane noticed Henry wince at the mention of Beulah. She knew her husband still reeled from Joe Tippett stepping down as the church's deacon.

"All Papa said was Mother was quite sick, and it'd be helpful if I came," continued Jane. "It's hard to measure someone's tone on the telephone, but he'd sounded worried, which, in turn, worries me. Bless his heart, for I know he was likely trying to spare me any burden."

"Well, you will be missed at home, but I'm glad we live close enough so you can see your parents. I know how much your mother loves Santa Fe and the mountains, but I do wish they'd stayed in town near us."

Henry turned and looked over at his wife, who, for the trip, had worn her navy slacks with a white button-down shirt, crocheted edging on the collar. How she always pulled herself together so seamlessly never went unnoticed by her husband. "I know you've gotten close to our newest member, Curtye Lee Logan, but she's not been at church much lately. How's she doing?"

"I think she's struggling with Blanche Preston's cold shoulder and just how slippery Willie Bob is to tie down. I think we all knew any long-term commitment was unlikely, right? It sounds to me like she and Willie Preston might be on the outs which is about true to the length of the boy's relationships."

"Sorry to hear that," said Henry. "Not much prospect of a future with that young fellow. In our brief visits with Curtye Lee, she's come across as a smart girl, though I know that's not how some see her. Miss Logan seems to have a generous heart. Let's hope she finds someone more suitable."

"Well, I'm afraid she'll return to Colorado, so Shelby and I keep trying to persuade her to stay. She brings a much-needed lightness and youth to Dalhart. God knows we need that. And at the church."

Henry smiled and reached over for his wife's hand.

"Maybe I'll stop by Sue Jones' boarding house for a visit one evening for some tea with Curtye Lee and the ladies," said Henry, his eyes on the depth of the road moving west.

The small adobe house at the northeast edge of Santa Fe welcomed Jane and Henry with its charm, but an odd stillness surrounded the house except for one old man ambling down the sidewalk. Jane wondered if the neighborhood was always this serene.

Henry took the suitcase and train case from the trunk as Jane walked to the door and knocked, and it took only a moment before her father greeted them.

"Oh, Papa," said Jane, hugging her father. "So good to see you."

"Glad you're here, Dear. Hey, Henry." The two men shook hands. "You're both looking well. I am sorry to drag you away from home, but the doctor doesn't give me much confidence of Mother's getting well, and I'm not sure I can deal with this alone." A glimpse of hope passed onto Jane's father's face. "Jane, your arrival will bring some light to the house."

"Well, Papa, speaking of light, it's terribly dark in here," said Jane as she walked through the front room and pulled the curtains back from a window to draw more sunlight into the room.

"Oh, I know. I've been spending all my time in the kitchen and our bedroom, so I don't even notice the house. Your mother's in the bedroom."

"What does the doctor say, Jon?" asked Henry.

"Later. We'll talk later," said Jane. "I'm going in to see Mother."

"I think she's awake," said Papa.

Jane found her mother sitting up in her bed, supported by pillows at her back, a book in her hand.

"How are you doing, Mother? I see you're still voraciously consuming novels," said Jane, taking the book from her mother. She looked down to see it was the new Daphne du Maurier novel, *Rebecca*.

"Ah, Mother, that's an excellent story. Can I get you anything? A drink?"

"No, dear. I recently read her novel, *My Cousin Rachel*."

"Really? Some women in a church group whispered about that novel. About it being quite racy."

"Yes. An interesting tale it was," and Mother smiled an impish smile. "I'm so glad to see you. I hate that Jon dragged you away from home. Did Henry come?"

"Yes, he did. He's talking to Papa, and he'll stay a bit before going home."

"I sleep a lot these days. Doctor's orders. I think my heart's turned old before my brain has pickled, and I'm not at all happy about that."

Jane hugged her mother.

"Is there any medicine?" Jane asked.

"Yes, but it's not a cure. Just gets me through the days, but look," and she pointed to the window. "Spring is in full bloom. At times, I go into the courtyard, and that is where I'm happiest. But you already know that."

"Yes, I do, Mother. After I unpack and when you feel up to it, let's go sit out there," said Jane.

Jane and her mother sat in the courtyard for part of the afternoon.

"Dear Jane, I'm so glad you're here. I wouldn't want to leave this world without seeing you again."

"Oh, Mother. Me either." Jane held back tears. Mother didn't need that. "I've been a lucky girl, having you and Papa as my parents."

Mother fell asleep in the chaise lawn chair as Jane read a magazine and breathed in the abundance of honeysuckle. She recalled her teenage years living here in Santa Fe and how vital spring and summer could be. It had become their respite from the horrors in the Texas Panhandle, and she had missed her friends left behind in the dust and sorrow. She recalled her best friend's letter recounting the death of her little brother and then her grandmother from the dust pneumonia. Over recent years, she'd been negligent in speaking of that with her friend and promised herself she'd do better. She remembered the summer days in Santa Fe, how the days could be hot but the nights frequently cool. And then, just as she'd almost finished high school, she'd gone off to Denton in Texas.

Henry walked out with two tall glasses of iced tea, one for her and Mother, but since Mother was asleep, he sat down next to his wife.

"It's pleasant here. I do understand why your parents love Santa Fe," he said. "Besides, he worked those years here, at the newspaper, and has all his old friends."

Jane wondered if Henry would want to live here but knew he'd never leave his church. His congregation he'd worked so hard to build. He'd come from back east, and she sometimes wondered why he'd settled for the small community and big skies of life on the plains. No forests. No fields of the Georgia sweet corn he talked about all the time.

"Well, Henry, if my parents had not moved back to Dalhart when the storms ended and when, at the same time, you so eagerly showed up to build that new church, you and I would never have met. Maybe it was fate? Predestined?"

Henry laughed his easy laugh and smiled at Jane.

"I believe it was God's plan all along," he said, "but you knew I'd say that." He winked at his wife.

Jane fixed supper from what she found in the kitchen and refrigerator, promising to go to the store in the morning, and Papa fixed a tray he took into his wife. Later, after Jane's mother had gone to sleep, Jane and Henry met in the living room with Papa. Papa was a distinguished-looking man, mustached and dressed in casual brown slacks, a blue challis shirt, and suspenders, a contrast to the well-worn suit Jane remembered him wearing when he worked at the *Santa Fe Examiner* years before.

"Ruby's doctor made it clear that there's not more he could do beyond the digitalis medicine. He said to keep her rested and limit fluids that could build up in her chest and impact her breathing. We've had our conversations." He paused, reached over and put his hand on Jane's. "Your mother's accepted her fate and, one day, mine to follow. We both know that we all have such a fate, and it is seldom well-planned. Or welcomed, but I don't know what I'll do without her."

The three of us sat silent, having heard Papa's somber words.

"Jon, you have us, and you know we'd welcome you in Dalhart when the time comes. Or, for that matter, both of you now, if you wish," said Henry.

"Oh, Henry. You are the son I wish I'd had, my only son, but this land became our home when we moved here in the thirties. It was salvation, and we were never as comforted as we were here, which is why we came back. Ruby wants to be buried here, as do I. I'm sorry, Jane, but that is our decision. There is something about Santa Fe that's spiritual. It comforts us."

Jane perked up at her father's words. She thought of her friends back home and their secret meetings and remembered the book she had brought with her, *The Art of Mysticism*.

"Well, Jon," said Henry, "I can understand that. It's important to feel at one with our Maker. As well as the land that loves us back."

Jane looked at her husband, a bit surprised at his words and filled with the love she carried for him.

Chapter 16

The day had finally come, a rodeo in Dalhart, and Curtye Lee dressed in her red ruffled skirt, even added her old crinoline, and her worn cowboy boots. She looked out her window to see if Willie Bob's truck had arrived, but no one was there. She'd left her hair down but tied a red bandanna at her neck in case she wanted, later, to tie up her hair, and she put on her rosy lipstick as she heard the engine of a familiar pickup.

"Willie, today's the day. To see ya ride that bull, but I don't wanna see it throw and stomp on ya. It won't, will it?" she asked as she settled into the front seat close to her beau. She'd be arriving early since Willie Bob had to be at the arena in time to check his schedule.

"I hope not—but surely, I'll hit the dirt a time or two at some point. Can't stay on them beasts forever." He leaned over for a quick kiss. "You're lookin' mighty purty."

As she'd expected, the stands were almost empty, but there was a lot of activity near the pens holding the animals. A costumed clown walked 'round the fences. She hadn't sat there long before Willie Bob's friend Colt showed up and sat next to her.

"How ya doin'?" he asked.

"Just waitin' to watch Willie ride."

"Oh, it'll be a bit. I'll keep ya company," said Colt. "Can't believe a girl as purty as you used to go huntin' in the mountains. Never been to the mountains 'cept when we'd ride a rodeo over in New Mexico. I know Willie Bob rides up there—in Colorado. That's how he met ya, right?"

"Yep."

"You're a brave girl, comin' all this way to Texas."

"Maybe foolish, huh?" Curtye Lee pulled her sweater tight around her shoulders against the morning chill of late spring.

"Ya cold?" He snuggled closer to her and put his arm over her shoulder.

"A little." She stood up for a minute, his arm falling away.

"Ya leaving?"

"No. Just stretching my legs." She sat, putting more distance between them. "Did you always live here, in Dalhart?"

"Born and probably die here. I help Pop at his farm. One day it'll be mine s'pose. Ain't sure I wanna be a farmer. Man, Pa works like a dog. Maybe I'll run cattle one day."

The bleachers began to fill, and the clown was joking around with the crowd. A calf he kept half-heartedly trying to rope awkwardly skipped about. Both of them put on a show.

"You're looking like a flower out here in that red skirt," said Colt as he adjusted the brim of his hat. "And ya haven't come out to the barn to visit us."

Curtye Lee wondered if she should even mention she'd been out at the barn and decided not to.

"That's where Theo lives, right?"

"Yep. A fine ranch."

"I've gone riding out at Shelby's ranch. The Hauser place."

"Oh, Jim. He works out at Welch's Grain Company. See him all the time. When I'm pickin' up supplies. He came down here—to Texas—when I was just a boy. With the gov'ment. Married the Garrigan girl. I knew her brother, Paul, when I was a runt. We were best friends 'for he died in those awful storms back then."

"Really?"

"Yeah. World was different. For a while, everything seemed ta shut down. Even the schools. Before they closed, we'd spend half a day sweepin' dirt out of the rooms. My pop kept his farm, though. Had saved enough to barely make payments when some couldn't."

"So many stories I hear from those times. Such grit in this small town—looking like it's at the end of the Earth," said Curtye Lee. The speakers came on to announce the first event coming up. Bronco riding.

"I gotta get over there to help gather up them wayward dogies," said Colt as he stood to leave. "Maybe one day you and me can go visit the barn. I'll take you riding." He winked at Curtye Lee as he turned to walk away.

Curtye Lee made no response. No loyalty in these boys, she thought, and she looked over to see Willie Bob watching her from a fence rail where he sat. When he saw her look his way, he waved. A fella in the arena was thrown from a bucking horse as the crowd moaned in unison, and Curtye Lee wondered why anyone would want to do this.

Willie Bob was the third rider out of the gate on a black bronco, and he held on for dear life. He held on longer than the two fellas before him, but in the end, he placed third. The sun finally came out, and she took off her sweater as she watched more events. Then, the bulls came out, one by one, with each rider risking life and limb. The clown would distract the bull after a rider fell into the dust, and once, when the clown flew over the fence and into a lady's lap, popcorn and soda pop flew everywhere as the clown's antics had the crowd roaring.

As the bell rang for Willie Bob's ride, the announcer called out his name and some of his awards. Willie Bob's friend, Theo, sat down next to her.

"Hey, Curtye Lee," he said. "Having fun?"

"Yes," she answered, wondering if he was going to ask her out too. She sat quiet, watching for Willie Bob.

The bull sprang from the gate, jerking up and down as if Willie Bob and the creature were one. Willie Bob leaned to the side, and Curtye Lee gasped. She stood up in fear, and then, Willie Bob righted himself on the bull. Three more times, that happened before he went flying up and landed in the dust like the others. Willie Bob got up and took a bow as the bull headed back for him, and the clown captured the beast's attention. The crowd was cheering, but Curtye Lee found it hard to watch.

"How do y'all do this?" Curtye Lee asked Theo, turning toward him.

"Oh, it's crazy. I don't ride the bulls anymore 'cause I like my bones unbroken. But the years I've been rodeoing got me friends and skills I can use at the ranch. Better understanding of the animals. Got me some respect. It's all about community."

Curtye Lee looked at him in a new light. Realized he was different than the others.

"Once, I was crazy 'nough to try bulldogging. See this scar here?" and he pointed to a scar along his hairline.

"What's bulldoggin'?"

"When you go down and dirty to wrestle a steer. Like a fool. Got all them wild oats out of my system so I'd be ready to settle down and make a life in these beautiful high plains of Texas." Theo looked at Curtye Lee. "Hope you stay. Here in Dalhart. It's a good life here."

They watched a couple more bull rides, some roping, bronco riding, and then more bull riding before Theo stood to leave.

"Was good to see you again, Curtye Lee." He walked away and greeted Colt who sat down next to Curtye Lee.

"Here, thought I'd bring you a Dr. Pepper," Colt said, handing the drink to Curtye Lee. "Only got a minute. Whatcha think of the rodeo?"

"Too much drama for me, I think. I expect there are broken bones sometimes, right?"

"Yep. Specially ribs."

Curtye Lee looked up at the pens at the end of the arena and saw Willie Bob standing close to some girl in a cowboy hat. He was nuzzling her neck. *Was he kissing her?* Curtye Lee was aghast and couldn't take her eyes off what was going on.

"Gotta go," said Colt, but Curtye Lee didn't even turn or thank him for the soda.

She sat there in the bleachers, fuming as the sounds around her were muffled by her thoughts. First, her beau's good buddy was hitting on her, and now, Willie's putting the moves on another girl. Right there in front of her. What was she doing, moving all these miles for a scoundrel like that? *Just who did he think he was?* But she'd been warned.

Sunday morning came with the smell of early summer as Curtye Lee and Willie Bob walked out behind the church, where sat a swing set and two see-saws.

"So, what did you wanna talk about?" asked Willie Bob.

"Us."

Willie Bob walked past the swings and sat on the see-saw. "Wanna risk it?"

Curtye Lee knew she should say *no*, but she held down her skirt as Willie Bob stood to level the board, and she climbed on.

"We good?" he asked, his voice a bit unsure, and he put his weight back on the seat, and Curtye Lee rose high.

"I think we're good to be friends. Ya know—I followed ya all the way down here from the north." She paused and looked into Willie Bob's eyes. Was regretting getting on the teeter-totter.

"Back in Colorado, I thought ya saw somethin' in me. Special. But you're no more loyal to me than your buddies are to you. I thought on it and decided I shouldn't be your girl anymore."

She watched him. *Would he jump off and let her fall?* He pushed his legs to balance the board. The two of them were level. Him standing, her weight on the board.

"Why?" he asked.

"Lots of reasons, but mostly 'cause I'm not your girl. Appears to me all the girls are yours. I'm not jealous." She smiled at him. "I'm just worth more."

"I'll do better," he said. "You're special to me."

"Maybe right now. What about tomorrow? I'm not bargaining, Willie. I made up my mind." With those words, he jumped off the board, and her seat fell to the ground, just as she'd feared.

"Dammit, girl." He looked at her, and she saw tears in his eyes. She'd not expected that.

"I'm still your friend, Willie," she said as she stood and brushed dirt from her dress.

"Ain't no one my friend."

"Willie, you're a charmin' fella. Not ready to settle down. But please—can't we be friends?" said Curtye Lee.

"Girls ain't friends. Ain't had a real friend. Not since the day Pa died," he yelled. "Since Ma drove him to that bullet in the barn. Every damned day she rubbished him. All I heard was fighting. How he'd go out to the 126 House and pay a woman to be kind to him. Then Ma would make him sleep in the barn for a week. Badmouth 'im the whole time."

His tears kept coming, and Curtye Lee walked closer to him.

"I loved him. Damn her. She made him leave, and now ... now, she drinks and brags on me to make herself shine. She took what I loved away from me. Ain't no home." He looked over at Curtye Lee.

"And now I got no girl."

"Well, I'm your friend." Curtye Lee wanted to hug him but hesitated. "I can see you might need one. Need more. There's plenty of girls to be your girl. Just pick one. Find your lodestar."

Willie Bob looked confused and said nothing.

"My pa always told me to find the lodestar. A star in the night sky that guides you, but it can also be a person or maybe a backbone. Find what—or who—grounds you, Willie."

He kicked the dirt. "You going home? Colorado?"

"I don't know yet."

He walked in a loop, loop after loop, shaking his head and landed on a swing. Curtye Lee sat on the swing next to him.

"Willie, I'm twenty-four years old. I need to start acting like a grown woman. And I'm gonna. Sounds like you need to make some such plans yourself if you're not happy where you are. I'm sorry about your pa."

He looked at her, his eyes swollen and red. A Texas breeze stirred up, and Curtye Lee hoped Willie Bob's face would clear before he met his mother at the truck.

"You can badmouth me to your ma if you want," said Curtye Lee. "Doesn't matter. She doesn't like me anyway, but I can see she doesn't wanna share you with anyone."

He said nothing. Knew she spoke the truth. The two sat for the longest time, in silence, gently swinging before Willie Bob stood.

"Gotta give Ma a ride home." He looked longingly at Curtye Lee. "I hope you stay."

Chapter 17

With Jane out of town and Willie Bob in her rear-view mirror, Curtye Lee had plenty of time to read and immersed herself in Edith Wharton's stories. She'd made it to the story titled "Fullness of Life" and was eager for the next meeting at the back of Crawford's store. She couldn't wait to tell Jane and Shelby how much she loved the story of the woman in a beautiful afterlife who turned away from the promise of eternity with the Spirit of Life to instead wait for her husband. Curtye Lee needed to finish the last stories and get the book to Shelby. It was unknown when Jane would return to Dalhart, so she'd likely not be able to read the book before their next meeting.

Curtye Lee wondered about Jane and hoped her friend's mother in Santa Fe was getting better. New Mexico was a place Curtye Lee had never seen, but had heard of its wonders and beauty, how the artsy people she'd met in Colorado shared how they were drawn there like moths to the light. Each night, Curtye Lee prayed for Jane and her mother, for her own pa and aunt, and, of course, for Shelby, who'd been so kind to her. Once in a while, she'd throw in a prayer for Willie Bob and deliverance from his despair. Suddenly, claustrophobia overtook her, having spent too much time in her room, and she laid her book on the nightstand and walked into the parlor where she found Sue Jones knitting.

"Join me, dear," said Sue. "Would you like some tea?"

Mrs. Jones loved her tea, thought Curtye Lee.

"Yes, I would. I'll make it. Don't get up," she said as she walked toward the kitchen. "Be back in a few minutes. Do you want a fresh cup?"

"No, Dear. I still have a bit," called Sue. "Thank you."

"What are you making?" asked Curtye Lee upon her return, sitting in the blue chair with the tall back.

"It'll be a sweater for my granddaughter," said Sue. "For next winter. She lives up in Kansas, and I imagine they'll come down for a visit this summer. Maybe a couple weeks."

Mrs. Jones always kept a large bedroom upstairs vacant for her family. Lost income, thought Curtye Lee, and she wondered if the old woman felt lonely with all these strangers living in her house.

"When did your husband pass, Mrs. Jones?"

"Oh, dear, please call me Sue. It's been ten years since Colin died. All of a sudden, it was. I still feel him. Here in this house. We'd managed to stay through the dust years, though the bank closed down a couple of times. He was a loan officer, you know, at the bank. Oh dear, those years were trying. Not just the weather, but the farmers going bankrupt, and poor Colin couldn't help them as much as he wanted to. Everything turned worthless except our survival, and I got that awful cough, but over time recovered. Not everyone did. We kept our house, thank the Lord. And the Conservation Corps that came to help us—those dear men. Oh my, I'm going on and on about the past. How are you doing, Curtye Lee? And that fella of yours, Master Preston?"

It felt odd hearing her call Willie Bob *Master Preston*. He wasn't master of much except riding and roping.

"We've broken up. He's always had eyes on all the girls, yet at the same time, he seems tied to his mama's apron strings."

Sue stopped knitting and looked up.

"I'm sorry, Curtye Lee. We all coulda told you, but we knew you wouldn't believe us, and that time itself would tattle on that boy. It always does. There's some nice fellas, young single fellas, here in town. A few, but those few are keepers. I hope this doesn't mean you'll be leaving Dalhart."

She resumed flicking her needles in and out of the dusty

blue yarn after she tied off the red.

"I haven't decided yet. I might return home, but Shelby's begging me to stay. Since I've got work—a salary—I figure I'll just go slow in deciding."

"Well, I'd hate to see you go. I've never been to Colorado, so I cannot speak to its beauty. Or its intrigue. But I've come to love the plains here, how vast the horizons and skies are. As if they go all the way to heaven. How they bloom at dawn and dusk, and the people all look out for each other." The sweater and needles dropped to her lap. "I do hope you stay, Curtye Lee."

"Oh, Miss Sue, thank you. I've got dear friends here in Dalhart. So kind to me while others shunned me as if I'm a foreigner or some harlot."

"Dear, you need to ignore them. We have too many dogmatists here in north Texas as if the winds blew them all in with the tumbleweeds."

"Well, I've heard of the tumbleweeds. And seen 'em this winter. But what are *dogmatists*?" asked Curtye Lee.

Sue laughed and picked up her knitting. Began flicking the needles again.

"I'm sorry. I learned those big words at college. A dogmatist is one who spouts dogma. In other words, they don't know what they're talking about, but pretend like they know everything."

"Oh, I've met a few of 'em," said Curtye Lee and, getting comfortable, she rested her legs up on the hassock. "Where did you go to college, Miss Sue?"

"Back in 1905, we lived in Waco, down south of Dallas. My parents sent me to the Texas State Normal School, down south of Austin, so I could be a teacher, and when I graduated, the school sent me here to Dalhart to teach. Just like Jane Connor, who returned to Dalhart after the bad years. When I was young, Dalhart was growing so fast. New farmers coming in and buying land, dirt cheap, and that's when I met my husband. When I went to the bank to open an account." She stood. "Give me a minute. I want to refill my teacup. Can I get you more tea?"

"No, thank you."

Curtye Lee sipped her tea, now lukewarm, as Mrs. Jones walked away, and the room turned silent. Curtye Lee wondered what it would be like to be a teacher. To go to college, a possibility never even spoken to her in Grand Junction. After high school, she'd found work as a nurse's aide at St. Mary's Hospital. It was tedious and thankless work where, after being on her feet and on the run all day, from room to room, she'd sleep soundly at night, only to be eager to leave Colorado when she met Willie Bob. She found that the small community and slow pace of Dalhart suited her well.

"You know," said Sue as she walked back into the room, "I taught Willie Bob's English class in high school. He wasn't much interested in literature, but I do remember he seemed to hold a dogged sadness beneath all that swagger. I imagine it came with his overbearing mama and the loss of his father."

The two sat together in the ticking sound of knitting needles as if a clock were counting away the seconds.

I can't be that boy's savior, thought Curtye Lee. *He's surely broken, an anguished soul chasing skirts, girls in cowboy boots. He charmed me, lured me to these treeless plains where it was up to me to find my own way. But I'm a girl who can find her way, and I have friends cheering me on, a pa who taught me to stand on my own two feet. To value my values. As sweet as Willie Bob can be, I will not save him. No one can but himself, and someday, he'll lose his mama and be naught but a boy adrift. Or maybe his anguish will bring him to stand up to Blanche Preston and go his own way. It won't be with me.*

Curtye Lee took in a deep breath, and her thoughts traveled back to that night when Willie Bob revealed the suicide of his father. And behind the church when she broke it off with him. She recalled how he had laughed one night before they broke up and said he'd made up the story to get her sympathy and get her back in bed with him. She'd been miffed at him for the terrible lie, but now she wondered about his antics and doubted his words. She remembered how his devastating heartbreak had spilled from him that night he bared his pain— and then, that Sunday morning when he broke down behind the church. She was certain it was the truth, and she knew he wanted no one to know the family's secret.

Chapter 18

On Friday, Curtye Lee called me about the book, and I dropped by the department store in the afternoon to pick up Edith Wharton's book.

"Shelby, I can't wait for you to read this. That Edith Wharton uses a lot of big words, and I had to look a lot of 'em up. Words like *hyaline* and *balustrade*, but the stories are magical. This author creates scenes that feel as if I'm standing right there in them," said Curtye Lee as she pulled the book from her satchel and handed it to me. "Have you heard from Jane?"

"No, I haven't. I'll ask Henry on Sunday. What does *hyaline* mean?"

"It describes something as glassy and see-through."

"Oh, well, now I'll know. Kinda like my husband Jim lately. Vanishing from around the house. Will you be at church on Sunday?" I asked.

Curtye Lee paused.

"I don't know. I miss coming, but I really don't want to deal with Mrs. Preston or Willie Bob if he's there. I'm thinking of going over to the train station for a ticket home."

"Oh dear, Curtye Lee, I hope you don't leave, but I'm certain you miss your family. You know you are welcome here in Dalhart by those of us who love you. Joe Tippett and his wife asked after you last week."

"Oh, please tell them I send my best. I do hope their granddaughter will be embraced back into the church when she returns, and I'm missing my rides on the trails out at your barn, but I have no desire to be around the boys, especially after Willie Bob and I parted ways. His so-called friend Colt made advances on me at the rodeo while I was still Willie Bob's girl."

"Well, enough of that. You come out and ride with me," I said. "I'll pick you up on Tuesday after lunch. You tell old Crawford I gave you the afternoon off."

After we laughed, I hugged Curtye Lee and left. As I drove home, past the Chevrolet dealer, I saw Jim's car parked out front and wondered what he was up to. He'd never mentioned wanting to replace his old pickup. I was missing my best friend Jane and knew I'd miss Curtye Lee if she left town, and when I looked at my watch, I decided to turn around and drop by the high school to pick up Lorene. I knew she'd probably prefer sitting with her girlfriends on the school bus, but we didn't get enough time alone together. She'd be a young woman soon enough, and, God forbid, she'd likely be having boys, with their souped-up old cars, picking her up for dates soon enough. Jim and I will need a united front to get us through that and out the other side with our family intact.

Lorene hadn't much to say on our drive home. I asked about her classes, and in her usual manner, her answers were short. At times, curt as if I shouldn't be asking or her life wasn't any of my business. Billy arrived on the school bus as we drove through the ranch's gate, and he jumped in the car with us.

"Gonna ride my bike when I finish my reading assignment," he blurted out.

"Okay. How about grilled cheese and tomato soup for supper?"

Billy agreed readily, and Lorene didn't answer. As the kids went to their respective rooms, I busied myself in the kitchen, setting the table. Canned soup it would be since the garden's tomatoes were just starting to flower. When Jim arrived, he seemed preoccupied and walked out to the barn for daily chores after changing into his work boots. I saw him yell at

Billy to come help him, and the boy threw down his bike on the spot and followed his pa.

"How was your day, Jim?" I asked at the supper table.

"Usual. Gonna' start up the plow tomorrow and get some crops started, so I'll get home early," he said.

"I saw you at the Chevy dealer when I drove by. You lookin' at new trucks?"

He looked down at his plate, picked up his knife and slowly cut his sandwich into quarters. I'd never seen him do that before.

"I did take a peek at one but just dropped by to make a payment on your Bel Air."

"I already mailed that payment, Jim. Since when do we make payments at the dealer?"

He stuffed a quarter of the sandwich into his mouth, and I held my eyes on him, waiting for him to swallow. Waiting for an answer.

"You checking up on me, Shelby?" He picked up his plate, leaving a half-full bowl of soup on the table, and set his dish in the sink. "I just want to pay the damn thing off early. I'll be in the barn."

I sat watching him go. I'm certain my mouth hung open, and Billy was watching the scenario with curious eyes. Even Lorene had a puzzled look on her face.

"Well. I don't know what to say about that. And, Billy, you left your bicycle in the dirt in front of the house. I've asked you not to do that. One day, the tractor or pickup will run right over it, so if you're finished, go put it up and see if your pa needs any help in the barn."

Just as I was done wiping the kitchen counters, the phone rang, and as I walked to the hallway, I prayed it would be a friendly voice.

"Shelby?"

"Jane," I yelled into the phone. "I'm so glad to hear your voice. Is everything okay?"

"No," said Jane, "Mother passed away yesterday. Her weak heart took her so quickly, and I needed to hear your voice. Though the doctor had prepared Pa for the outcome, he wanders about the house as if searching for her. I've been on the phone with Henry. He's driving over here on Monday for a small service and the burial. I'll be home by the next Sunday."

"Jane, I'm so sorry. What can I do to help? Can I get anything for you or Henry? I'm assuming she is being buried there, in Santa Fe."

"Yes. Pa made it clear that's their wish. He won't be coming back with us, though Henry and I have extended our welcome. He's done with Dalhart and determined to stay here. I hate the idea of him being alone here, but it's obvious he's not alone. He's got more friends than I can count, so he'll be fine as long as he's healthy."

"Tell him I send my love."

"I will. Are you okay, Shelby? You said you needed to hear a friendly voice. Is everything alright?"

"Well, things seem a bit tense here at the house, and I'm not sure why. My teenage daughter only speaks to me in one-syllable words. Curtye Lee broke it off with Willie Bob Preston, and I hate the thought of her leaving Dalhart."

"Is she leaving?"

"She hasn't decided, but I'm afraid she might. I think I'll schedule our group's next meeting for the Tuesday evening after you're back. We need to get together. We need to give Curtye Lee a reason to stay."

"That sounds good, Shelby. I'll call you when I get back. We can do coffee. Curtye Lee, too, if she can get off work. Have a blessed week, friend."

"I'll be thinking of you, Jane. And I'll see Henry at church before he leaves. Bye, dear."

After the kids were in bed and Jim had gone off to shower, I sat in the living room, looking out the window toward the horizon, the sky lit with stars and the slight crescent of a moon. Under those stars, far to the west, sat my best friend, mourning her mother. Comforting her father. I began to feel sorry for myself. Like a failure who could not even keep her own family joined together. Only Billy seemed happy, and I dug deep to understand. Jim had never been a romantic man. There'd been no trips or dinners for just the two of us. He'd always loved the ranch, but now, he seemed distracted. Tomorrow, after supper, I'll suggest we saddle up our horses and ride the ranch. Hopefully, he won't be too worn out from plowing the fields. We can watch the sunset. I'll encourage him to come to more of Billy's baseball games, though the school year was nearing its end. It all seemed so petty when I thought of Jane and her loss and even Curtye Lee and her struggle to choose her life's path.

Chapter 19

It was a somber beginning to our next meeting at Crawford's store. As it happened, we were all a mess, but the deepest sadness was Jane's loss.

"Thank you both," said Jane. "Shelby, for the lovely flowers you sent to Mother's funeral. And Curtye Lee! The most kind and sweet letter awaited me here at home when Henry and I arrived. You do know how to lift a friend's spirit. Papa and I comforted each other, and we know Mother will always be with us, in our own ways, for we still need her and, especially when we don't even know we need her, but we do."

We hugged each other as each of us spilled our pain and shared it with the ones we loved and trusted in this dim and disordered room full of us.

"Curtye Lee, I hear that you broke up with Mr. Preston and might return to Colorado," said Jane.

"Well, I've mulled it over, back and forth, for I love both of you. Your kindnesses. Including me in this group. I've cried all the tears I'll ever cry over Willie Bob Preston. So many more than he deserves. He has a lot of growin' up to do. But I've also grown used to the big skies and the tumbleweeds that scratch my legs when the winds blow," said Curtye Lee. "And yesterday, I went over to the depot to purchase a train ticket, and when I dropped some money at the ticket window, the gentleman standing behind me picked it up."

A twinkle appeared in Curtye Lee's eyes, A mischievous twinkle. And she continued. "When I turned, he handed the money to me and I looked into his eyes, eyes lit up with a smile. I'm certain I blushed. I purchased my ticket home, and as I walked out the door, the man caught up with me. Asked me to lunch. And there was a gentleness about him, and his smile, that made me say *yes*."

Jane and I looked at each other and then squealed.

"Does that mean you'll stay in Dalhart?" I asked.

"Most likely. For now," she answered. "Not because of him, but because of that little miracle and all my blessings here in this Texas town. Like maybe God was telling me somethin', and I should be listening."

Like a couple of schoolgirls, Jane and I asked about the new beau. Curtye Lee said he wasn't a beau. We asked our friend what she and the gentleman she called "the new young man" talked about at lunch. Where was he from? How long had he lived in Dalhart, since both Jane and I were surprised that we'd never met him in this small town.

"Slow down. It's only been one lunch. Yet, I must say, there was such an ease as we talked and talked for so long that he was late getting back to his office. He's a tall man. I'd guess a little over six feet, tall and thin. His hair is dark brown, almost black, yet his eyes are a piercing blue. He works at the bank, a loan officer, he said."

"Oh dear," I said. "Isn't that the position Ed Jones, Sue's husband, had at the bank?"

"Might be," said Jane.

"Well, his name is George Breville. Doesn't go to our church. But of course, you'd know him if he did. Said he's Catholic. He's thirty-one years old and moved here from ... guess where? Colorado. Two years ago, from Denver, but he said he'd been born in Tyler, Texas, and his parents had moved to Denver when he was twelve years old."

"Wow," I said. "Sounds like some heavenly intervention."

Jane smiled. "Yes, I suspect that might be true."

"Well, calm down, girls. I'm not jumping into anything after letting my heart muddle my brain about Willie Bob. Though I must say, George seems much more mature than Willie Bob.

Something this lost girl needs. A good thing for any girl wanting to settle down. I'm keeping my train ticket home for the time being, but y'all are stuck with me."

"Well, I did bring a jug of sweet tea and some fresh-baked chocolate chip cookies with pecans, so grab a cup and a napkin." I unsnapped the lid on the thermos, and what with all the talk of the evening, it crossed my mind that I should've brought whiskey. I'm sure there'd already been plenty of moonshine pass through this back room.

"Shelby, did you get to read any of Edith Wharton's ghost stories?" asked Curtye Lee as I poured tea into the cups.

"I did. A lot more interesting than the books we checked out in Amarillo. Still can't say I believe in ghosts, but her stories did draw me in."

Jane reached into her bag and pulled out *The Way of Mysticism*. She handed it to me as I sat down at the table.

"Sorry you've had this checked out for so long, Shelby, but it was some comfort to me over in Santa Fe. And Curtye Lee, you were right about the many expressive quotes it held inside. I made a few notes to share with Henry. Thank you, both."

"I'm so glad," I said. "Now I want to take a quick look through it before I get it back to Amarillo, to Esther. And since we're working our way through confessions, I'm fixin' to share something I don't want to leave this room." I paused, gathering my courage to say the words out loud. "I'm starting to suspect my Jim might be seeing someone. A woman. There's something he's hiding from me. He's been absent from home and the kids' functions so much more than usual. Distracted. When I did laundry last Friday, I smelled perfume on his shirt that was nothing I ever wore, and when I asked about it, he got angry. Not a good sign."

"Oh dear," said Jane. "What will you do? Does Henry need to speak with him?"

"Well, do you think he'd be more truthful with Henry

than with me? I'm not so sure. If he's cheatin', I suppose our marriage is shaky. Never thought we'd end up like that."

"The church frowns on divorce. But nothing can heal without truthfulness," said Jane. "I'm just going to tell Henry you are worried about Jim, and he'll likely ask Jim discreetly if everything is alright. Henry has a way of getting people to spill their secrets and miseries."

"We've been together so long: the kids, all the work Jim's put into the ranch. If he'll just be honest with me, maybe we can work through it," I said with about as much certainty as I could muster. We'd come too far to let it all go. "I'll pray on it, Jane."

Curtye Lee reached over and squeezed my hand. Here, we all sat in the back room of Crawford's Department Store. Each of us with our own loss. Mine, only a suspicion at the moment, was nothing compared to Jane's. Sweet Curtye Lee had stood strong in hers, and, by God, she'd found hope just when she thought there was none. Deep inside, I believed there was surely a way forward for me and Jim.

It was nine o'clock, and we'd not even spoken of ghosts, though the room seemed full of them. It was as if spring had broken open the Earth to release them all around us. So, we sat and ate cookies and sipped tea as if the world was ordinary, and then Jane spoke up.

"I do have a tale to tell," said Jane in a voice near a whisper. "One that surprised even me. Two nights ago, I could not sleep and tiptoed into the living room on the way to the kitchen. I saw nothing but darkness and a few rays of moonlight when suddenly I smelled a familiar fragrance, my mother's cologne, that came with a chill. I slowed my steps almost to a stop. Baffled." Jane stopped and looked at us as if she weren't sure if she should continue. Curtye Lee and I sat wide-eyed. "Then there was the faint touch of fingers running down my arm and enfolding my hand with a gentle strength. For a moment, I was terrified, and then, suddenly, I felt an unmeasurable sense of comfort. A faint pressure on my hand, so indistinct I was unsure if it was real or my imagination. It was all so unnatural to everything I understood, mysterious, but I felt as if I was with someone I knew or had known. I believe it was my mother, yet at the same time, I've never believed in ghosts." She paused and looked up at the bookshelves.

"*As if a phantom caress'd me. I thought I was not alone walking here on the shore.*"

And after a moment, as if she suddenly remembered we were in the room with her, she looked at us. "Walt Whitman from *Leaves of Grass*. I doubt you'll find that book in our little library."

Curtye Lee and I sat in silence, and in the quiet of the room, I wondered if the bulb in the lamp had flickered. When Jane began speaking again, the softness in her voice held us all spellbound, as if she herself were a ghost in the room.

"It was moments filled with a tenderness I'll never forget, and I sat in that moonlit room for a long time, unable to explain away the experience because of the solace that came with it. The kinship of my mother's presence."

Curtye Lee and I sat there just looking at Jane, our words held captive in our throats and our eyes large. We could not interpret it or understand it, but we all believed.

"Did you tell Henry?" I asked.

"Heavens, no," exclaimed Jane. "You know, we are meandering nearer the taboo. The supernatural. Henry would have thought me mad." After a short pause, Jane continued. "I must say that there's a part of me that wants to tell Henry. It was such a soulful experience that I feel has changed me. Makes me more a believer than I was before. Makes me see God a bit differently, and I wonder if Henry would appreciate it. Perhaps, one day."

"Well, Jane, I think you should share it, but of course, you know your Henry best," said Curtye Lee. "Your story outshines Edith Wharton's stories, though I liked her tales. Oh, to have that experience, Jane. I would love a visit from my mother, but it'd likely scare the bejesus out of me. I don't really know what *bejesus* means, but Pa used it all the time."

We all laughed, and I wasn't too sure either. *Where did bejesus come from?*

"Jane," I said, "I think your visitation's a gift, no matter how it came to be. Mothers make us feel protected, and I wonder if it might happen again."

"Mother always protected me when I've needed it," said Jane. "Maybe too much, sometimes."

"Well, I do hate to interrupt the discussion. We can always come back to it, but let's get down to the book before it's too late," I said. "My favorite story was the 'The Pomegranate Seed.'" I chuckled as I realized the story reminded me of my own story about Jim and me thinking he might be cheating.

"Because of Jim's absences," I continued. "Could that be why I liked it? Why it rang true to me?" I turned to Jane, who hadn't read the stories. "It's a story of a woman who thinks her new husband has a mistress, but eventually it comes to light that the gray envelopes coming to the house appear to be from his dead first wife, and then, the woman's husband disappears, and it was assumed he went to join his dead wife. The story implied hazy edges between life and death. So, the mistress was really a ghost."

"Whoa," said Jane. "That's eerie. Makes me want to read her stories, but I'd best not have the book lying about the house. As I recall, Edith Wharton died, right?"

"Yep. In 1937, I believe," said Curtye Lee. "Shelby, can I borrow the book again? Since it's not from the library, I want to read a couple of the stories again, including your favorite. There's a part of me, Jane, wondering if you would have noticed the chill, that connection with your mama if we hadn't been discussing spirits here. I think our talks have eased us into seeing happenings around us, payin' more attention."

"Curtye Lee, that's so true. We really don't look or listen. We don't see. Even that fragrance pulled me into those moments with my mother," said Jane. "Child, you're wise beyond your years."

"It's 10:15," I said. "I think we could go another hour or two, but the cookies are gone, and it's late. Henry'll think we've kidnapped you, Jane. And maybe, with any luck, Jim might wonder where I am."

We gathered our things and hugged each other before I locked the storefront. With the moon waning, the skies twinkled above us as we all went our way.

"I'm going to walk home, Shelby," said Curtye Lee, pointing toward the heavens. "Look at the night sky. The clusters of light."

I waved goodbye to her, imagined her eagerness to see her new friend George again, and I was glad she'd found a nice man, even if he were a Catholic.

I drove home slowly, seeing only one car on the road, and it passed me in a flash. Before our meeting, I had stopped by Mother's house. Took her some cookies, and I shared how the kids were doing and updated her on Jane and Curtye Lee. I'd said nothing to her about Jim and my worries. As I drove toward home, the late-night sky was clear above Dalhart. Tonight's meeting had evolved into our griefs yet had been uplifting, and the bright stars were like friends watching over me. I thought of my young brother. My brother who'd never seen the rest of his life. Who and where would he be now? I wondered. I wished him a star of his own up in that deep sky and suddenly felt thankful for my own life, no matter the roadblocks. Life always holds its ups and downs, and at that moment, I did not feel alone on the journey.

Chapter 20

I fretted all day Monday. Jim had been gone most of Sunday afternoon after church services. Said he was doing some visitations for Henry, and I wondered just who he was visiting. He'd said little at the supper table last night and had even been curt with me at breakfast before he left for work. Part of me wanted to check out the Chevy dealer at lunchtime, but I didn't want to become that woman. I'd seen the blonde at the dealership's front desk, though I didn't know her name. She was a tall girl with long hair dyed that champagne blonde color, and she certainly was under thirty, at least eight or nine years younger than Jim.

I knew I was jumping to conclusions. *He might have something troubling his mind, problems at work, but why hasn't he talked to me?* It had never been like him to hold things in, to miss the children's activities so often, and now they were at that age when they needed his attention and guidance. He and I needed to talk, but he'd been resistant. Agitated. Or maybe it's me. Had I distanced myself too far from him with all the time I'd spent with my friends? Was I neglecting him? Our relationship? The phone rang.

"Hello."

"Dear, it's Jane. I might not be able to make it for coffee tomorrow."

"Oh. I really needed to talk to you, Jane. But that's okay," I lied. I knew she had other obligations, but I needed to speak with my friend. To someone who could lend a kindly ear and, perhaps, good advice.

Here, I was being greedy about my friend's time and realized that I'd been feeling sorry for myself all morning. There were chores to do.

At supper, Jim gobbled down his food and disappeared into the barn.

"What's Daddy doing?" asked Billy.

"Not sure, son. Probably at his workbench fixin' something," I replied. "Have you finished your homework?"

"Yes'm. Done."

"Well, it's gettin' late. Go upstairs and take a bath. Get ready for bed, and then I'll tuck you in. You know, you'll be out of school for the summer soon, and I need to sign you up for Bible Summer Camp. You still want to go, right?"

"I do. Is Lorene goin'?"

"I doubt it. She hasn't wanted to go the last two years, but I'll ask her."

After supper, I walked out to the front porch, sat in a rocker, and lit a cigarette. Clouds had settled near the horizon, and the falling sun lit them like a kaleidoscope, shades of pink, orange, red, and yellows. Swirled in bright and pale hues shining in the west. Darkness would settle over us in minutes, so I inhaled and exhaled slowly and watched the day's exit. Waiting for my husband to come in from the barn.

In the dim darkness of dusk, Jim sauntered toward the house, and I saw the pause in his step when he looked up and saw me in the shadows. I saw his apprehension as if it were a thing I could touch.

"You missed a beautiful sunset," I said as I crushed the stub of a second cigarette in the ashtray.

"Really? Probably from all the dust blowin'," he said, still walking toward the door.

"Do you want to sit for a bit? Enjoy the night sky before the heat of summer comes. Keeps us indoors?"

"Need a shower." He paused. "Oh, hell, I'll have a smoke before bed." He sat in the other rocker, pulled a Camel from the pack in his shirt pocket and lit it.

The tension was thick between us, so I sat quietly. He said nothing.

"There's a concert at Lorene's school tomorrow night. She's singin'. The end-of-the-school-year performance. I put it on the calendar taped to the icebox. Can you make it?" I asked.

Jim bent forward and put his elbows on his knees. Took a deep draw of his Camel. I stayed quiet, waiting.

"I'll try," he said. He tossed the half-smoked cigarette butt out into the dirt and turned his boot on its heel. The clouds had covered the moon, and the sky held no light.

"Gotta' get that shower," he said and rose. "See ya upstairs."

The screen door slammed behind him as he went inside, but I stayed in my chair and lit another Viceroy. The moon reappeared. I rocked the chair back and forth as I looked across the shadowed fields and felt the animals in the barn, the chicken coop, and even the few cattle left in the pasture, all stilling themselves for the night. I tried to imitate them, stilling my mind. I struggled to put aside the doubts I'd wrestled with all day, putting away my worries and remembering night was for rest. The animals knew it.

On Tuesday, I set two glasses of iced sweet tea on the table. Jane picked hers up and took a sip. Her schedule had allowed her to come for lunch instead of our usual morning coffee.

"Thanks, Shelby. I need to wet my whistle."

"Just a second, and I'll get some chips to go with the chicken salad." I turned to grab a bag from the cupboard.

"How are you and Henry doing, Jane?" I asked as I added a handful of chips to our plates. "And how's your father?"

"We're doing okay. Papa usually calls me on Sundays, and I call him on Wednesday evenings just to check on him. Sometimes, he doesn't answer, and I take that as a good sign that he's getting out with his friends, like he used to before Mother turned ill."

"And Curtye Lee," I said. "I do miss her at church, but I understand why she doesn't come anymore."

"Well, I saw her at the store yesterday. She said she has a dinner date with her new beau this week. I'm sure he won't be coming to our church, and since she's no stranger to the Catholic faith, she may not be back at all."

"Remember. She said George wasn't her beau," I said, and we laughed. I stood to grab the plate of cupcakes I'd made, white cake with early strawberries mashed and blended into white icing. I set the plate on the table.

"I do hope she stays in Dalhart. And in our little group, specially since she's the one who was so curious. But, Jane, I reckon I need to talk to you about Jim. I'm afraid we're coming apart." I put both my hands on the table. Looked at them as if they weren't part of me. "He won't talk to me. He just busies himself with work and chores. He said he'd try to come to Lorene's choir concert tonight, so that's good. Not sure if he'll show up, and I really don't know what to do. He gets annoyed if I talk about it."

"I did tell Henry about Jim being withdrawn and asked him if he'd noticed," said Jane. "As if something was bothering him and told him you were worried, so I'm sure Henry will chat with him. If I hear anything, I'll let you know, but you know Henry. He'll be discreet, so I may learn nothing. Do you really think he's seeing another woman?"

"Maybe. There's been those signs, but I'm not gonna follow him around like some schoolgirl. Sometimes, I feel like I'm somehow neglecting him. They always say a man strays if he's not getting what he needs at home, but I don't know what I'm doing differently. If I went out and bought some racy negligee, he'd likely laugh or worse, get irritated. It'd be so out of character for me. Maybe that's the problem. We're in a rut, and he's bored."

I picked up the pitcher of sweet tea from the counter and put it on the table so we could refill our glasses.

"Stop blaming yourself, Shelby. No matter what's in his head, he should talk to you. Listen to you. It's not your fault. I've never even seen the two of you argue."

"Well, we did have a fight a couple weeks ago. He got really mad when I mentioned the odd perfume on his shirt. Half teasin', half not. Angry words went flyin', and that's not like us. How do you keep Henry's interest? I know. Way too personal a question, right? Which it is."

"Not between friends, it's not. But remember, Henry's a pastor and the whole community is watching him. Watching us. People are different, and what drew Henry and me together was that we both like to read, have discussions, and enjoy walks before the sun sets. We both like our space and quiet time. And, of course, my art keeps me distracted and busy while Henry is out and about comforting people and organizing events. Right now, he's busy recruiting and training teachers for summer's Bible School, so when the weather's nice, I go out on the roads and sketch the silos."

Jane poured more tea into her glass and picked up a cupcake.

"We give each other space. Sometimes we cook together," continued Jane as she pulled paper from the cupcake. "I'm not sure what to tell you, Shelby, because you and Jim are different than we are. From what I see, Jim likes things like farm work, carpentry, and tinkering on his truck and tractor. Maybe you need an activity you enjoy doing together. But, if he wants to stray, there may be nothing you can do to stop it. So, please don't blame yourself, Shelby, because I can hear that's what you're doing."

"I know. But it's what I do. How can I fix this problem or that problem? Always the mediator. The skill and flaw of the middle child. I know I need to confront Jim, but I don't see it going well. I imagine I'm just stalling, hoping this is a passing thing and will go away. That it's only my imagination."

"Well, ignoring it never works. If it doesn't go well, you tried. And then, you might suggest he should talk to Henry. My goodness, Jim's a deacon. He should already be doing that if he's troubled."

I forced a weak smile and indulged in a cupcake.

"By the way," Jane continued, "Henry and I talked about Joe Tippett, and I think he's going to ask him to return to the deacon position. Poor Joe is devastated about his granddaughter, and she won't be back to Dalhart until late summer or later. Joe's given so many years to our church, helping Henry and everyone in need. He's like family, and I told Henry we should be treating Joe like family. We had a long talk about forgiveness."

"Oh, dear. Forgiveness. I wonder if I can do that if Jim's really cheating. If I find out. If he even wants forgiveness. Or will he want her instead of me? Assuming there is another woman. If so, it's either a fling or it isn't. Oh dear, I don't even want to think about it. Look how it's making me crazy talk."

"Shelby, all will end up as is God's will. We don't always see that right away. Things are either gonna' make you stronger or carry you to a better place in the storm. And I hope it's with you and Jim together."

Jane stood and carried her dishes to the sink.

"Oh dear, I've been around Henry too long. I'm sounding like the preacher, but you know, I do believe we always end up where we should be. Look how Mother lived her last days in a place that was a sanctuary to her and Papa after those horrid years that drove so many west."

I fixed sandwiches for Billy and Lorene, and then I went upstairs and changed into my challis shirtwaist and my shiny black pumps. Unbraided my hair and twirled it into a French twist, fastening it with pins. Just as I poured Billy a glass of milk, the phone rang. It was Jim.

"I have to work late. Can't make the concert."

"Really?" I answered after a long pause as I swallowed my disappointment. "Lorene will be sorry to hear that. I'll wrap your sandwich and put it in the icebox," and I hung up before he could respond.

It was almost ten o'clock when I drove through the Texas night toward home.

"Lorene, your choir was better tonight than I've ever heard y'all. Such great songs, and even the first-rate backup with the wind ensemble in tune. All the practice is showin'. I do wish your father could have heard you, but he had to work late."

"As usual," said Lorene. "But thanks, Mom. I think I'll sign up for choir in junior year."

"That's music to my ears," and Lorene and I laughed. I imagined our words had gone over Billy's head or, more likely, he'd already dozed off.

After I locked the gate, I drove down the lane to our house and saw that Jim's truck was nowhere in sight.

Chapter 21

The temperature was pleasant for a June day, a day of heavy clouds of gray stubbornly holding rain as I picked up Curtye Lee at the department store on Denrock Street. Promptly at noon, as we'd agreed. She was quieter than usual on the drive out to the ranch, which struck me odd, for I was accustomed to Curtye Lee's bubbling demeanor. The break-up with Willie Bob Preston had whittled away her sunny nature, but she'd worked through that and had been seeing that new young man that Jane and I had yet to meet.

"You know, Curtye Lee, Jane and I will be glad to give your new beau a once over, the necessary interrogation for someone dating our best friend," I said, turning to see her face and finding a brief smile. "How did your dinner date go with George?"

"It was a fine dinner." Unlike Curtye Lee, she failed to share the details and feelings so often eager in her face and gestures.

"Well, I thought at our next meeting we might talk about prayer, perhaps some of ours and some from the church you attended in Grand Junction. Maybe the prayers. Or maybe chants you've heard around the Indians. Whether or not they are answered. Does it even matter?"

"Hmmm," said Curtye Lee. "I'm intrigued. Did you mention it to Jane? I imagine she would enjoy that as well."

"Not yet, but I reckon she'll jump in," I answered. "She always brings a unique take at the meetings. So, let's do that. I'll schedule a day later in June. But for today, I baked a Danish, a strawberry Danish to be exact, since I have oodles in the garden, and we'll indulge in that and coffee after we ride. I thought we'd ride out into the fields. See if we can find some cattle roaming, the few we've got left here. Jim sold some and sent some north because of this drought. He planted cotton, but only one field this year, so we'll ride around and past that."

I parked the car near the house so Curtye Lee could run inside and change into her riding pants and boots, and I walked out to the barn and began saddling the horses.

"How long does it take cotton to grow?" asked Curtye Lee as we rode the edge of the crop.

"Well, I reckon Jim won't harvest it till late fall. It's a good money crop, so I don't know why Jim hasn't planted all three fields. Probably cause there's been no rains," I said.

"Are things better with the two of you?" asked Curtye Lee as we rode slowly through the tall grasses.

"Let's go slow. The rattlers stir this time of year. Going slow. Being loud gives them good warning and time to slither away. Maybe we won't see any." I tugged Molly in the direction of the creek, thinking that we might find the cattle there, near water and shade. "Not much different with Jim, to answer your question. Not sure how this plays out, but I need to confront him, which I reckon might make things worse, so I'm dragging my feet. Past weekend he went to Amarillo and didn't even tell me he was going. Told me later he'd visited his uncle. Of course, I must admit, that's what he told me. For all I know, he might not have gone to see his uncle. Maybe he didn't even go to Amarillo at all."

"I'm sorry, Shelby. It's always the unknowing of what might come that's the hardest. Y'all have a nice place here, and I'm hoping you don't have to leave it."

"Curtye Lee, the ranch still belongs to Mother, so that won't happen."

"That's good. As for prayers, I'll send one up for you and

Jim. You asked about George. He was quite attentive at dinner. Took me to a fancy restaurant in the De Soto Hotel. Told me all about his family, but what impressed me most was how he seemed so interested in me. Not only asking about my family, my childhood but listened to my every word." I reined Molly and we dismounted, leading our horses as Curtye Lee reached down and ran her hand through the wildflowers. "And George took me to the matinee to see that movie *Shane* at the La Rita Theater on Denrock. He treats me like I'm special, and I feel good about him, but I'm wary of my judgment after being so easily smitten with Willie Bob. With Willie's flash and charm. But I'd like you and Jane to meet George."

"Well, I reckon we'll figure out how to get that done. It won't be at a church supper, for sure."

"Probably not." Curtye Lee said.

I pointed my hand toward the creek and a copse of cotton-woods and black willow. "Look at the birds. Watching us."

In the kitchen, I poured some sweet tea for the two of us and served the Danish. We shared gossip, including the story I'd heard that Blanche Preston and Peggy Brown were seen and heard in a tiff at Porter's Grocery last week. "I heard Peggy started it with some fault-finding remark about Willie Bob."

"Well, when I'd visit their house, I think Blanche indulged in spirits a bit much. Like it was medicinal or something. She seems an unhappy lady to me."

"Oh, Curtye Lee, I'd not call her a *lady*. Though she does behave as if she's royalty."

"She's surely unhappy and, I believe, deep down, so is Willie Bob, but he won't ever let that show." Curtye Lee paused a moment. "Instead, let's talk about George. Too bad Jane isn't here," she said. "I've already told you how good-looking he is. When he listens to me, really hearing me, and I look into those captivating eyes of his, so intent on me, I think I could just fall in love. And, perhaps, I will if I haven't already."

She took a swig of her tea and went on.

"I've told ya he came here from Denver after being offered a job at the bank and once he'd proved himself, he got promoted to the loan officer job. Told me he has two brothers. George is the youngest, and he told me the oldest one moved back to Tyler, Texas. His father works for the Post Office in Denver, and his mother works part-time as a nurse."

"Well, young lady, seems you can manage your own interrogations. He sounds like a nice young man."

"I asked about his faith, him being Catholic and all. He goes to St. Anthony's parish. Said it was in a renovated building from the old Army and Air Base. Guess I didn't know there was such a place. He told me the parish was welcoming and eager for new members. His great-grandparents had come to our country from Canada, Catholics from the outskirts of Montreal. Shared there'd been a strong Catholic community in Tyler when he was young. Said their community had come up from a place called Nac'doches, which I've never heard of."

She took another drink of watered-down tea as the ice had melted.

"Look at me going on and on. More than you ever wanted to know," said Curtye Lee.

"Oh no, Curtye Lee. Sounds better than any background investigation we could do." I laughed. "I can tell you really like this George."

"Well," Curtye Lee continued, "When I told him about Willie Bob and how I'd followed him down here to Texas, he said I was courageous to do such a bold thing. I told him it was the dumbest thing I'd ever done and then, he said it all happened so I could meet George Breville. Can you believe that? Is he too good to be true?"

"Maybe," I said. "I'm always leery of 'too good to be true.' But time will tell. He sounds solid. And I reckon he really likes you if all his talk was the truth."

Curtye Lee smiled and said no more about it.

Jim arrived home just as I arrived back at the ranch after tak-ing Curtye Lee home, just before the school bus was to arrive with the kids.

"Are you fixin' to seed another field?" I asked, wondering why he'd come home so early.

"I am not. But we need to talk. The two of us."

"I reckon we do. Such as that perfume I've been smelling on your shirts. It's not mine. And why are you always getting' so angry when I've mentioned it? I hate you being so secre-tive, Jim."

Jim sat in my favorite chair and began pulling off his boots. I remained standing.

"I've met someone," he said as the second boot dropped. "And it's turned serious. Not somethin' I expected to happen like this, but it has."

Silence.

"That's all you got to say?" I yelled when I found my senses and my voice. "You're telling me this. Just like that? After all the years we've worked this ranch. The children."

I walked back and forth and then dropped onto the sofa. His words were more a dream than real. Like I was sitting in some movie picture.

"I've filed paperwork," continued Jim, "through a lawyer in Amarillo. It's a separation, and once it's signed at the court, I'll move out. That's why I went to see Uncle Joe last week-end."

"More deceit," I snapped, not knowing how to respond to any of this. "When did ya start lyin' to me?"

"Well, the ranch is yours, of course. Your mother's, to be

exact. God forbid, not owning my own home was emasculatin' enough. I don't expect any of it except profits on sale of those cattle, the ones here, and the cotton I planted. The cattle I moved up to a Kansas pasture won't have much profit, and then there's the kids. I want to see them ...."

He kept on talking, but all I heard was the word *separation*, a word holding out hope, and the word *emasculating*, which held blame. As his words continued, I wasn't hearing any more of what he said. I'd heard enough. The tension in my spine collapsed into the pillow on the sofa. My face fell into my hands. Everything I'd feared was materializing right in front of me, like a horrible nightmare. Like I'd dreamt this moment into being.

"We could meet with Henry. Work things out." The words crept out of my mouth. My brain heard them and how they sounded pathetic.

"I feel I'm a young man when I'm with her. Dixie makes me feel needed. I haven't felt needed in a long time, Shelby."

Why did I even want the man sitting in front of me? Saying these hurtful things? We were always a team. How could he not feel needed? My husband was a man I always knew would be loyal to me. Never cheat with another woman. The one committed to his family and the church. Had I truly been so clueless? Or had I taken him for granted all these years?

"I'm not gonna bargain, Shelby. I've gone through the struggle in my head long enough and made up my mind. I'll meet with Henry tomorrow morning. Resign as deacon," he mumbled those last words, as if ashamed, and looked over at me. "I'm not sure what's to work out, except for the property and me seeing the kids. My lawyer said I needed the separation filed before I can move out, so I'll make myself scarce."

Jim stood and climbed the stairs. I felt my eyes water but fought tears with all my might as the kids would be walking into the house any minute. Then it came to me that Jim had planned it that way. *When had he turned so conniving?* I needed to hold it together. All I could think of was the years behind us, our building up the ranch, our babies being born. He's just gonna walk away.

I wanted to fly into him. Pound sense into his head. Break all the plates in the kitchen. Spoon rat poison into his morning coffee. I wanted to tell him I knew it was the blonde down at Tom's Chevrolet. *What did he call her? Dixie?* I wanted to remind him of our vows, but I had to hold it together. Billy and Lorene had no idea. After Jim showered and dressed, he left the house as I stood dumbfounded in the kitchen. As if I didn't know how to prepare a meal. Jim walked out of the house carrying a duffel bag and drove away, his pickup stirring dust up into the air just as the school bus stopped out at the road. I walked through the routine moves of making dinner and small talk with the kids. I helped Billy with his math homework. I showered, went to bed, and cried myself to sleep.

Chapter 22

Jane set the wooden box on the dining table and sat down in front of it. Her Papa had given it to her back after Mother's funeral.

"Your mother wanted me to give this to you after she passed. I don't know what's inside, but she'd said it was important to her that you have it. You know, she always felt she'd failed at being the mother you deserved. She was always reserved, just as her own family had always modeled. Holding her feelings within. Maybe you didn't know, but I suspect you saw that as a girl. I assure you—she loved you mightily. Always wanted the best for you, and we've both seen that you've found it. In your teaching. In your marriage to Henry."

Papa paused after saying those words to her.

"I know she loved me, Papa. I know."

"Jane, your mama will always walk beside you. You'll see the world through her eyes, and she will see what you see. She's not gone from us. I know she'll be with me. And with you—because she loved us. We'll be fine," he'd said, and Jane had wondered, at the time, if he was trying to convince himself or her.

But she already knew Papa's words were true. She'd had that visitation in the middle of the night here at home in Dalhart. She knew Mother was with her, and it filled her with confidence and comfort.

Gratitude filled Jane, gratitude for her friends who'd pushed her to further open her heart to possibilities beyond understanding, and she wished her husband could experience the same wide-eyed interest. *Would he ever be open to more than the stern rules of his church?* But it was her church as well, and she struggled to find ways to twine the two together.

In the quiet of an afternoon, Jane tried to lift the hinged lid of the box, stained hickory, but it resisted with all the years it had remained closed. Once open, she found a small stack of envelopes tied with a brown cord. Each envelope was addressed to her in her maiden name and her old address in Denton, Texas. Some to The Cottage and one to her dormitory. Not one had been postmarked, and Jane unfolded a note written in Mother's hand sitting next to the bound envelopes and cushioned by a pair of delicate gloves and a small blanket.

My dearest Jane, these letters contain words I sat and wrote you after we'd sent you away when you were only seventeen. Sent to you at The Cottage in Denton, and then the last letter sent to you at the Teachers' College. I worried about you, yet I agonized about mailing the letters. I was torn between right and wrong until, too late, I found it was I who was wrong. You were always loved, and I should never have felt shame for your misstep with young Gad, for we all make our own mistakes. The blanket: it's a baby blanket I crocheted when I finally realized just how much the gift of a grandchild would have brought to all of us. The last letter was one of sorrow when you lost the baby, and I've come to understand that the students you taught all those years in Dalhart became your family. They were fortunate for your guidance and your example.

I'm sorry I could never say these words to you when you needed them when I was still here on this Earth, but know you were loved and are worthy of all God has blessed to you. The gloves were crocheted by my mother and worn on the day I married your father.

As I've told your father, always think of me in the next room. For all my years past, I would speak to my heavenly mother as if she were still here. I needed her support, and those chats gave me comfort, even when I thought I'd failed you. Love, Mother

Jane opened and slowly read each letter and cried as she took in the words of her mother's struggle, disappointment. Of her regret and sorrow. Mother had always been eager for her daughter, her only child, to have the education denied her and had never swayed, even with Jane's unexpected pregnancy, from encouraging her daughter through college. Jane gently fingered the baby blanket and the gloves, and then she folded each piece, placed it back in the box, and put the box on the top shelf of her closet beneath an old quilt.

She washed her face, washed away the dried steaks of tears, changed into a cotton sundress, and pinned her hair into a loose bun. All the while, she thought of Henry and why she'd never told him of that year in her past. She'd never believed he would judge her. No one in Dalhart knew, though Jane never intended to be clandestine, only to hold her experience sacred and as her own. The shame and loss, so young in life, had revealed to her that life's trials were lessons and motivated her to bury herself in her studies, intensifying her desire to teach. Perhaps it was shame that kept her from sharing it, except for that one day she drove down to Denton to visit with young Janet Tippett.

She touched drops of her favorite cologne onto her wrists, shook off the sadness that had filled her, and went to the kitchen, determined to hold the past close in her heart, at least for now.

Henry walked into the kitchen as Jane set the small drop-leaf table for two.

"What's for supper?"

"I fixed a pot roast with potatoes, onions, carrots, a bit of celery. Be on the table in a few minutes," said Jane.

Henry took off his tie and draped it over the back of the chair, washed his hands at the sink, and sat down. Jane set a glass of iced tea in front of him.

"How's your papa doing?" asked Henry.

Jane put the pot roast on the table and sat down.

"I talked to him last night. He's been getting together with a few other widowers he knew at church and an old friend from the newspaper, and it's clear their bond sidetracks his grief. He said three of them went bowling on Monday and that he used muscles he didn't know he still had. How about if we go over and visit him at the end of summer or early fall? Maybe spend a week seeing the sights. You know, like a real vacation."

Henry smiled.

"Well, I'm all for that. I'll find someone to cover the sermon for one Sunday in September. I think you're right. It's time we treat ourselves. Life's short."

Jane looked at her husband as if, for a moment, she didn't know him, but her mother's death had been a reminder to both of them that life is fragile. Fleeting. Her husband's putting himself above the duties of the church both flustered and pleased her.

"Wow. I expected that to be a mediation. I'm pleased you see the value of our spending that time with Papa as well as some time for just us, away from the demands of the church. But you and I both know that God will follow you wherever you go. I will hold you to it, Henry. Might start packing tomorrow," she joked.

"Well, every day teaches me something new." He winked at his wife. "Our tomorrows are often unpredictable. About time I take some of that advice I hand out." He reached over and squeezed Jane's hand. "I'm sure you're missing your mother."

"Not so much, Henry. I find she's with me each and every day." Jane paused and smiled a moment before going on, "And I'm a bit surprised by that." Jane sipped her tea. "Does that surprise you?"

"Nothing surprises me anymore."

Minutes passed in silence as the two finished their meal.

"I didn't mean to be so curt in my answer, even though the truth," said Henry. "God does bring us peace in different ways. Yet I'm surprised your mama is spending time here in Dalhart." He paused and smiled at Jane. "I'd say it's a gift that you feel her presence. I can't say I had any such feelings when my father passed, but we weren't close. Ma was the same as Pa; both focused on the farm work, but she's got grandbabies to care for now. I don't even know if she's proud of her son who became a preacher, but Proverbs has taught me that pride goeth before a fall, and I suppose I'm vain to crave it. Ma did her job and sent me on my way."

Jane watched her husband, surprised at his revelations. He'd never talked much about his family from back East.

"I won't say I'm proud of you if pride must come to a fall, but, Henry, I will say that I am grateful to God I found you. Grateful that you're the good man that you are."

Henry helped his wife clean the kitchen, and after he'd dried the last dish and placed it in the cabinet, he walked over to Jane and kissed her, his hand gentle at the back of her neck.

In a whisper, he said, "Jim Hauser came to visit me this morning. I can't say much more, but he resigned as deacon." Henry kissed her on the forehead. "I think you should check on your friend Shelby."

She stood wide-eyed and without words, and Henry walked away, saying he'd be at his desk for a bit.

Jane called Shelby's number. It rang and rang until Jane hung up, determined that she'd visit Shelby first thing in the morning. She went to the bathroom, undressed, and walked into the shower, intent on washing away the burdens of the day.

Chapter 23

I woke up Wednesday morning to rain pelting the roof and windows. Still, in denial of what happened on Monday, I dragged myself out of bed, knowing I needed to make sure the kids dressed for the wet weather, and after breakfast, I'd drive them up to the road to meet the school bus. They didn't need to go to school all muddy just 'cause I was miserable. The rest of the day I'd be free to either wallow in self-pity or to come up with a plan. I'd still not called my mother. I'd not called my friends. I'd not called a lawyer but knew I needed one, yet I could only think doing so would banish all hope.

I pulled a robe over my nightgown. Looked in the mirror and just sighed before going downstairs.

Yesterday, I'd managed to feed the children before school. Jim came by around noon to pick up some clothes, and his only words to me were to ask about taking Lorene and Billy to Amarillo on the weekend to his uncle's farmhouse. I said Lorene may not want to go, and he should check with them.

I stood in front of the kitchen sink, full of dirty dishes, and could do nothing but stare out the window, thinking how, after all these years and in the midst of a family crisis, those few words uttered on Monday were all we had to say to each other. *How did I get here?* The kids were asking questions, and I knew they'd felt tension in the house even before the day the weight of the plains had fallen on me. I'd held them at bay, for now, by saying their parents were working out some disagreements, but in my heart, I knew they knew better.

With the kids gone and the dirty dishes still in the sink, I sat in a trance with my second cup of coffee in front of me. A sip proved the coffee to be lukewarm, and the sound of crunched gravel announced a car. I looked out the window to see Jane's car and that the rain had stopped. I wasn't dressed yet, and sadly, I didn't care.

A quick knock preceded my front door opening and in walked Curtye Lee and Jane carrying a box.

"Just as I thought," said Jane as she put the box on the kitchen counter. "You're wallowing in your misery. I'll bet you haven't even called your mother. Or had a proper breakfast."

I stared at her, unable to answer because she was right. I deserved time to wallow in this self-pity.

"Oh, Shelby," said Curtye Lee as she hugged me and then walked toward the kitchen sink. "You should have called us. You need your friends." Curtye Lee began filling the sink with soapy water and looking for a dishrag.

"It's under the sink. On a hook," I said. "How did you know? I've told no one. Not even Mom."

"Shelby, we live in Dalhart. Of course, we know." Curtye Lee smiled at me and started washing dishes. "Why didn't you call us? You were there for me when Willie and I broke up. When I was aimless and considered running home."

"Did he leave, Shelby?" asked Jane. "Henry didn't tell me. Only that Jim was no longer the deacon, so I knew it was bad."

I stood and walked to the percolator, handed the pot to Curtye Lee to fill with water. I filled the pot's basket with coffee grounds.

"He's gone, for now. I'll make the coffee. We can sit down and talk," I said as I set the pot on the burner and lit the flame beneath it. "I truly feel lost. Haven't told the kids a thing. He's leaving me for that young blonde over at the Chevy dealer. I don't even remember the name he called her. Dixie, I think."

I yanked a dish towel from the drawer and started drying the dishes Curtye Lee had washed.

"I don't even have anything to offer y'all with the coffee," I said.

"We don't care, Shelby," said Jane as she yanked the dish towel from my hand. "You go sit down. We picked up donuts, and I brought a casserole from my freezer." Jane pulled a cold dish from the box and handed it to me. "Put it in your icebox to warm up for you and the kids tonight." Jane pulled down two more coffee mugs from the cupboard and set them on the table.

"We'll sit and talk for a bit. Then you're going upstairs to wash up and get dressed. Does he have a lawyer?"

"Yes."

Jane sat at the table.

"Do you think he's just mad? That maybe he'll come to his senses? Come back home?" asked Jane.

"No," I said. "I kept praying for that all night as I lay wide awake. Like this all ain't real. But he sounded like he's been plannin' this for a while. Like it's arranged and ... no. I don't think he's coming back."

"Shelby," said Curtye Lee as she turned from the kitchen sink, "don't you be so easy to forgive your Jim. He's been up to no good for all this time, and don't you make it easy for him to treat you like this."

"Damn," said Jane, and her friends turned to look at her, unfamiliar with such language from their friend. "I've got to agree with Curtye Lee. Look at all that spunk we've drilled into her, Shelby." Jane smiled. "And I'm sure you haven't called a lawyer, have you? We need to fix that. Today. If Jim hired Lawrence Elliott here in town, we're gonna have to go down to Amarillo and find you a lawyer."

"He hired someone in Amarillo."

"Good. We'll call Lawrence today," said Jane. "They're members at the church, but it's only his wife who usually comes to Sunday service."

Curtye Lee turned off the burner and lifted the percolator.

"Sit down, girls. Here comes the coffee," she said as Jane set the plate of fresh donuts on the table. "I'll get the cream and sugar."

"Good," said Jane. "Shelby needs some sugar." And there was chuckling that wiped the frown off my face.

"Are we still having our meeting Tuesday night at Crawford's?" asked Curtye Lee.

We all looked at each other in silence, worry in our eyes.

"Perhaps we should put those meetings on hold for a bit," said Jane. "We'll just get together here or at my house when we can."

By lunchtime, I had a lawyer, Lawrence Elliott, and an appointment with him the following morning. As Jane had ordered, I'd showered and dressed, and just that act alone had raised my spirits. Gave me strength I hadn't felt the past two days. My friends had left, had gifted me back some confidence and left a casserole for supper. I decided I would talk to the kids after we ate.

After my visit to the lawyer's office, armed with a list of questions and instructions Jane had drawn up for me, I stopped by Mother's house and told her everything. Everything that I knew, which I felt wasn't much at all. I knew that the Rosenbergs, a man and wife committed to each, were executed for treason somewhere in New York this very week, but I still had a ranch to care for and my young son feeding the animals. Me, cleaning out the stalls. I could use a farm hand but doubted I could afford one, and that would be a question for the lawyer, including the disposition of the cattle, which I assumed Jim would take care of.

All the fuss and the details of the days distracted me but didn't soothe my heart. I'd never doubted Jim's devotion, his loyalty, and now I wondered if I'd taken him for granted, just as it came clear to me how he'd taken me for granted. When did we stop being the lovers we'd been in the hard days? Those days, in the beginning, when we thought all was lost to storms, drought, and the depression. Then the war. How could

Jim walk away so easily after all we'd been through? I suddenly felt I didn't even know the man I'd always believed I'd grow old with. Suddenly, life seemed fickle, just like the skies of the high plains, where we were never ready for the curveballs or the swift bolts of thunder.

Chapter 24

"Mom, I'm not sure how to move forward. It's not that I can't. I'll have to. I just … just don't know how. It's that we'd always been a team, weren't we?"

"Shelby, you were a team. Look at what you did with that ranch out there. At the two beautiful kids you've grown," said Lizbeth. "I can't say what's got into Jim's head, but I suspect the day's gonna come when he has regrets. Ain't gonna end well for him. The key is you need to take care of yourself."

I'd gone to the lawyer's office before coming to Mother's house, and Lawrence Elliott had made a list.

"What's the name of the woman he's seeing?" he'd asked, and I just stared at him.

"I don't know. I think he mentioned Bonnie at one point. No. It was Dixie, and she works at the Chevy dealer."

Lawrence told me we needed to protect the property and get financial support for the kids. When I told him about the cattle, he paused, then reminded me that I was entitled to at least half of any profits.

"No worry about the property. The deed's in my mother's name. I doubt there'll be much profit to come," I'd said. "He can have what profit there is 'cause he's gonna have to take care of those cows till they're sold. And there's a few fields needin' harvesting. Cotton and sorghum."

Lawrence Elliott said he'd work out the details, and he asked me about investments and pensions. I'd never even thought of such things and told him I wasn't sure. He planned to call Jim's attorney about the separation agreement and a statement of assets and would expedite the paperwork since I didn't need Jim coming and going at the ranch, but I said Jim could come until the cattle were sold and the harvest done.

"I'll call you when I get the separation papers so you can come in and sign them. Oh, and once the separation agreement is signed, call a locksmith to change the locks at the house."

"Really?"

It all seemed too easy. The dissolution of a marriage. A life.

"Mom, I wouldn't mind if you came out and stayed with us a few days. If you want to. It'd give the kids some continuity. They didn't take it well when I told them about the separation last night. I told them Jim had moved out and might not live with us again. Billy got mad, and Lorene was tearing up as she left the room. Not sure if Billy was mad at his father or at the whole situation."

"He'll be fine. It's probably a bit of both, dear. And I'd love to come out for a bit. Is it okay if I come in the morning?"

"Of course, Mom," I said. "You're being there is not just for the kids. I reckon I need someone near to keep me strong. I don't know why you don't just move out there. It's been your and Daddy's ranch since before I was a baby. Looking back now, I reckon it was a good decision that Jim and I leased the land from you. I'd hate to see the courts give him the ranch. Or be told I had to sell it. Don't know how I'll manage, but yesterday, the girls came by, Jane and Curtye Lee. Brought food. Made me get dressed. Helped me get a lawyer." I smiled at my mother. "I reckon I do have a support team."

"Sounds like it. As for me coming to the ranch, I'm glad to come, but you know I love being in town near friends. Where we all get together, and I can walk to the bank and the grocery store. I won't move in with ya permanent till I'm bent over and on wheels." Mom winked at me, and I laughed, trying to imagine Mom in such a state. The lightness of our talk put me at ease.

"By the way, how's that Curtye Lee?" continued Mom. "I've heard gossip she's dumped Willie Preston and is seeing someone from that St. Anthony church. What's it called—Padua?"

I shook my head. Gossip in Dalhart is still flourishing.

"Well, Mom, Curtye Lee did end her relationship with Willie Bob. As usual, he's always wantin' to move on to his next girlfriend, and Curtye Lee saw the bad choice she'd made to follow him down here. Saw he wasn't husband material. A life lesson, she calls it. But when she went to buy a train ticket back to Colorado, she met a young man from the bank. Yes, he's Catholic, and Jane and I have not yet met him. I think she's had one dinner date with him."

"Well, you seem to like the girl, so I'm sure she's a sweet young woman. You know the church people love talkin' about her, especially now that she's stopped bein' a Baptist. And I don't have to tell you they'll be talkin' about you and Jim, too. I'll keep you informed."

I shook my head, and Mom sipped her coffee, set the cup on the coffee table, and turned to hug me.

"I'm sure there'll be whispering in the pews on Sunday," I said. "And Curtye Lee is more like sunshine than sweetness. I'm sad she might not be a part of our church anymore because she sure livened things up. I'm prayin' this new man might just keep her here. In Texas."

I walked into the kitchen and refilled my cup.

"I'm drinking too much coffee these days, and now I'm not sleeping at night. Worrying," I said. "A bad cycle."

And then, out of nowhere, I just started crying. Mom brought me a hanky and sat near me, her hand on my knee, and all of a sudden, I felt like a little girl. Tears still dripping onto my lap and Mom's shoulder to lean on.

"I just don't understand it. How he can just leave? Walk away from everything. For some peroxide blonde who surely knows he's got a family. How, Mom?" My head fell into my hands, elbows resting on my knees, and Mom moved her arm around me.

"It's all crazy, dear. No explainin' crazy."

We sat quietly for a few minutes, me wiping my eyes and blowing my nose.

"It's not gonna end well for him, but Shelby, that doesn't help you any. You just need to work through it all. Find your own way. Keep the kids busy. Will ya have to get a job?"

"Don't know. Lawrence Elliott will help me figure that out. There'll be some financial support for the kids. Probably not much. I'll figure something out—maybe part-time if I can. Still gotta' feed the horses and keep the car runnin'."

As I left Mom's house, I decided to go get the kids at school, and the three of us stopped at Super Dog for cheeseburgers. They were delighted with the treat, and I didn't have to worry about what to cook.

"Grandma is coming to stay for a few days," I said. "I can use the company, and besides, she's a good cook. Can't wait for some of her biscuits."

It felt good not to be moping but lifting spirits, and as soon as I thought of the word spirits, I remembered our secret group and how we wouldn't be meeting.

"I hope she'll not be kicking up a fuss about the length of my skirts again," said Lorene.

"Well, Lorene." I was distracted back to the present moment. "Let's get along. I'm certain one day in the future you'll be old, and God knows how short your granddaughter's skirts might be."

Billy couldn't contain himself at the thought of Lorene being old and roared in laughter as Lorene rolled her eyes and took a bite of her burger.

"How am I gonna get to Bible school if Daddy ain't takin' me?" asked Billy once he'd calmed down.

"Well, I suppose I'll need to get up early and take you," I

said, realizing that this would last the next ten days. "At some point, we need to sit down and figure out what you kids will be doing this summer. Billy, you'll be in charge of feeding the horses, but you've pretty much been doing that anyway. We'll figure it all out." It was too soon to tell the kids I might have to take a job. God forbid I had to sell the horses.

I welcomed the soothing silence that sat with us as we finished our burgers and sodas.

Driving home, I couldn't avoid passing the Chevy dealer, nor could I resist checking out the parking lot. Jim's car was not there. Lorene turned on the car radio, and I turned down the volume. I wished I could read that girl's mind as she gazed out the window like she was somewhere else.

The sky held a haze in the late afternoon, and as I drove toward the ranch, the murky sky made me think I was suddenly in a whole different world from the one I'd known. Everything around me was a different time and place I'd never been before.

The following morning, I found Mom's car parked near the house when I returned from dropping Billy at Bible school.

"Mom, I'm back," I yelled as I entered the front door.

"It's good I had a key 'cause Lorene was still sleeping, like the dead, when I got here." Mom walked into the kitchen. "Did you get some breakfast before you left?"

"I had a bite of scrambled eggs when I fed Billy. Had to take him into town, to the church."

Mom filled a mug with coffee I feared had sat too long in the pot, and I followed her into the living room and sat on the sofa.

"Well, I heard some gossip last night. First, Maureen at Corbitt's Beauty Shop mentioned that Jim Hauser was leaving my daughter, and my son-in-law, the cad, was sleeping around with some young blonde. Sayin' all this as if I wouldn't know." Mom shook her head. "As if she was breakin' some scandalous news to me. News don't sit still long in Dallam County. And then, one of the women at my card game said you and your friends are said to be having secret meetings in the back room of old Crawford's store. Something about witches and apparitions. I said that couldn't be true. For God's sake, Jane's married to the pastor, and then the women snickered. Good Lord, Shelby. Tell me that's not true."

"Oh, dear God." I reached for my handbag, dug out my pack of cigarettes, and lit one. Took a deep draw.

"Well, Shelby, the good Lord will be eager to hear about this. As will I—so cough it up. Has that new girl, Curtye Lee, put y'all up to no good?"

"No, Mom. She didn't. We all wanted to study the unseen. Mysticism, which, might I remind you, is closely related to some religions and faiths."

"Not my religion," interrupted Lizbeth.

"Mom, there were no witches involved, no Ouija board or seances, though there were cupcakes and a bit of talk of the Indian healers. It was all just curiosity, and you know Jane. Being a teacher, she's always wantin' to learn new things."

"Well, dear, you should keep in mind all this might muddy your divorce, and you know how the ladies at church are—both your church and mine."

My head fell into my hands. Again. Just when I felt I was managing a crisis, a new one popped up. I wondered how we'd been found out and wondered if Curtye Lee had shared something she shouldn't have. Maybe with old Crawford, her boss, or that new fella she's seeing. Then I thought of Billy and Lorene at school. I knew how young kids overhear things and mimic their parents. Dear Lord.

"I guess I need to let Lawrence Elliott know. We decided to back off these meetings for a bit what with Jim's leavin', Mom. But all we did really was read and discuss some books. Poor

Jane. Henry won't be happy about this gossip."

I went to the kitchen, emptied out the percolator, and started a fresh pot just as Lorene wandered into the room, her hair askew. She walked past me to the pantry like the walking dead.

I sat in the old easy chair near my mother.

"We're glad you're here, Mom."

Chapter 25

Henry sat stone-faced at the supper table. It was Friday evening, two days before the Fourth of July, and Jane noticed her husband's demeanor as she set a plate of sautéed sliced ham and a bowl of mashed sweet potatoes on the table. What appeared to be the weight of the world seemed to sit on his shoulders. It was unlike him to withhold what worried him, and she wondered if he was concerned about Jim and Shelby.

"Does the Ladies' Group have a luncheon at the church before the fireworks?" asked Jane, hoping to open a conversation.

"I think so. There's a lot going on," said Henry as he cut a slice of ham into small bites. Jane sat down and poured tea into their iced glasses, and she caught the stern look in his eyes as he looked at her.

"I fear the church is coming apart. Clearly, I've lost control of things. Perhaps, it's more than I can handle."

Jane sat quiet and puzzled, hoping her husband would elaborate, but silence ensued. Finally, Jane broke the silence.

"That can't be, Henry." The colors of a July sun fell toward the west and lit the window in shades of summer, and Jane watched the colors fall across her husband's face. "Our attendance is good. I've heard no stirrings except, of course, our loss of Jim as the deacon. I think you're doing a fine job at the church."

"Jim's departure may be the least of our problems. Appears Janet Tippett, well—she's now Janet Campbell, returned to Dalhart this week, with an infant and a shiny new wedding band. I'm just glad young Bruce Campbell managed to graduate high school before taking on a family." He paused, looked at me with what seemed judgment. "Now, with Joe back in the deacon's position, this might cause some conflict in the congregation. As if everyone hadn't known all along why that young girl was said to be finishing her schooling with her aunt near Fort Worth."

Jane couldn't remember ever hearing her husband sound so cynical. So pessimistic. The news of Janet Tippett's return with her infant was music to her ears. Twice in the past week, she'd spoken to her friend Shelby and was glad her friend's mother was going to join the family at their ranch for a while. The gossip at church, as well as Shelby's grief at the end of a marriage, had kept her away from church the past two Sundays, but Jane hoped to see Shelby and the kids at the fireworks on the Fourth.

"Well, I'm glad the Tippetts will have a new grandchild, though it'll be a hard road for the young couple."

"You know that's not how many of our members will see it."

Again, she heard the sharpness in his voice. Jane felt her throat tighten, and she squirmed in her chair.

"I made dessert," said Jane, hoping to lighten the mood. "A strawberry tart."

"None for me," Henry said as he picked up the pitcher and refilled his glass with tea. "Hadley Brown's wife, Gina, came by to see me this morning about marital problems. I fear this might become a larger problem. I'm going to meet with the couple. And then, after lunch, Gene Crawford and I had a meeting."

Henry stopped for a moment and looked at his wife as if expecting some retort or, perhaps, a look of guilt.

"Apparently, Jim Hauser's lawyer, trying to dig up dirt on your friend Shelby, has been snooping about town and found out about illicit gambling in the back room of Crawford's store."

Jane folded her hands in her lap before looking up and, again, saw the unyielding look in her husband's eyes. To avoid his stare, she picked up her fork and knife and looked down to cut the last piece of ham on her plate. *Had they been found out? The secret meetings are just the kind of story Jim and his lawyer would want to spread around town, taking the spotlight off Jim's misdeeds.*

"Is there anything you need to tell me?"

Oh, God! He knows.

"I assume you've found out that Shelby, Curtye Lee, and I have been meeting in Crawford's back room to discuss books," I spurt out the words before they were swallowed and disappeared. I put down my fork and looked directly into his eyes.

"Yes, appears the rumors of such are rampant," said Henry. "And there's more that I'm hearing."

Jane pulled in a deep breath and gathered the empty plates, carrying them to the sink. She turned to face Henry.

"Yes, we were curious, Henry. About mysticism. About spirits and healers. Yes, I know that's frowned upon in the church, but still, it's all around us. A desire to be close to those we've lost. It was not Curtye Lee who led us into sin. We were all curious, so don't go blaming the new girl as I'm certain will happen at the church."

The room went silent. Jane was shocked she'd been so blunt—accusatory—and she saw her words had ruffled Henry. *Had she gone too far?* She waited and watched her husband gather himself.

"Gene said you were reading about ghosts and talking about shamans. Said he'd seen your books, overheard some talk." Henry shook his head. "I believe he used the word witchcraft. How do you think I can explain that to the church? Jane, I'm the pastor, and people are talking as if my wife, you, are an unbeliever. And when did I ever say Curtye Lee instigated this endeavor?"

A tear escaped Jane's eye as she saw the disappointment heavy in Henry's face, in his eyes searching for explanation. She should have, at least, told him. Though curiosity had always driven Jane, lead her to finish college, she suddenly realized she had neglected to consider Henry in this scheme with her friends. The same recklessness that had led her to Denton, Texas, all those years ago.

"I'm sorry, Henry. Being curious doesn't make us nonbelievers. If anything, we were all searching deeper to understand. So, I'm not certain our curiosity was wrong, but it was wrong for me to keep a secret. You and I have always talked things through, and I never expected such consequences. I'm not sure how to make it right. Never did we talk of witches or the occult, and I'm certain the rumors will fade with new ones, but it's for me to help make it right at church, Henry."

Again, the room went quiet. Jane began to fill the kitchen sink with water just to veil the all-consuming silence.

"I'm going to go work on Sunday's sermon," said Henry. "A new one, truly. Never have I needed more to find all the right words." He stood and walked out of the kitchen.

On Sunday morning, Jane sat in the third pew from the front next to Curtye Lee Logan. Jane had called Curtye Lee and said she needed reinforcements and told her about the budding rumors around church about their secret group. She hadn't bothered Shelby about it because their friend had enough worries in the midst of her divorce, and Shelby had skipped church on this Sunday. Blanche Preston, a small navy-blue hat dressing her brown curls, sat in front of the two women, and Curtye Lee breathed a sigh of relief that Willie Bob was not with her. Just like that day of Curtye Lee's first visit to Victory Church, whispers and muffled snickering echoed in the pews.

After opening prayers, a hymn, and announcements, Henry walked to the pulpit, his face held down and somber.

"Good morning, everyone."

Whispers ensued behind the two women, and then Henry's worn Bible hit the lectern with a thud, clearly meant to wake the dead, and he looked out at his congregation with unflinching eyes. He looked eye to eye at one after another of his church members, and Curtye Lee thought she could hear rustling in the seats behind her, something akin to fidgeting on hardwood.

"Oh, *mon Dieu*," whispered Curtye Lee, and Jane reached for her friend's hand and squeezed it. Jane wasn't sure if her gesture was to distract a giggle or, perhaps, a shudder.

"This book is my solace and my weapon," said Henry. "You and I might well use our Smith and Wesson when we cross a rattler out in the fields, but this book...." He lifted the Bible high above his head before it would land again on the pulpit. "This book is my weapon against the devil, against evil. It's counsel, my scabbard against hate and mudslinging.

"At the same time, most of you may know life comes with struggles, and not one of us is excused of life's struggles. You all know that Jim Hauser is no longer our deacon. You know that our friend Joe Tippett has returned to his old position, replacing Jim, and today he is here with his family, including a new grandchild and a new son-in-law, Bruce Campbell. We welcome Bruce and Janet, and we look forward to getting to know their new daughter, Laura Jean Campbell, our newest member. Our Father has sheathed them in mercy and his goodness, and I have no doubt we will all embrace them in our church, for they are one of us."

Henry stopped again, his stern eyes passing over the people sitting before him, and his grim look lingered a moment on Peggy Brown.

"Others in our congregation have new struggles. Some have long-held struggles and have come to me for guidance. Most of us don't know what tomorrow will bring. I'm here to help. Not to judge. Certainly not to gossip. I'll start with words from the book of Proverbs: *A froward man soweth strife; and a whisperer separateth chief friends.* I know. The Good Book uses some hard words at times. *Froward* means contrary, and we know there's some of that in the church, along with the whispers. Now, let's get to the meat of the matter. Turn in your Bibles to Luke chapter six, verse thirty-seven: *Do not judge, and you will not be judged. Do not condemn, and you will not be condemned. Forgive, and you will be forgiven.*" Henry looked up. "It's the golden rule, isn't it? Not one of us here is without flaws. That's why God sent Jesus to us. God's Son walked this Earth and showed us how to forgive. How to accept those who are different than us, for aren't each and every one of us different from the other? That is how God made us. Verse forty-one."

Henry looked up as if to make sure everyone was listening.

"Stay with me. Verse forty-one: *Why do you look at the speck of sawdust in your brother's eye and pay no attention to the plank in your own eye?* God's words. Now, when you judge another, do you not also look in the mirror? See your reflection? Your own shortcomings? We can do better. Like Jesus, we can embrace all, for we're all flawed. Should we not lend a hand to the needy and the judged, for that was our Lord's example?

"Now, in your Bible, turn to Second Corinthians, chapter twelve and verse nine." Henry paused for those using their Bibles, allowed a minute for them to find the page.

"*Three times I pleaded with the Lord to take it away from me. But he said to me, 'My grace is sufficient for you, for my power is made perfect in weakness.' Therefore, I will boast all the more gladly about my weaknesses, so that Christ's power may rest on me. That is why, for Christ's sake, I delight in weaknesses, in insults, in hardships, in persecutions, in difficulties. For when I am weak, then I am strong.*" Henry paused and looked up at the people watching him, faces full of anticipation. "I want each of you to think about these words. Take the words home with you and ponder them, like a school assignment, for I want you to remember that you, too, are flawed, at times weak. Like my wife, Jane. Like me—yes, even me—and our dear Hadley at the piano. Each and every one of us." Henry saw Peggy's mouth tighten, and she looked down while a muffled titter echoed in the pews. "I hear the sniggers." Henry paused and looked around, happy to hear the squirming on wooden seats. "If you're laughing, you are the ones not looking into the mirror. Like many of us—there but for the grace of God, go I. If you can't reach out to help your neighbor, who will reach out to you through God's love in your time of need? Think about that, won't you? Who?"

Again, Henry gazed, somber-faced, at his congregation. He looked long at Blanche Preston and then old Gene Crawford who looked down at his shoes. Then, Henry's eyes met Jane's and softened as his wife sat in wonder at Henry's stalwart fervor. He swiftly moved his gaze on through the crowd as if he awaited an answer from some brave soul in the pews.

"Who?" Henry repeated.

Curtye Lee turned toward her friend Jane and smiled, but Jane saw or heard naught within the walls of that church but the sound of her husband's love.

"Now I know," continued Henry, "that I'm running long, and y'all have dinners to go to and perhaps a baseball game to watch, but one more thing. The Book of Peter. Go to chapter three, verse eight. *As you go forth today and tomorrow and all your tomorrows, remember Peter's words: Finally, be ye all of one mind, having compassion one of another, love as brethren, be pitiful, be courteous.*" Henry looked up. "For our God is watching. *The light of the body is in the eye*, said Matthew. Do not see the world with the evil eye of darkness, for I, your pastor with all my own flaws and the weakness of mankind, is watching. God is watching. Your own children are watching. You are their example."

Henry stood silent and watched the people before him. Watched them long enough to make them uncomfortable. "God be with us. With each and every one of you through the week. Through your good days and your bad days, may you receive the mercy of an extended hand. Peace be with you. Amen."

A great silence held the church as Henry signaled to Hadley to play the piano, and Curtye Lee lifted her hymnal and turned to the page number posted on the hymn board before she rose, sharing the book with Jane. Piano music filled the room as Hadley played "Send the Light," and Curtye Lee's voice rang silvery with "There's a call come ringing over the restless wave," as one by one, the congregation joined in.

Chapter 26

In the turmoil of a divorce, amidst the town's gossip of Jim's infidelity with the girl Jim had called Dixie, the phone at the Hauser ranch rang on Sunday night. Lorene answered it.

"Mom, it's for you. That Mrs. Brown from the church," she said as she handed the phone to me. I rolled my eyes, and Lorene shrugged her shoulders as she walked away.

"Hello, Peggy."

"Oh dear, Shelby. I've just heard the most terrible news, and I just knew it couldn't be true. The women at the salon whispered that you and Jane—of all things, the pastor's wife—and that new girl from the mountains have been studying witchcraft." I inhaled deeply and knew I should have expected such calls after what Mother had shared with me. "I had to call you to make sure such horrid stories were untrue."

I was so taken by surprise by Peggy's bold accusation that I could find no words. I began stuttering before I could compose myself, for I knew Peggy Brown was the bullhorn of our church.

"Oh, Peggy, what silliness. Are you listening to gossip again? My friends and I had a small book club, just the three of us, where we discussed books and things that interested us. Henry knew we had a book club, but nothing we talked about was ever discussed with him. Let's not get carried away about witches and such." I paused, knowing well of our very deceit and seeing how it was being inflamed. "I'll talk to Henry about it. No gossip here, Peggy, but thank you for the heads up. You know, what with Jim's straying and filing for divorce, my hands are full of misfortune, aren't they?"

"Well, dear girl, I'm sorry about Jim. I've heard about that girl over at the car place, and I do hope Henry's hands are clean in this other matter. I'd hate to see him leave our church. What were you girls thinking? And that wicked girl from Colorado. I'm certain she led y'all astray." As she talked, I envisioned her face all flushed with the thrill of scandal. "Perhaps your idolatry is why Jim abandoned your family and the church," said Peggy. "Now, dear, you take care of yourself and those children. Beg Jim for forgiveness, and he might come home." She hung up before I could say another word or before I could defend Curtye Lee, and I could just picture her dialing her phone to spread the news.

The talk of the town turned from Jim's cheating to my brazen detour from the righteous rules of the church. I was now the wayward woman, and I'm certain Jim and his lawyer were counting their blessings. My prayers that night were for me. For myself and the kids, and I begged God to keep them with me. Mother had said it would be a fine punishment for Jim to get custody, but I could not abide that.

"That young floozy he's chasing surely hadn't planned on feeding and getting two kids to school events," Mom had said. Though I agreed with Mom, I wanted the children to stay at the ranch. With me.

Who had revealed our secret? It had to be Curtye Lee, now being squired around town by a handsome Catholic man. I'd even heard gossip calling her a gold-digger, but that only made me laugh because a bank employee is no rich man, though Mr. George Breville would have a steady income. You have to own the bank to be a rich man. Curtye Lee had been so eager about our discussions—and now she's going to the Catholic church across town. I imagine she'd shared our secret with this new George.

On Monday morning, Mother had left to meet her friends in town, and then, Jane showed up at my doorstep, dressed in a crisp cotton dress, her hair pinned with a barrette. I saw her eyes were red and swollen.

"What's wrong?" I said, and Jane began tearing up. "Sit down and we'll talk. I've been hearing our meetings at Crawford's have been discovered. Is that it?" I started a fresh pot of coffee, and we sat at our usual meeting spot in the kitchen.

"Shelby, I cannot tell you how sorry I am. For what I've done."

"What do you mean, Jane? What happened?"

"You don't know?"

"No." I poured the coffee and handed a cup to my friend.

"It was me," said Jane. "I'm the one who told Henry. About our group. He insisted I tell him what I knew about the meetings. Someone in the church, one of those poker-playing geezers, confessed to the poker games over there, and then old Crawford told Henry about us meeting in that back room. Everyone's trying to shift the guilt. Then Jim's attorney got wind of all the talk. Now everyone knows what we were up to. I'm so sorry, Shelby." Her eyes were wet with tears, and her hand brushed them away.

I sat in dismay, overwhelmed at all the walls crumbling and disappointed in myself for being so quick to suspect Curtye Lee. Our yearning to understand more of the world around us had come crashing down.

"You are my friend, Shelby, my best friend. Henry's not happy about any of this, and I don't know how to help."

"Jane, God is not confined to that clapboard building with

the big oak doors. He does not sit on those pine pews surrounded by hymns. He's not likely listening to the ladies' gossip in Bible class or at the salon. God's bigger than that. You and I know it; we know He created a universe greater and filled with more wonder than we can even begin to understand. Just like that night your mama visited you in the spirit. He's in you and in our Curtye Lee over at that parish confessional and, I hate to say it, even in Jim."

I'd never seen Jane so keyed up. I assured her all would be okay in the end. Besides, that's exactly what we'd told Curtye Lee when Willie Bob Preston showed his true colors and she'd ended the relationship. And she's doing just fine. I even suggested we meditate. But when I said those words, Jane began to cry, and suddenly, she was laughing hysterically. I looked at her and, realizing the absurdity of the situation and my suggestion and then, began laughing with her. I told my best friend about the phone call from Peggy Brown, word for word, and we laughed and cried and then laughed some more.

"Shelby, you should have seen Henry on Sunday morning. Curtye Lee went to the service with me for support, but I didn't need it. Henry gave the congregation what for because of all the gossip. And to top it off, young Janet Tippett came with the baby and her new husband. Henry welcomed them back to church and then proceeded to put the gossipmongers in their place. I'd never seen him so upset. You know—how Henry gets upset, with all his arguments lined up in a row."

I smiled and refilled my coffee cup.

"I'm sorry I missed that. Did Henry's Bible land on the lectern like a gunshot?" I asked, and as before, laughter ensued.

"Mother's staying here with me for a bit, and she told me about the gossip," I added.

I reached for my pack of Viceroys and lighter at the edge of the table where the newspaper lay folded with its bold headline of the execution of the Rosenbergs, more affirmation of what was called the Cold War after we'd fought the real one. I lit a cigarette.

"Shelby, I wish you wouldn't do that. That smoke's no good for you. I know, I know, I sound just like your mama."

I propped the cigarette in the amber ashtray and reached over for Jane's hand.

Jane smiled. "You, Shelby, are the best friend one could ever have. And you know what? All that gossip be damned! I know you will always be with me."

"Sure 'nuff. Always, Jane," I said, squeezing her hand as my cigarette turned to ash in the amber glass.

After Jane left and I heard the kids begin to stir upstairs, I walked outside and breathed fresh air, walked toward the barn and past it, on toward the flowered pasture next to the plowed field Jim had planted. I stood in the stillness of it all, and in the distance, that dreaded sound of crying cattle came and took me back to those years when the government had rounded up cattle too weak to be sent to slaughterhouses and shot them. That awful sound of the ones who hadn't died still rings in my ears. The sound of agony had filtered for days in the dusty skies of the plains until all I, only nineteen at the time, could do was cover my ears and cry. And I realized I felt the same way now, all these years later, as I faced putting my life back together.

I looked into the sky, holding only the empty promise of rain. A grayness hung over the land as far as I could see, and I knew nothing but this place where I'd grown up. Nothing but these wide skies full of voices spoken in the spin of clouds or their very absence, like songs in the heavens. I knew there'd be no storms in the sky today, only the ones stirring all around us.

Chapter 27

Jane woke to a sunny Tuesday after spending half of Monday with her friend Shelby as she'd offered all the support and apology she could. But today, she had another mission. With the breakfast dishes washed and put away, she walked into Henry's home office.

"I'm going over to visit the Tippett family. Really, Janet Tippett and see that new baby up close," she told her husband as he shuffled through papers on his desk as if looking for something.

"Thank you for that," said Henry as he paused from his task. "I'm certain they'll be in a better place with more of such support. They have a struggle ahead, and this community's rebuke can undermine that young couple. Tell them I'll visit in a week or two. When they're settled."

"I will. I'll have the car back in an hour or two in case you need it," she said as she picked up the car keys and left.

The teenage couple was living with Janet's parents, and the girl's mother answered the door. Jane hoped for some alone moments with Janet, and as she entered the living room, she saw the young mother rocking her daughter toward sleep.

"Oh, hi, Mrs. Connor. Bruce is out on a job interview over at the grain silo."

"Please sit down, Mrs. Connor," said Janet's mother, wearing a house dress and apron and looking a bit disheveled.

"Please call me Jane."

"Let me put Laura into her crib," said Janet as she stood and walked away.

"Oh, Janet, can I hold little Laura for just a moment? I'll try not to wake her," Jane pleaded, and Janet gently transferred the infant to Jane's arms. Jane sat quietly, holding baby Laura, watching her. The encounter was too short, yet Jane sat in a different world for those moments as she gently rocked the baby. Taking in the sweet sleeping face and breathing in her fragrance, she closed her eyes for just a second. When she stood to return the child to Janet's arms, she saw young Janet's eyes had watered, and she smiled at the girl before she walked away with the baby. "Thank you, Janet," Jane whispered.

"Make yourself comfortable, Jane," said Janet's mother. "I'm doing some baking for the week. Janet'll be right back." Janet's mother returned to the kitchen, and Jane sat alone in the small living room that felt dreary with so little sunlight from one curtained window. She imagined the young family of three was sharing one bedroom since the younger Tippetts also had a fourteen-year-old son. Joe Tippett, Janet's grandfather, had a larger place at the edge of town, and Jane wondered why the couple had not moved in there instead. Joe was so generous, and Jane was certain he would have offered. Janet walked into the room and offered Jane a cup of coffee, and she left again to return a few moments later with coffee for each of them.

"I can't seem to get enough coffee," said Janet, "what with the baby keeping us up at night, but sometimes Mama helps with a bottle feeding."

"Well, thank you for letting me hold her for a spell. I can't tell you how happy I am to see you back home. With the baby. Back at church. How's Bruce doing with all of this?"

"First, Mrs. Connor," whispered Janet, "you were so kind-hearted to come visit me in Denton. Sharing your story. It opened my heart in a hard time and helped me make this decision. Along with Bruce. I know we're young, but he, like me, didn't want to lose this child. We'll find our way. I'm sure." Jane saw the maturity, a hard-learned maturity, rare in a girl almost eighteen. "And, yes, Mrs. Connor, Bruce has been helpful and eager to get out and make a living, and my parents are happy to see that in him. I took classes in Denton and will get my diploma when all my grades are added at the school." The girl smiled, reflecting a sense of accomplishment. "And Mrs. Connor, you were my only visitor in Denton until Bruce arrived. Thank you," she whispered.

"I was glad to come, dear, and glad for your news. And, I must say, Henry and I look forward to watching little Laura grow up in the church. Your grandpa is such an integral part of our community."

"Yes, Grampy was happy his great-grandchild came back to Dalhart, and he's glad to be deacon again. Pastor Connor's sermon on Sunday was encouraging, but I suppose Bruce and I will have to prove ourselves worthy of support."

"For me, Dear, you and Bruce have proved yourselves to be a brave and loving little family. I'm your cheerleader, you know."

"Thank you," she whispered again, "and I appreciate your encouragement, just between us."

Jane smiled.

"I'll go and leave you to grab a nap while your baby's sleeping. Thank you for the coffee, and you must tell me or Henry if you need anything. I'm sure Henry will be by to visit."

Jane rose, reached for Janet's hand and squeezed it before she stopped in the kitchen with her empty cup and to say goodbye to Janet's mother.

On the way home, Jane stopped by the department store to pick out a gift for Bruce and Janet's baby, with the ulterior motive of checking on Curtye Lee. At the store, she waved at Curtye Lee across the way as she scrutinized the infant goods and chose some sleeping gowns and a lilac-colored cotton blanket for tiny Laura. She smiled at Curtye Lee as she approached the register.

"How are you, Curtye Lee? What with all the new rumors about our mischief?" asked Jane.

"I'm okay. A couple of customers gave me the cold shoulder. But seems no more than usual," and she rang up the items for Jane. She leaned over the counter and whispered, "I heard old lady Brown told Shelby we were a bunch of witches."

"Yes. But who's stirring the pot? Or perhaps the cauldron. Can't you just see Peggy Brown in a witch's hat?" Jane shook her head. "Are you still seeing your new beau?"

"Yes. S'pose we can call George my beau. We're an item, and I've made a much better choice than the one before. I'm not sure what I saw in Willie Bob. He's all flash and good looks." Curtye Lee put the baby gifts and receipt in a bag and handed it to Jane. "And maybe some swagger, but swagger doesn't hold much weight in crossin' the struggles and joys of life, does it?"

Jane laughed. "No, it doesn't. I just visited with Janet Tippett and her new baby. And, Curtye Lee, I want to thank you for going to church with me last Sunday. You, Shelby, and I are a team. I saw Shelby yesterday, and in spite of everything, she's doing well. Now, when do we get to meet this fabulous George?"

Curtye Lee walked with Jane toward the exit.

"I'm sure he'd like to meet y'all 'cause I talk endlessly about the both of ya, but I doubt I can get him to come to Victory Church."

"Well, let's do a dinner. Maybe at my home, but I think it would be a good distraction for Shelby out at the ranch. I'll arrange something but will check the date with you. Okay?"

"Perfect," said Curtye Lee as she hugged her friend goodbye.

It was the following Friday night when Curtye Lee and George Breville drove up to the Hauser ranch. The children had left to spend the weekend with their father at his apartment in town, and Shelby's mother, Lizbeth, greeted the couple at the door.

"Hello, hello. I'm Lizbeth Garrigan, Shelby's mom." She looked Curtye Lee up and down. "Sweetie, you're cute as a button, just like Jane and Shelby told me. I'm so glad to finally meet you. And this is your beau?"

Jane and I walked over just as Curtye Lee was introducing George.

"Come sit down, both of you, in the living room. Do you want some sweet tea?" asked Shelby.

"No, thank you for me. I'll wait for supper," said Curtye Lee.

"Yes. I'll have some," said the tall man with blue eyes that beamed, as Curtye Lee had described to her friends.

"I'll get it," said Jane and she walked away.

"Well, George," I said, "I cannot tell you how grateful Jane and I are to you for keeping our Curtye Lee here in Dalhart, Texas."

The man smiled and immediately, I saw what Curtye Lee had seen that day she met him at the train station.

"It was a lucky day for me to run into this sweet girl." He ran his hand up her arm and back down before taking her hand into his. "She's making Texas look brighter to me each time I see her."

"Mother is fixing most of our supper," I said. "It's been nice to have her here at the ranch for a bit." Jane handed a tall iced tea to George.

"Yes, Lizbeth made a big pot of country ribs, sweet potatoes, cornbread, and green beans from Shelby's garden," said Jane.

"Wow, that sounds like better eatin' than any fine restaurant 'round here," said George.

The five enjoyed an easy supper filled with laughter and revelation, but as Curtye Lee and Lizbeth began clearing plates from the table, I leaned toward George and, in the hush of my church-talking voice, said, "George, we all love Curtye Lee Logan. If you break this girl's heart, you'll never be welcomed in Dalhart again. But if you love her like we do, you're one of us."

I saw a moment of fear in those crystal blue eyes, and then, he smiled at me and whispered back, "I don't think that'll be a problem. I'm very much in the fan club."

Chapter 28

July was coming to an end, and the bright blue skies of the Panhandle showed little mercy and no rain as Henry sat in his church office and waited for Gina Brown, Hadley's wife, to arrive for her appointment. When she'd first called him, she'd mentioned marital problems. After that last appointment with Jim Hauser, Henry wondered if Hadley was having an affair, but he'd known the piano player for a long time and could not imagine such a scenario. Marital issues were tricky, and he was not fond of giving advice on such matters.

Henry called out, "Come in," when he heard the soft knock at his door. Gina Brown was a soft-spoken woman, tiny, with a brown bob haircut and tortoiseshell glasses. She wore a plaid skirt with a matching green cotton shirt, and Henry recalled that he didn't often see her smile. A serious young mother and wife.

"I ... I'm embarrassed about coming to you with this, Pastor Connor."

"Don't be embarrassed, Gina and you and Hadley have known me long enough to call me Henry." He fidgeted with his pen and lay it down firmly, pushing it to the side of his desk to calm himself. "I'll do whatever I can to help. At times, even Jane and I have our own issues to work out, so tell me what's going on."

"Something's come over Hadley. He's always been a quiet man and found solace in his work and music. But he's become more withdrawn, and the loneliness I feel is unbearable. My house would be like a tomb if I didn't have our daughter, Alice, to talk to. And ... I'm uncomfortable saying this, but he shows no desire for me anymore. I can't even remember the last time he kissed me, and I don't know what to do."

Henry squirmed in his chair. This wasn't the first time such topics had come up in his office, but he felt so inadequate at discussing another's intimacy problems. It seemed better advice to come from a mother, but he wasn't sure of Gina's background.

"Well, have you expressed your desire to be closer? Have ... have you talked to Hadley about it?"

"Yes. To no avail. As a matter of fact, it seems to distance him even further."

"Does he know how you feel? And as I ask you that, I imagine his being withdrawn is its own answer to that question." Henry thought of writing some notes on the matter, but it all seemed too personal to record on paper, so he left the pen lying where he'd put it. "Does he know you've come to see me? It might be helpful for you to come in together, or perhaps better, I should speak with him first if he's willing."

There was an uncomfortable silence as if disappointment filled the room. When Henry looked up, he saw tears rolling down Gina's cheeks.

"Henry, I've not told you everything, and I'm reluctant to expose any question of Hadley's character. I've known for years that Hadley is not attracted to women. We've always been compatible. It was like our unspoken agreement. The best of friends. But I know he's more troubled than I've ever seen him, and I do think he could use your guidance. And no, I've not told him I've come to talk to you."

Henry struggled to hide his shock at Gina's words. At their implication. Yet suddenly, he realized his ignorance, his failure to see things happening before his eyes and now, made him doubt himself. He'd always seen Hadley's gentle mannerisms. How he'd handled his music and polished the piano on Sunday evenings, but he'd never given it much thought. He'd seen and heard the teenage boys at church make jokes and chuckle when Hadley played at some potluck suppers. He was the pastor and wondered how he could have missed all the details. *But isn't that conjecture—and making judgments?*

Henry pulled a tissue from the box and handed it over to Gina.

"I think Hadley and I need to have a talk, especially if he's troubled. It sounds like you want to save your marriage, and we'll do what we can to that end. Is your daughter doing well?"

"Yes, she's like me. Likes to read novels. She wants to go to university, and Hadley encourages that. I'm happy at my job, but not like Hadley, who loves his music and his art at the shop."

"Gina, I suggest you take up a hobby that you love, like Hadley loves his music. One day, your daughter will be gone, and creating things with our own hands is a fulfillment we all need. That's some advice I need to take for myself, I must say. We'll talk again, and I want you to give me a call if things get better or get worse. Okay?"

It was the first week of August when Hadley walked into Henry's office.

"Henry, I was afraid it would all come to this. Gina told me she'd come to see you. She told you."

"Sit down, Hadley. I just want to talk."

"I thought I was being dismissed."

"No. But we might need to iron out some concerns. As I'm sure you know, Gina is worried. And lonely. But I imagine you may be lonely as well."

Henry turned silent, his silence urging Hadley to open up. Time passed, but Hadley didn't budge.

"Why did you think you were being dismissed?"

"Well, I think Gina told you, and I know the church frowns upon such leanings. Lately, I've felt more lonely. It's just ... I've always been who I am," Hadley paused. His reluctance to say too much was obvious. "I don't want Gina to be unhappy, but she expects more than I can give. Wants me to be her version of me."

"Well, everything aside, that's a common issue in marriage. But what is your version of you?" Again, Henry noticed he was fidgeting with his damned pen, and he set it down. Placed his hand flat on the desk to still it.

"I don't show a lot of emotion," said Hadley, looking down. "Since I was young, I've always been drawn to men, not girls ... or women, I should say." Hadley looked up and looked Henry in the eye. "I know what the church says. I've tried, and succeeded with all my might, to follow its tenets, but that doesn't change who I am. I feel like I live a deceptive life, but I don't. I love Gina. Being a father. Never wanted to disappoint my ma."

Henry thought a moment of Peggy Brown and what a force she'd be at finding this out about her son. Peggy Brown was enough to keep anyone on the straight and narrow.

"But recently, I lusted after a young man who visited my shop." Hadley paused a moment. "I know the man would haughtily reject my feelings, but I never acted on them. Such behavior would destroy my mother, who struggles to barely accept me as she thinks I am. It would undo my place in this community, our church. My worst nightmare, yet it weighs heavy in my mind."

Well, Henry thought, there it is. Right out in the open.

"Hadley, you know the Bible says it's a sin. You made a commitment all those years ago to Gina, and I know you care about your family. Seems you have a path to choose, and I'm not sure how to help you with that."

"I know, sir. Gina has, over the years, been accepting of who I am."

"Maybe she's changed. We all change in time. Does Gina have family here?" asked Henry.

"No. Her parents moved to Abilene during the war. Her

dad took a job at the Army Air Field down there. Gina and I turn to each other for friendship and support. And she has her high school friends here. That's our bond, and I'm grateful for it, but sometimes I feel like an imprisoned man."

"Well, the church hasn't, yet, demanded your ouster, but you know these desires you speak of are abominable to God. I want you to stay at the church, and I advise you to pray on this matter."

"I will, Henry, but don't think I haven't spent years doin' just that."

"Well, I want you to visit with me again in a couple of weeks, and we'll see where you are, if you've made peace with God, with yourself, and, I hope, some comfort to Gina. Okay?"

After supper that evening, Jane walked into the living room to find Henry sitting in the dark.

"Henry, are you okay?"

After a brief silence, "I don't know," was his response.

Jane sat on the arm of the chair and put her arm around his shoulders. She could feel how tight his neck muscles were and started to rub them gently.

"Can I help?"

"Well, rubbing my back seems to help." Through moonlight spilled through the window, she could see him look up at her with a meager smile. "The church seems to be treading water, Jane. Why can't I get the congregation moving forward instead of sideways? I feel like a failure. I know God's path is often through the struggle. I know I'm going against my practice of not sharing private conversations, but Gina and Hadley have come to me with problems that may be beyond me. Did you ever think there was something different about Hadley?"

"Yes, I have. He's a dear and creative man, but there are boys at church I've heard call him a *pansy*, and though that's a lovely bloom, the term is meant to belittle. On the other hand,

I've always felt that he and Gina were solid. Hadley's built a solid life."

"Well, you've been more sharp-eyed than me. It's funny. You used the same words Hadley used when we met, and I don't know how to tell him to be someone else. Even if it's God's word that he does so. Yet scriptures say there's no other way to the Lord."

Chapter 29

Porter's Grocery was more crowded than usual on an early Friday evening, the first Friday of August, and Curtye Lee tagged along with George to pick up some items for a home-cooked meal he'd promised her. As she picked out three firm tomatoes and put them in the cart with the pasta and fresh parsley, George ran his hand gently down her bare arm, sending a tingle into her core. Her new man touched her often in a way that made it clear she was always on his mind, and she knew she was falling in love. At last, she was in love with a man that deserved her.

As the couple walked down the canned goods aisle, Curtye Lee heard a ruckus in the store. It sounded like someone was singing and yelling at the same time, and when Curtye Lee heard the name Willie, she knew right away it was the voice of Blanche Preston.

George was pushing the cart. "Follow me," said Curtye Lee, and she walked toward the noise.

Near the refrigerated section, she found Blanche Preston standing over an open carton of eggs, shells broken and egg white and yolks seeping across the floor.

"This is my ... family. This mess on ... the floor," yelled Blanche to a gathering audience, "oh, the floor is moving." It came clear to Curtye Lee that the carton had been thrown to the floor.

Curtye Lee had never seen Blanche Preston look so scruffy, her dress with buttons unmatched to corresponding button-holes and some not buttoned at all, and her hair looked like it had been pinned up, but pieces had fallen loose about her face. The woman's fondness for the potions she kept in glass decanters had not gone unnoticed by Curtye Lee, and now, Blanche's unsteadiness and disheveled appearance revealed right away that the woman was drunk.

"Oh, look," yelled Blanche, pointing at Curtye Lee. "It's Curtye Logan, Curtye Lee … Logan, that tramp from some mountains up north. Tried to snag my boy. That no good boy of mine, Willie Bob, just like his daddy who shot himself in the head."

Curtye Lee heard gasps behind her. She looked over at George, his eyes wide in disbelief at the sight before them. The Preston secret was a secret no more, and Curtye Lee wondered if Willie had revealed his discovery. If he'd told his mother that he'd found the death certificate about what really happened to his pa.

"Willie's Pa," and Blanche hiccupped and stumbled. "Was a good-for nothin'. A loser. Bill Preston. No good for nothing. And Willie's the apple. Fell from the tree … he did." Curtye Lee reached out to grab Blanche's arm as the woman began stumbling and almost fell into the slime.

"Get your hands off me," she yelled at Curtye Lee. "You're a devil woman. Deviled. Like them broken eggs."

"Mrs. Preston, you don't want to be saying these things. We should get you home." At that moment, Blanche yanked her arm back and fell into the mess on the floor. George reached down to help her up.

"Oh, a fine man. I don't think we've … met." She allowed George to help her up. "Hey, good lookin'," she began singing the new Hank Williams tune to George, her words slurred and slow. "What ya got cookin'? Don't ya wanna take me home?" and then she started crying.

"Yes, ma'am. I think we should get you home," said George.

"Home," she sang out the word slow and long till it faded.

Quite a crowd had gathered around the scene, including the young store manager standing there bewildered, but

George managed to get Blanche upright and, leaving the groceries behind, the three headed for the door as Blanche kept talking nonsense and badmouthing her husband and son. Curtye Lee couldn't help but wonder what had happened between Willie Bob and his mother to upset her so.

"Tell me where she lives," said George after they were all in the car. Curtye Lee, in the back seat, gave him directions to the house, and she was grateful it took just a few minutes to get there and get Blanche to the front door. Curtye Lee prayed Willie Bob was home because she wasn't sure his mother could even find her key, but when George knocked, the door opened. Willie's eyes went wide at the sight of his mother, all askew, standing there with Curtye Lee and a man he did not know.

"Your mama needs some help, Willie," Curtye Lee said before Willie Bob could think of what to say. "She's had a bit much to drink, and she fell at Porter's. She was yelling and told everyone about what happened to your pa."

As Willie Bob helped his mother inside, Curtye Lee saw both puzzlement and shame on his face. He wouldn't look Curtye Lee in the eye, and before any more words were said, George closed the front door, leaving the mother and son behind it to deal with their pain. At the car, before Curtye Lee slid in, George pulled a rag from the back and wiped down the front seat where egg whites were congealing.

Once in the car, George turned to look at Curtye Lee.

"What was all that about?"

"You know I used to date Willie Bob. He's why I moved here, and his mama never was friendly to me. I always suspected she might like the liquor a bit too much, which appears to be true, and one night, Willie told me the secret of his papa's suicide back in the days of the storms. He told me his mama didn't know he'd found out and, clearly, she was shamed by it and kept it secret."

"Well, Curtye Lee, all considered, it was utterly kind of you to help her as you did tonight. What with how she was talking to you. Now I know I'm dating the devil woman." He grinned at Curtye Lee, and laughter filled the car.

"Well, perhaps. Thank you for being so understanding," said Curtye Lee, reaching for George's hand as he was about to put the key into the ignition. She stretched over and kissed him on the cheek, and he turned to kiss her more deeply just as the front porch light at the Preston house went out.

"Let's go back and get our groceries. We have a dinner to cook, and I'm hungry," said George as he started the car and drove back to the store. "I've heard from my co-workers about the awful times, the storms you mentioned, in the thirties. A terrible time. He wasn't the only suicide as all those farms went under. So I've heard."

As usual in Dallam County, word of the incident at Porter's Grocery spread faster than chicken pox at a birthday party, and Shelby called Curtye Lee early the next morning.

"Oh, my God, Curtye Lee, what happened at Porter's? Tell me everything. I heard Blanche Preston was drunk last night. As drunk as them fellas who hang outside Pete's liquor store, I heard," said Shelby.

Curtye Lee told Shelby the play-by-play of events from the night before, and its retelling sounded just as sordid and dramatic as it had been under those fluorescent lights on Friday. Curtye Lee knew it would be the talk all through Victory Church on Sunday, and she was glad she wouldn't be there. For certain, she would've been asked to retell it a hundred times.

"And your George was there?"

"Yes, he was, Shelby."

"I'm surprised that scenario didn't scare off the poor fella," said Shelby.

"No. He even helped poor Blanche Preston up off the floor. Shelby, I'm beginning to believe I've found my person."

"If anyone deserves that, it's you, Curtye Lee, but don't hang up. I've heard more about Willie Bob," said Shelby. "Peggy Brown called me, and probably everyone else, to share that Willie Bob married a girl down in Lubbock this week, and then she told me the new bride is five years older than Willie and has a six-year-old daughter from a previous marriage. I can't imagine."

"Well, that explains some of what happened. I knew something had happened for Blanche to speak so ill of her darling son. Now, it all makes sense. There's all kinds of thoughts spinning in my head, Shelby. All the possibilities of Willie's action to do such a thing on a whim. You and I both know that's not like him, but I'm pretty sure somethin' happened between him and his mother that's driving him away. I think that'll shatter her."

A short silence passed through the phone line before Shelby spoke.

"Well, that's sad. I think we should be praying for them instead of gossipin'. Set an example for the whole damn town."

"I agree, Shelby. How are you doing is what I should be asking."

"I'm okay. The divorce hearing is coming next month down in Channing. And the courthouse in Dalhart hired me, part-time, to do some filing. Keeping records. I reckon that'll be a help and keep me out of trouble, for now. I do miss our meetings at Crawford's, and I want you to come out to ride with me when you get a day off. Take care, Curtye Lee."

"I will, and I love ya, Shelby."

Curtye Lee wondered how things were going at the Preston home, and in spite of all the history between her and Willie Bob, she couldn't help but feel sorry for the two Prestons. She wasn't so sure either had the heart to help the other, and now there were two new beings involved, but Curtye Lee knew, without a doubt, that she'd ended up in a good place.

Chapter 30

I sat next to Jane on Sunday in our usual spots in the third pew from the front. As a buzz of conversation rose and fell behind us, the seats in front of us, where Blanche Preston usually sat, were empty. I wasn't surprised.

"Henry went over to their house last night," whispered Jane to me. "Willie Bob answered the door and said his mother wasn't feeling well, but Henry chatted with the boy for just a bit. Found out he was moving on down to Lubbock, and Henry encouraged Willie Bob to keep a check on his mother."

"How sad. She'll be lost without him," I replied in my soft church voice. Henry walked onto the platform and took his seat as Hadley started playing the piano.

"I imagine her drinking won't stop what with her son gone," Jane said in a hushed voice, and we both sat up straight as Henry stood at the pulpit.

Henry looked tired as he spoke to us. It was almost like his heart was not in the sermon spilling from his mouth. What with Jim gone from the church, him finding out about our meetings at Crawford's, and now this mess with Blanche Preston, I suddenly had a fear we could lose him at Victory Church. I knew that the Baptist Association of Virginia had provided the initial support to Henry to open Victory Church, and they could likely find a replacement for him if need be and if they chose to continue to support the church. I feared members could be lured to the church downtown.

After the service, as Jane and I leaned against the wall watching the room, certain a few congregants were watching us,

I turned to Jane.

"Is Henry alright?"

"I hope so, Shelby. It's been a tough time ever since Mama died and demands on Henry from the church. One crisis after another, including our mischief at the back of Crawford's store."

As she looked at me, I saw the creases in her face and a new sadness in her eyes. Here, the two of us stood, almost outcasts in our own church, while my soon-to-be-ex, Jim, was out cavorting with his new woman. I'd heard he'd taken her to services one Sunday over at the First Baptist Church at the corner of Fourth Street and Main, but I knew enough about Dalhart to know they'd be privy to all the town's gossip and not look kindly on the two of them. Our divorce had been worked out between the attorneys and filed, but it was not final yet. Jim could have made a bigger fuss about all the work he'd put into the ranch over the years of our marriage, but he was so eager to be done with that life and move on to life with Dixie that he abandoned such a battle. We were scheduled to go before the judge in September for the final decree to be signed and issued.

And there was Curtye Lee over at the Catholic church with her beau and her future looking bright. When I drove to Porter's Grocery this last week, I saw George walking into the Leder's Jewelry store, likely for some shiny trinket for Curtye Lee. I needed to get a grip. I'd been part of this community since the day I was born, and I could do better than I'd been doing.

"Jane, how can I help? You and Henry?"

"I don't know. I try to be supportive because I know Henry's feeling a bit overwhelmed. He loves this church, but you and I both know the people here can be downright stubborn and unforgiving. Henry can't fix everything, and it hurts me to see him trying so hard for so many who are ungrateful."

"Well," I said. "I think I'm gonna' invite Bruce Campbell to do some work at the ranch for me. You know I can't keep up with it all. Jim's sold most of the cattle we had, but he's still got to harvest those fields he planted for his profit, and I don't imagine there'll be much of that with the drought. I just don't know what to do with the ranch. It's been in the family too long for Mother to sell it. Sure wish I could keep it for Billy, but he's way too young for me to even think of that. It's time Mother and I have a long, hard talk about it."

"Don't you even think of moving away, Shelby Hauser," said Jane, just as Peggy Brown walked up to us.

"Well, Jane," said Peggy, "do you think that Blanche Preston will grace the church again with her presence?"

"Peggy, I'm certain she will. She's one of us, just like you. Just like Hadley and his wife Gina. Excuse me. I need to refresh my coffee." Jane walked away, leaving Peggy standing next to me.

"Well," said Peggy. "What's this church coming to? And y'all out there in Crawford's old poker room studying Satan, and Henry's still letting Crawford come to church. I think we might need a new preacher to get this place right again."

My eyes met Peggy's, and I held my gaze on her. "Mrs. Brown, this church is full of good people trying to do the best they can, and I've heard Henry preach how we should reach out to help each other. Seems he's talking to a wall. Jane and I, and even our friend Curtye Lee, have never lost our faith in the Holy Spirit. So, tell me who you've helped this week, Peggy? Pastor Connor's out there helping so many he's done worn out, and I wonder who here is gonna help him."

And with those words said, I spun and walked across the room to join Jane at the coffee pot, where I found her baby-talking to young Janet Tippett's new daughter wrapped in a lavender blanket.

As I drove home, Billy sat quietly in the back seat. Lorene had decided to spend the night at her friend's house in town.

"What are you thinking about, Billy? So quiet back there."

A minute passed before he answered.

"Why Daddy doesn't want to be at church with us anymore?" he said in his serious voice, and a bit surly. "I know. I know. He told us he loves that Dixie girl. She's so girly. Nothing like us, and Daddy'd be happier on the ranch. At our church, where he used to work with Pastor Connor."

Now it was my turn to be quiet for a moment, taking in my son's words. His hurt feelings.

"Honey, I don't think I can answer that. Everything you said makes sense to me, but your Daddy is chasing his happiness. Or, maybe, his youth. Both are mysterious things, like chasing a butterfly."

"Maybe he won't catch it. Maybe he'll come back."

"Maybe," I answered, knowing full well that such an outcome was not at all likely. "But we're going to keep living. And you're gonna keep growing and learning, and we'll shine in all these big Texas skies."

I heard his giggle from the back seat. It had been less than a week since the war in Korea had ended with an agreement to split that country into two. Seemed everything was coming apart. Beneath the blue sky of a Texas summer day, I saw the gate to our ranch in the distance. The gray roof of our house. The refuge of home.

Chapter 31

The skies above Dalhart had been stingy with rain through the summer, impacting the town's economy, but on this Sunday in August the skies had parted and brought on merriment in the morning service. A couple of farmers stood and walked to the windows to see it up close, as if unbelieving. Flashes of lightning across the skies were not seen as God's wrath, but as a song of celebration. Praises were lifted, and Henry pulled hope for an end to this drought into his sermon.

It was early afternoon as Jane fussed in the kitchen, cutting vegetables for a stew, and Henry sat in the living room stewing over all the dramas and struggles erupting in his church. Hadley's dilemma continued to baffle him, but it was Blanche Preston and her downfall that left him without answers. He knew the doctrines would not tolerate Hadley's urges or any abandonment of his vows to his wife. He had seen the anguish on Hadley's face that day in his office, the man's struggle to fit into a world at odds with his desires. That moment of Hadley acknowledging, out loud, his affinity for men to his pastor had been painful, and Henry wondered if the man had ever said such words in his past to anyone.

Then, what do about Blanche Preston? Not an easy person to deal with on a good day. Now, she'd acknowledged her husband's suicide in public and was losing her only son, who'd been her sole reason for living. Not to speak of Willie Bob's unusual behavior. He couldn't imagine getting Blanche to open up about any of this, but it was the only way to help her. Henry didn't often involve his wife in such matters of the church, especially personal matters, but she was a wise woman, and he decided to run his concerns past her after dinner.

His musings were interrupted by two rings on their phone.

"Hi, Henry," said Jon, Jane's father. "Just calling to check in. How y'all doing?"

"We're well, Jon. Let me tell Jane you're on the phone," said Henry, and he called to his wife in the kitchen. "I'm doing alright. The church is keeping me busy. Out of trouble, I think. And you? I imagine it's pretty quiet in the house, but I hope you're getting outside and spending time with your friends."

"Absolutely. My friends are like the national guard, swept right in to my rescue. I've never played so many games of dominoes in my life. Has the drought eased up any there in Dalhart?"

"We got rain today, but I think we'll need a flood to fix it all. Here's Jane. You take care, Jon." Henry handed the phone to his wife.

After dinner, Jane and Henry sat in the living room, hoping to watch the sunset, but the rain continued to pound at the window. Lightning flashed through the room, but Henry knew it was a godsend and hoped there'd be more such days.

"Jane, I'm still struggling with Hadley's dilemma and what to do about Blanche Preston. And all that on top of Peggy Brown, and likely a few more, calling for my removal as church leader. But no matter what, regarding Hadley and Blanche, I'll do what's right. If they chose to fire me, so be it, but for now, I could use some of your wisdom. You always see things in a different light, and that perspective seems, often, to guide me to a solution."

"I'll try, Henry, though each issue is tricky, and I'm not sure I know the answers. Hadley's dilemma is all about the church's doctrine, which makes it easy. But ...."

"But we care about Hadley and his family. That's the problem."

"Exactly, and that's why I love who you are, Henry." Jane smiled at her husband as the couple rested in the moment.

"Let's start with Blanche," said Jane. "Such a looming problem. I worry about her state of mind, and she's resistant to any help. You know, it's possible we can't help her." Again, a pause of silence and then a clap of thunder made Jane start.

"But we'll try," continued Jane. "That's who we are. The trick with Blanche is to find the way to get her to open up. And to listen. Once that happens, we can help her. My advice would be to enlist the help of her closest friend, but there is no one I know of. Sadly, her closest friend was her son." Sadness filled the space of the room. "Henry, this will sound crazy to you, but I have this urge to send Curtye Lee on this mission."

Jane saw the surprise on Henry's face. "I know. I know. But Curtye Lee has this way about her. Like, no matter the hardship, the only way she sees it is love. Corny, right? Oh, Blanche will resist. Be sure of that, but look how Curtye Lee got Blanche out of Porter's when she was drunk. At least that's how I heard it happened."

"Really? You think that'll work?" asked Henry.

"Yes. I do. I even think it's our Hail Mary ... to borrow a Catholic phrase."

"Well, I trust your judgment. Maybe we can start with that if Curtye Lee's willing to do it. Really, there's nothing to lose in trying it if Miss Logan can bear the tirade she'll likely face. So, we'll do that if we can, and if it works, Curtye Lee can encourage Blanche to meet with me. A visitation. And do you think Curtye Lee might get Willie Bob and his mother to come toward a reconciliation? Yes, I know that's asking an awful lot of your friend, but if you're right about her, she might do it. You and I both know Blanche will never be right again without her son in her life."

"That's true. It sounds like a good plan if Curtye Lee can get through to Blanche. God works in mysterious ways." Jane smiled mischievously at her husband, knowing he'd come to grips with her delving into the mystic.

"I made a pound cake. Let me go cut a piece for each of us. Do you want some coffee?"

"That would be perfect. And I'll sit here and think on what we've talked about. Your insight's like gold, Jane. I'm a blessed man." Before she walked away, she saw her husband wink at her, and she knew how lucky she was that the two of them had found each other.

"This is delicious, especially with this pineapple sauce you've never made for me before," said Henry, all full of smiles. "Why've you been keeping this secret?"

"Ha! I just thought it sweet enough to cook it down to a sauce. It works, doesn't it?"

"Yes, ma'am. If only it'd sweeten all those problems at church. What are we going to do with Hadley?"

"We're going to keep him," Jane said, taking another forkful of the cake and a sip of coffee. "Henry, he's a believer, a musician, and a man struggling with who he is in this world. I cannot turn my back on him, and I believe neither can you. He'd never walk away from Gina and their daughter, bring shame on them, so what he needs, Henry, is a way to find peace in that."

Silence sat between them. The rain had stopped.

"That's all we can do," continued Jane. "Help him. He knows what the Bible says, the disdain our culture holds for such. But I know the good Book is full of dichotomies. 'Spare the rod and spoil the child' and then, 'a father should not invoke his son's wrath.' And John says 'no man hath seen God at any time,' but in the book of Genesis, Jacob says 'for I have seen God face to face ....' And so on."

"God's word's clear," said Henry, "in its condemnation of men with men. Right or wrong, the people of the church would drive him out for such leanings, certainly for such conduct. Yet it was never the way of Jesus to turn away the troubled. On the other hand, you've brought it to my attention that Hadley's tendencies may not be so secret, what with the young'uns mocking him behind his back. Making me notice, at last, for myself."

"Well, teasing is just that, Henry. It's not knowing. Plenty of men are neat about their appearance or papers, play wonderful music, or are delicate in their touch. They are still men. It does not mean they are homosexual because of their habits or their talents. And I imagine the opposite is also true. Besides, there are plenty of sign-makers. I'm sure they're not all homosexuals. Those boys at the church are making assumptions based on ...."

"I don't know."

"Henry ...."

Words suddenly stuck in Jane's throat. Henry turned at the tremble he heard in his wife's voice and saw the serious look in her eyes. He waited.

"Henry, I'm going to tell you something. Something I've never told anyone. About me. Long ago."

Henry set his plate on the coffee table and moved to the edge of his chair. His attention intent on Jane.

"When I was near finishing high school, I was a girl in love with a boy called Gad, the same age as me. His mama was Nambe Pueblo, or maybe part Navajo, and she'd imparted a tender character to her son. We loved each other. My papa had big plans to send me to the college in Denton after I graduated. I wanted to be a teacher, but something happened that sent me to Denton early. I found out I was pregnant."

Jane looked over at Henry's face. Looked for judgment in his eyes but saw none. She saw only sadness. He reached for her hand, but Jane pulled back.

"Let me finish," she whispered, "before I lose my courage." She looked into Henry's eyes, her face full of resolve. "I went to the Cottage, the same place they sent young Janet Tippett. Papa drove me because Mother asked him to. I remember that trip. Papa was so full of sorrow, and he left me there and told me I'd finish college later. Mother had said the baby would be adopted, and we never told the boy. Mother was ashamed, and, in turn, I was ashamed. In Denton, I studied and finished my final exams to graduate from school. Papa wrote me letters and twice sent me a book, *The Rim of the Prairie* and Pearl Buck's *The Good Earth*. I have held the memory of those novels because Papa sent them when I needed his love the most. *The Good Earth* still sits on my bookshelf here in this room. In Denton, I buried my loneliness and disgrace in all the books I could find."

Jane took a deep breath. Downed the last of her cold coffee.

"Then, in August, just before classes were to start over at the college, the baby came early. Too early. They could not save him. I'd only been at the Cottage for seven weeks, and I thought the loss was punishment from God. But I've seen enough since those days to know the punishment is in handing away one's baby, never to see him again. That's why I went to visit Janet at the Cottage in April. Yes, I did share a bit of my story with her so she wouldn't feel so alone, and now we're all glad she kept her daughter."

Jane stood.

"I need to refill my coffee. I'm certain I won't sleep tonight. Do you want more?"

"No," said Henry. He knew she had not finished her story. "But I'll take another piece of that cake." Jane smiled at him.

"I'll be right back, and we'll talk."

After she handed the cake to her husband, she sat down. Henry relaxed back into his chair. "You know I love you, Jane. Unconditionally and forever."

"I know. But let me continue. Upstairs, there's a box in my closet with a crocheted baby blanket and letters, unmailed letters my mother kept, unbeknownst to me, from the time I was in Denton. Papa handed me the unopened box after she died, and it took me a few weeks before I could even open it. I always wonder what would have been. But I threw myself into college classes, and then, teaching here in Dalhart. Then I met you. We all have our secrets, Henry. Our scars. Just like Hadley. Poor Hadley, who lives every day hiding who he is."

"It breaks my heart that happened to you, Jane, and that you felt you couldn't tell me. It breaks my heart that you never held your baby."

"Yes. And it's clear Hadley can't tell the world who he is. It came clear to me long ago that all my young students, over the years, some needing more comfort than others, were my purpose. There are all kinds of ways to mother. What happened to me all those years ago taught me, so young, life is seldom what we expect. There are no straight lines through it. So, let's help Hadley."

"Well," said Henry as he looked at Jane and paused. "What can I do except remind him of God's word? Words, I'm sure, he's read them more than once. I guess he's no more flawed than the rest of us." Henry smiled at his wife, his eyes full of love for her. "I'll continue to encourage the church members to judge less and reach out more. You know, he's hidden this from his mother his whole life." Henry paused and shook his head, "I suppose some marriage counseling might help the couple come to see all the good in their relationship. Beyond that, it's in Hadley's hands, isn't it?"

"Yes, Henry. Exactly, and regardless, we can still love him."

He set his empty plate on the table and stood. Walked over to Jane, took her hands, and pulled her up to him. He kissed her.

"Let's go out and look at the stars like we used to when we met. Make a wish if we see a shooting star."

"What would you wish, Henry?"

"I'd wish the skies weren't cloudy so we could see the stars." Their laughter rang in harmony as they looked out at the foggy skies. "I think I'd have to wish that I was as wise as you, Jane. You always find the way to the heart of any problem I bring you. What would you wish?"

"I don't know. The rain's come, so there's no need to wish for that." Again, they laughed. "If there's a shooting star behind all those clouds, I might wish to return to teaching again."

"Really?"

"Yes, if I can find the right schedule. Maybe a history class and a couple English classes. Maybe four hours, four or five days a week. Plus, grading all the homework and tests. We'll see. You know, Shelby got a job at the courthouse."

"That's good. She'll likely need the extra money, and it'll get her out around people. I don't know how they keep that ranch. Even with Jim there, it wasn't profitable," said Henry. "It's late. Let's go to bed."

Jane put the two plates and cups in the kitchen sink, leaving them for the morning, and walked through the house, turning off the lights, Jim trailing her.

"Jane." He continued following his wife toward the bedroom. "One day, I'd like you to show me the box your mother gave you. Only if you want to. It's time we all start healing our wounds, and I'm coming to learn that it's our differences and the scars that make us who we are."

"And one day, I'll show you the box from Mother," she responded.

He kissed the top of her head and walked into the bathroom.

As she readied for bed, Jane felt as light as a thrush soaring in the clouded sky. Her secret was revealed to the man she'd loved from the day she'd met him and who, God willing, would grow old with her.

Chapter 32

Curtye Lee couldn't believe she'd accepted this mission if that's what one would call it. It felt like a walk to the edge of a cliff. But she understood why Jane and Henry had asked it of her. The community had to bring Blanche back to the church, back to her everyday life, or maybe a better one, before she drowned herself in liquid spirits. They couldn't let her wither within her home's walls. Could not let her follow her husband to the grave, for it seemed she'd been widowed a second time with this loss of her son. Losing her son to another woman and, of all things, one she'd never even met.

Curtye Lee knew she was the lightning bolt needed to light the fire. Blanche had rejected help and hidden in shame, but she'd respond to Curtye Lee. Not in a godly way, but it was the spark to open the door.

Then, like icing on the cake, Jane had asked her to call Willie Bob to wile him home and convince him to talk to his mother and mend their rift. Curtye Lee had called him. Three times she'd called before he'd answered, but she'd managed to sweet-talk Willie Bob to come home. To talk to his mother. He said he would come on Saturday, but today, she'd confront Blanche Preston, and it wouldn't be pretty. She rang the doorbell twice, and finally, the door opened.

"Well, well, well. Look who's here."

Curtye Lee could tell by the lilt of Blanche's voice that she had likely had a drink or two since sunrise. She stepped just inside the door before Blanche had a chance to shut her out.

"Barging in, are you? Looking for Willie Bob? I'm sure you've heard he's found the love of his life, and it's not you."

Blanche's voice shook and no longer held the venom it had held the other night, and Curtye Lee knew Blanche would have been happier if Willie had married her than that divorced woman in Lubbock with a child. But it was the new bride that Curtye Lee felt sorry for.

"Blanche," said Curtye Lee, feeling odd calling the woman by her first name, but she'd decided to try anything that might work. She kept her voice firm as it trembled inside her. "I care about you. I know you don't think so, but I do. I don't know if you remember, but it was me and my friend who brought you home from the store that night you fell. I don't like seeing how you're shut in here, seeing or talking to no one, and I don't know how to help."

"You? Help?" Blanche, still standing near the front door in a bathrobe, and her hair unbrushed, streaks down her cheeks from tears that had fallen and dried. "You drove him to that hussy, ya know," she spit out through new tears. "You."

Curtye Lee, without any welcome, closed the door behind her.

"Maybe. Maybe I did. Can we talk, Blanche? Can I make you a cup of coffee?"

At first, Blanche said nothing. Just glared. But Curtye Lee could tell the woman had turned helpless. Unraveled. And then Blanche nodded, and Curtye Lee took her hand and led her to the kitchen.

"Sit down here." Curtye Lee helped her into a chair at the small kitchen table, an old drop-leafed table. It appeared to be oak and handcrafted, thought Curtye Lee, and she wondered if Blanche's husband had built it. "I'll make a pot of coffee if you tell me where you keep the grounds." Blanche pointed to a cabinet.

Once the coffee began percolating, Curtye Lee sat down at the table. Intermittent soft sobs were the only sounds as Blanche's face lay in her hands, elbows on the table.

"Blanche, we're all worried about you. You didn't come

to church on Sunday, and I know you're lonely here without your son."

Another sob came at the mention of Willie Bob. Curtye Lee stood and grabbed a dishtowel. "Here, Blanche, wipe your face." She put the towel in Blanche's hand. Like a small child, Blanche wiped her face and through swollen eyes, looked at Curtye Lee.

"What did I say? At the store? Tell me. What did I say—what did I do?" asked Blanche.

After Curtye Lee told her, more tears flowed until her sobs waned. Curtye Lee touched Blanche's shoulder and poured coffee, setting the mug in front of Blanche.

"Do you want cream or sugar?"

"No, Curtye. I need it bitter right now." Blanche looked up at Curtye Lee. "Thank you."

Ah. Breakthrough, thought Curtye Lee. Then she proceeded to tell Blanche about what Willie Bob had told her—about finding his father's birth certificate, how suicide stood black and bold as the cause of death, how it had crushed him, mostly the secret of it.

"I cannot imagine the wreckage of the storms and how your husband's sudden death must have crushed you. How you wanted to protect your son, Blanche. Was this what brought on your falling out with Willie?" asked Curtye Lee, apprehensive of how her question might stir more emotions.

Blanche sipped her coffee, her eyes vacant. "There are some powdered donuts in that cupboard over the sink. Get them, and we can have them with the coffee."

Curtye Lee rose and got the package, opened it, and placed the pastries on a small plate. Set them on the oak table. Blanche took one, grabbed a napkin, and pushed the napkin holder toward Curtye Lee.

"There were words. Between us about that damn courthouse wedding in Lubbock. Harsh words. I wasn't even invited, but I know why. What was that boy thinking?" Blanche looked at Curtye Lee as if she might have an answer to the question. "Then he spilled his anger at me about his pa's suicide. Said I gelded his pa, like a horse. And about me keeping the secret."

Curtye Lee sat quietly, listening and finishing her coffee, which had turned lukewarm. She had Blanche talking, and she wasn't going to interrupt.

"But how could you tell a little boy a thing like that?" continued Blanche. "What's the purpose in his knowin'? Even now. But he does. Now—now he's gone. Of all places. To Lubbock."

One more tear snuck down her cheek. She looked long at Curtye Lee.

"He shoulda married you."

There it was. Curtye Lee knew, what with all that's happened, Blanche would have preferred Willie Bob had married her. The wayward, bedeviled girl from Colorado. Her preferred daughter-in-law.

"Let's have another donut," said Curtye Lee as she reached for her first one. "Blanche, there's something you can do for me."

"What?"

"First, I'm gonna call you every day to make sure you're alright, but I want you to come back to church. I'll even go a couple of times if you like. With ya. Anyone stares at ya, we'll stare right back at 'em."

Blanche laughed.

"And I want you to talk to Henry 'cause he's terribly worried about you. Okay?"

Blanche raised her coffee mug, and the two women toasted to an agreement.

Henry visited with Blanche the following evening, but Willie Bob never showed up to visit his mother. Curtye Lee was glad she'd made no mention of his coming to Blanche, but she knew Henry had made a suggestion to Blanche to invite her son to visit her and one day to invite his new family.

Time would tell, but on the following Sunday morning, a hot late August morning, Curtye Lee chose the cotton dress she'd worn to church on that very first day and applied her ruby-colored lipstick. She walked into Victory Church with Blanche Preston, arm in arm like the best of friends. Heads turned and chattering came to a halt as the two women stood proud and walked down the aisle to the second pew and sat in front of Shelby and Jane. From behind, Jane touched Curtye Lee's shoulder, and she turned to smile at her friends. Things had come full circle.

Chapter 33

It was Tuesday morning, and Gina and Hadley Brown were arriving in thirty minutes for their first marriage counseling session. Henry recalled his earlier meeting with Hadley, where he revealed homosexual leanings. As he waited and fretted about this meeting, he reached out to move a stack of books from his desk to the bookcase behind him. Rearranged papers into neat stacks.

Hadley knew God's word, or at least the intent after translation upon translation of the original writings two thousand years ago. Hadley knew the culture of Texas and beyond. Henry had advised him to pray on it, but most of all, Henry had advised Hadley to be the best person he could be.

"Your talents, Hadley, are a legacy," Henry had told Hadley at a second meeting. *Choice is a big word,* he'd thought as he'd counseled Hadley. "You're a gift to our church. Your creations color our city—on signs at curbsides and hanging over entrances of local vendors and diners. And your family. Look at them. You give so much, Hadley. Be proud of all you do."

Hadley had smiled at the recognition. Recognition that was rare and unfamiliar to a quiet man in a small town. "You mean I can stay at the church? Play the piano?" he'd asked.

"Yes, Hadley. Of course. As for the rest, you will have to choose. Including the consequences that choices bring. But I want to help with the present and help you see the worth of the life you've chosen for whatever reasons. I'll work with you and Gina to strengthen your bond. Like any marriage, even my own, we must hold our common bonds strong. Nurture them."

Hadley had agreed. Expressed his gratitude for Henry's continued acceptance.

"Remember, Hadley. God made us and loves his creations."

Now, I sat at my desk, waiting for the couple to arrive, when I heard laughter in the hallway just before they walked through the door.

"Good morning. Just the sound of your laughter echoing down the hallway has already lightened my day," said Henry.

"Mornin', Henry," said Hadley, and Gina smiled. Her eyes were brighter than the last time she visited, and her hair was pulled back from her face, a style that flattered her. Henry's heart quickened at the promising start to their meeting.

After offering coffee to the couple and their declining, Henry jumped right in.

"I want to start this off by saying, as I'm sure you both know, that I'm not a marriage counselor. But I know the Lord, and I consider you both friends and valued members of this church, so I'm going to do everything I can—everything you ask for—to suggest ways you can make your life and your union better. Please, please, both of you, be open about what you need from me."

"Thank you, Pastor," said Gina.

"Please call me Henry, Gina. We're family here."

"So, to start, the first thing I want you each to tell me this morning is what drew you to each other. Let's start with you, Hadley. I want you to share what you saw in Gina that made you want to know her better. Tell me about it."

"Well, it's been a while. If I remember right, she was shy. Like me. Met her in junior high when I saw the swing of her ponytail and heard her laugh with her friend. I was almost in high school before I found the courage to talk to her."

"I love that. Tell us more, Hadley."

"Gina was kind. I liked that right away about her, and we became friends."

"Turn and say your words to Gina," said Henry.

"Like a soulmate I could talk to, 'cause I had no friends before that. No brothers nor sisters. We'd fret about the storms, especially about Gina's life at the farm, and in the end, her pa lost it. We'd talk about the stories we'd read, even after the dust storms shut down the schools, about a shared dream to one day see the ocean, and about my piano music."

"Did you play the piano for her?"

"I did. When she came by the house and at the church. Back then, Mama wiped the dust from the piano every morning so I could play, and Gina sat and watched me. Made requests."

"Like what?"

"Oh, she loved me to play 'Georgia on My Mind' and that hymn 'Morning Has Broken.' That hymn is an old Gaelic tune we both loved."

"And 'Somewhere Over the Rainbow,'" said Gina.

"Oh, yes," said Hadley, and they both laughed.

Henry loved hearing their laughter. "What about the ocean? Have you gone?"

The room turned silent at Henry's question.

"No," said Hadley, breaking the silence.

"I'm not going to ask why because I know life gets in the way of such things. But my first assignment to the two of you is to start planning that trip. East or West. Atlantic or Pacific. It's a common dream, so start working on it. Together. And whether you'll go as a couple or take your daughter."

Henry saw Hadley reach for Gina's hand, and she smiled awkwardly. Henry had not imagined things going so well as this, and he wanted to believe it was his doing, but he knew better.

"Okay, Gina. Your turn. What made Hadley stand out to you all those years ago?" asked Henry.

"Well, I'd noticed him, so handsome," she said. "Wore his hair like Ricky Nelson. Once he spoke to me, he became like a best friend. We talked and talked. He listened. Spoke to me in a way that showed he saw beauty in me."

She turned to look at her husband. "I miss that."

"Okay," said Henry, hoping today's discussion and assignments might change that. "We'll address that. But, today, tell me more of what you found desirable in Hadley when you met him."

"Well," said Gina, clearly searching the memories held in her mind. "Like I said, our conversations. And I discovered, just before we married, that Hadley's a great cook."

"Does he still listen to you, Gina?"

"Less."

"Okay, so I'm hearing a couple issues we need to work on. You, Gina, want him to see you, hear you. And if there's something you need from Gina, Hadley, speak up. We'll talk about that next time we meet. I gave you one assignment. Now, here's one more. For the next two weeks ... and beyond, I hope ... I want you each to focus on those traits that drew you to each other, what you've mentioned today. I hear a strong friendship that may have fizzled in daily routine and obligations. I want you to make seeing each other important. Let's see how that works before we talk again. Any questions?"

The two looked at me, their eyes wide with what appeared as singular fear.

"This will be good," said Henry. "See you both in two weeks, same time, same place." When he stood, he saw a single tear creep from Gina's eye and wasn't sure what it meant.

As the sun set in the west, a day-is-done brilliance edging to the horizon, Henry sat at the dining table where he always found comfort and contentment in the meals with Jane at the dusk of each day.

"How did your meeting with Hadley and Gina go today?" asked Jane, knowing her husband had fretted about being able to help them.

"I'm not sure." He wet his mouth with a gulp of sweet tea.

Henry's mind wandered to a long-ago memory of an older brother who'd left home at seventeen and never returned. On a farm where a family worked from dawn to dusk, not much had been said about the boy's departure, and now Henry wondered what had happened to him. Someone once said he'd heard Henry's brother was seen in New York City, but no one in the Connor family spoke of him. As if he'd never existed.

Henry looked over at Jane and thought how his wife embraced everyone, unconditionally. She never judged. He realized that Jane was a better example to follow than the very judgement he often preached. Perhaps, as described in the book of Hebrews, she was an angel sent to him on that destined day when he first saw her come into his church with her parents.

"At first," said Henry, returning to the conversation, "I felt the three of us were sailing smoothly, but by the end of our meeting, I was a bit worried. Then, as the couple left, I saw a tear in Gina's eye. What did that mean?"

Jane smiled at her husband.

"Honey, that could mean anything. Perhaps worry or doubt, maybe some guilt, but it could just as likely be hope."

"Hope," sighed Henry.

Chapter 34

The school year was upon us. I was glad to be home after a morning shopping for school clothes and notebooks. On the way out of town, I'd stopped at Langhorne's barber shop and had Billy's hair clipped to a flat top. We'd just gotten home from town, where I'd purchased Billy and Lorene each a new outfit, a black taffeta skirt for Lorene's choir performances, some extra pants for Billy since he'd grown about four inches, and a pair of new shoes for each of the kids. Jim had been stingy with the money for school clothes, but Mom jumped in to help. Lorene would be a junior in a week, and Billy was about to begin the second grade.

The kids had run upstairs with their goods when the phone rang.

"Shelby. It's me. Curtye Lee. I'm engaged. We're getting married."

"Oh, dear, Curtye Lee. That's wonderful," I said. "Have you told Jane?"

"Yes. I called her first. She's so excited for me."

"Are you sure, Curtye Lee—that he's the one?" I said, moving the phone receiver to my other ear, where I'd already removed my earring. "The forever one?"

"Oh, Shelby. He couldn't be any righter. And we're taking the train to go see my pa. And Aunt Mabel."

"Are you moving home?" I asked, afraid of her answer.

"Oh, no. George just wants to meet my family. We'll get married here. In George's church, and I'll have to finish the catechism first. I've done some of it before, up in Grand Junction, but never been confirmed. We're making Dalhart home."

"Oh, I'm so happy for you, Curtye Lee. And for us."

"I want you and Jane to come. George and I decided to have a small ceremony, a mass, at St. Anthony's parish. I haven't figured it out yet. Don't have a dress. Maybe you and Jane can help me choose one. Or maybe Aunt Mabel. I'll meet George's papa when we change trains in Denver."

"I bet your pa and aunt won't be happy about you marrying here in Texas," I said.

"Probably, but George loves his church here and wants to start our life in our hometown." She paused. I could almost hear the wheels turning in her head. "Imagine. Me saying this is my hometown. And George, too."

"You can go whenever to visit those mountains up north," I said. "We're gonna have to get together. You, me, and Jane. When are you leavin'?"

"In a couple weeks. I still have the train ticket I purchased on the day I met George. He bought one to Denver and then on to Grand Junction. The wedding's in October," said Curtye Lee.

I walked out to the barn to make sure Billy had fed the animals. The chickens were roosting on their perch, and I let the horses out to the pasture and wished I still had a milk cow. We'd had one up until about three years ago. Now, the milk came in bottles. A part of me missed the early morning milkings, and Lorene had spent about three years doing milking duty. Until she turned too ladylike to do such a thing.

Once inside, I called Mom, who was back at her house in town, about Curtye Lee's news.

"Oh, dear," said Mom. "Those girls at the hair salon are still talking about that Curtye Lee. You know, the pastor over at the Baptist Church said all those Catholics are going to hell. Worshiping all those saints and idols."

"Mom, stop it. You know better. Why do you repeat all that talk?"

"Well, they're probably sayin' the same about the Baptists over at the Catholic church." I giggled at her down-home view of the world, and I knew she likely spoke the truth. Mom just lived for chin-wagging in Dalhart, especially at her dominoes games. I had to wonder if she played gin rummy. Or poker, knowing full well her church would tell her she'd go to hell.

I told Mom about the kids' new outfits and thanked her again for her help. Said I'd see her next week after I dropped the kids at school and reminded her that my divorce would go before the judge in two weeks.

"Would you go with me, Mom?"

"Well, yes. If you want, I can take the day off."

"Sounds good, Mom. It's not a show. At least, I hope it won't be. I planned for Jane to pick up Lorene and Billy after school and reckon she'll bring them out to the ranch."

"I think your cousin Esther knows one of the judges in Channing. Maybe she can get you a good outcome at the courthouse."

"Oh, no, Mom. Don't you do that. Jim and I've already worked out the details. Really, our lawyers did. Our agreement even has Jim paying the legal and court costs. Just let the dogs lie where they are."

On Saturday morning, I sat with Jane and Curtye Lee around the Connor's maple dining table. We'd decided to meet at Jane's house before Curtye Lee had to show up at Crawford's at noon. Henry had gone to the church, so it was just us girls, all excited at the prospect of a wedding.

"A simple wedding," Curtye Lee reminded us. "George is spending money on the reception, and I asked Hadley to play the piano. At the wedding and the reception. All his friends and my friends. I invited Blanche Preston."

We all started laughing. "I assume the reception will be dry," I said, and we couldn't stop laughing. Blanche Preston at

Curtye Lee's wedding reception. Never would I have dreamed of such a thing.

"Well, it's at the church," said Curtye Lee. "There'll be wine, and I'll keep an eye on Blanche if she comes. I think she will. She seemed surprised and happy that I'd asked. She'd talked to Willie Bob once on the phone, but he ain't visited from Lubbock yet, and Blanche still hasn't met her new daughter-in-law."

"Mercy," I said. "Who would've thought that could happen? I do feel a bit sorry for her."

"She'll be fine," said Curtye Lee. "If she'll lay off the liquor. I'll send out my invitations this comin' week before George and I leave for Colorado. I need to get addresses for George's friends."

"What's the date again?" asked Jane.

"October fifteenth. I've gotta finish my formal confirmation first. Wish I'd done it in Grand Junction."

"I'm gonna' invite you and George for supper out at the ranch after you get back," I said. "Does George know how to ride?"

"Yes. He'd ride in Colorado. Let's do that one day," said Curtye Lee. "Shelby, why don't you board some horses to make a little extra income. I bet George would like to get a horse but would need somewhere to keep it."

"Maybe," I said. "Don't know about the need here, what with all the ranches and homesteads. But don't know of anyone doing boarding. An interesting idea, Curtye Lee."

Jane brought a plate of cinnamon rolls to the table along with a stack of paper napkins. I walked into the kitchen to refill my coffee.

"Well, what're we gonna do about your gown?" I asked. "I think we need a trip to Amarillo."

Chapter 35

As we piled into my Bel Air in front of Jane's house, the joyful colors of the sunrise bled into the blue sky, and a dark cloud hung in the distance, threatening rain. No one north of San Angelo ever complained about any promise of rain. It was Monday, Curtye Lee's day off, and at the courthouse, I'd asked for time off in trade for a full day's work on Tuesday. We were on a mission.

Levine's Department Store on Polk Street in Amarillo would open at nine, just before we would arrive. Curtye Lee didn't have much to spend, and George had given her some extra money—not much, what with the upcoming trip to Colorado, but Jane and I had already conspired to chip in more to get her the best. This girl expected so little and was happy with what God had given, but if ever a girl should be showered on her special day, it was Curtye Lee. She'd brought the light of her smile to Victory Church, to Dalhart, and likely over to that Catholic church.

"And with that shiny smile of hers, she brought a generous heart," Jane had said, turning to wink at Curtye Lee.

Yes, I thought as I drove south between fields of cotton growing toward harvest. That recent Sunday when Curtye Lee had walked into the church arm-in-arm with Blanche Preston had shown the church what charity looked like. She'd been the very example of a big heart.

"Are you and George going on a honeymoon, Curtye Lee?" asked Jane.

"I don't know. Probably not, since we're spending all our money on a wedding and the trip to Colorado. And George is thinking of buying a house."

"Maybe you should get married and then go to Colorado. Make it your honeymoon," I said.

We drove under a dark cloud, and I wished for that storm cloud to open up and drop a bit of rain. The fields looked so dry.

"Shelby, that's a perfect idea. Maybe we should consider it," said Curtye Lee. "I'll talk to George. And we could take some snapshots from the wedding for Papa to see."

"Any ideas for your dress?" asked Jane as she pulled a compact mirror from her purse and freshened her lipstick. A soft pink.

"Not really. I've seen pictures of a gown with a bateau neckline. I like those. I don't think I want it long. Maybe mid-calf. What's that called?"

"A waltz length," said Jane. "I think."

"Well, I hope they have some choices. I keep thinkin' we should have made one for you," I added.

"Y'all would do that?"

Jane and I looked at each other and laughed.

"Of course we would," said Jane.

"You know. Maybe we should go by Esther's first. Then to the store. Esther knows everybody, and I'll bet she'd knows the best stores or a seamstress. The best fabric stores."

"Yes," said Jane. "That's a good idea. I haven't seen Esther for years. When was it?"

"I think it was just before you married Henry, and you and I went shopping at Levine's."

"Like today," said Curtye Lee. "I can't wait to meet this Esther. She got all our books for the club, right?"

"Pretty much," I said. "If there'd been more, I reckon she'd have gotten them too. I'm sure she'll know the best place to find a dress for you, Curtye Lee."

"Does she know we're gonna spring on her?"

"Yes," I laughed. "I called to tell her we're coming today,

but since it's early, let's go by Belmar's and get some dough-nuts," I said as we crossed into the city, and the click-click of the blinker signaled our first turn since we'd left Dalhart.

We all sat in Esther's kitchen, drinking coffee and eating glazed doughnuts, and as always with Esther, laughing.

"My Lordy, Curtye Lee, you're everything Shelby told me you were," said Esther, "and more. I'm so happy you found the right fella for you. I met that Willie Bob once, back when he was in high school. Mother and I were up in Dalhart visitin' my aunt. He weren't the right fella for you or any girl less he's grown up."

"Well, last month, he married a girl in Lubbock," said Curtye Lee.

"Lordy, that ain't gonna end well. How's his mama doing?"

"Better," said Curtye Lee. I saw Jane roll her eyes, and we laughed.

"Curtye Lee is our fixer," said Jane. "She can smooth over any awkward situation, and Henry and I wish she'd stayed at our church. She's like the bright colors of stained glass we wished we had at Victory."

"Wow," said Esther. "I'm not surprised. This girl clearly has wiles."

Curtye Lee blushed.

"Well, we need to get her a dress," said Esther. "A weddin' dress. Go to Levine's and see what they have. If the right dress ain't there, you go to Marie Cohen's house. I'll write down the phone and address. She's one of my friends who goes to the synagogue over on Taylor Street. She's a wizard with a sewing machine. I'll call when you leave here to warn her you might visit on the spur of a moment."

"Thank you, Esther," said Curtye Lee.

"Oh, sweetie, I'll make sure you have it on time. But, in return, if you find one at Levine's, I expect y'all to come by on your way out of town, and you model it for me," said Esther, pointing at Curtye Lee.

Laughter filled the room. All the doughnuts were gone, with help from Esther's husband, and we were on our way.

It was two-thirty when we stopped back at Esther's place for Curtye Lee to model her choice for the wedding. To be honest, Levine's didn't have a large choice of wedding gowns, but when she tried on the first one, with its full skirt swallowing tiny Curtye Lee, the woman helping us shook her head.

"Dear, this isn't gonna do," said the woman sporting a strawberry-blond bob and rhinestone eyeglasses fastened around her neck with beads. "You just disappear into that dress. Are you open to some suggestions?"

Within thirty minutes, we'd been on our way, and Curtye Lee walked from Esther's bedroom, where she'd changed her clothes and sashayed into the small living room, dressed in an ivory suit of a brocade chintz with the palest-of-pink crepe blouse trimmed in an ivory lace. She'd put on the new ivory pumps as well.

"Oh Lord, girl. Lordy. Even the priest at that wedding will have his jaw hanging open when you appear. What a shrewd choice, Miss Curtye Lee. No weddin' gown would have shown off your curves the way that fitted skirt and blouse do, and with the jacket, it's just enough to make you proper."

Curtye Lee giggled. "I'll pull my hair up and fasten it with the opal barrette my aunt gave me."

"Oh, honey, no one's gonna see that barrette."

Shelby and I bent over laughing, as quietly as we could, at Esther's reaction. We'd felt the same way at seeing our friend in the suit. She couldn't have looked any more beautiful or more like Curtye Lee Logan.

"Do you have a seamstress in Dalhart?" asked Esther. "I'd take that skirt hem up just a bit to fall proper at your calf, and perhaps the waist needs to come in a bit, but your hips fill it out just right. That bit of color in the blouse is perfect."

"I'll ask Suzie Johnston from the church. She's a reliable seamstress," said Jane.

"Well, all that outfit needs is a small hat with a veil," said Esther.

I turned to the square box on the chair and pulled out the palest of hats—slight with velvet bands coming to a point at the sides, points trimmed in pale satin leaves with delicate mauve voile flower petals sprinkled through the hat and embellished with a few well-placed pearls, the edges trimmed in a pale cocoa velvet. Just a touch of an ecru veil stitched to the front. Enough to cover Curtye Lee's eyes till George kissed her but scarce enough to leave it down or pull it back, as she chooses.

"Well, that could not be more perfect," said Esther. "I'll want some photographs of this bride. As a matter of fact," Esther raised her voice just enough for her husband to hear her, "Hank and I will pay for a photographer."

Curtye Lee hugged Esther with all her might.

"I could not have found better friends in this state of flat lands and big skies." Curtye Lee's eyes watered. "Y'all are gonna make me cry."

"Dearie, don't you cry," said Esther as she stepped back, holding Curtye Lee's hands. "And it's not all flat. You haven't seen the Palo Duro Canyon yet, have you? One day, we'll go. I'll bet that fella of yours hasn't seen it either."

We ended up having an early supper in Amarillo. Esther insisted we eat with them, and Jane called Henry to let him know.

"We'll get that skirt over to Suzie to hem as soon as we get back," said Jane as we sat around Esther's table, stuffing ourselves with her fried chicken and mashed potatoes with gravy. Harry, Esther's husband, couldn't handle all the chatter and giggling and left the table for his workshop when he finished his chicken.

Esther refilled our glasses with iced tea, and we all toasted the day.

"This was the best day," I said as we clinked our glasses. "And we're finishing it off with supper with you, Esther."

"And you and Hank are invited to the reception," said Curtye Lee to Esther. "I hope you can come. I'd better get the invites mailed. And I'm gonna talk to George about taking our trip up north after our wedding instead of before."

"Well, see what that Willie Bob Preston did for you, Curtye Lee?" I said, raising my glass again. "All this happened because he lured you to our Texas Panhandle."

As the sun edged toward the west on our drive north, it colored the evening clouds with vibrant hues. Vibrant hues like frosting on a joyful day. Everything seemed to be changing too fast. Curtye Lee getting married, my marriage ending, uncertain futures and Mom getting older. I wanted to slow it all down. Enjoy the moments, big ones and especially the small ones, with family and friends. I missed our secret meetings at Crawford's, but clearly, those meetings were no longer a secret. Now, with Curtye Lee and me working, our coffee klatch has faded away. I was walking a slippery line between all I wanted to hold onto and the unknown future. To be sure I held onto these dear friends, I mustered all the moxie within me.

Chapter 36

The drive to Channing was only thirty miles. The journey made me think of our trip only two weeks ago when my friends and I had the best time in Amarillo. Full of dread, I accelerated my shiny blue and white Bel Air, the one Jim had bought me only two years ago, my destination, the courthouse. The same Bel Air Jim had purchased at the dealership where he'd met Dixie. *Is that when it all began? With the purchase of this car? The lies and betrayal?* A new spring in his step that had gone unnoticed by me.

Inside, I was angry, yet my hands trembled on the steering wheel. *How could it have all been so easy for him? How could I have been so naive?*

"Are you okay, Dear?"

"Yes, Mom. I'm just thinkin' how this day came upon us so quickly and how I never saw it comin'."

Mom turned off the radio in the car.

"Billy is having a hard time with it all," I continued. "And I have no answers for him. I just tell him we'll be okay, and then I feel like I'm lying to him."

"You're not lyin'. You're comfortin' the boy, and everything'll turn out fine, Shelby. I'm just glad I followed your dad's advice and kept the ranch—the deed—in our name. On the other hand, it's a weight to keep up that ranch, isn't it? Did Jim harvest those crops yet?"

"Yes. I think he wants to keep the tractor, but he'll have no use for it. Probably sell it," I said.

"You keep it. You never know if you'll need it. Maybe someone'll come along who can put in some crops. No point all those fields going to fallow," said Mom. "Shelby, let me remind you my will leaves the ranch to you. Let's keep it in the family."

I looked over at Mom.

"Oh, I don't mean you can't sell it if you want. But don't turn it over to the kids before they know what they're doing. Your papa was right about that." Mom looked down to check all the buttons on her dress, always fidgeting. "Are ya feelin' strong enough to face the new-and-less-improved Jim in court? I see you're wearing those diamond earrings Jim gave ya."

I laughed. I turned and looked at Mom. Smiled.

"Yes, Mom, I am. I wanted him to see how good they looked on me with my navy shirtdress. My girlfriends have convinced me I deserve better, so let's get it done." My hands still trembled, but the anger had faded.

After the hearing, I walked back to the car, mulling over just how quick and easy it was to dissolve a marriage. To dissolve years of sweat and struggle, of lovemaking in rumpled sheets or in the barn, to dissolve bonds of love and family and children. Those bonds gone like a runaway calf in a thunderstorm.

"I'd say let's go get a soft ice cream and then drive home," said Mom, "but this darn town is getting smaller by the minute, so let's get out of here."

I started the engine and headed north to retrace the route back to Dalhart. A soft September rain started to fall, and it seemed quite appropriate.

"I think having that young fella, Bruce, who married Tippett's granddaughter, around might be a good thing," I said. "Billy needs a man around, and I'm sure Jim's not likely to be around as much as Billy needs him. He's already made excuses on a couple weekends. I pay Bruce to clean the barn out and do a few other chores every weekend 'cause, God knows, that young couple can use the money, and I can use the help."

"You know, dear," said Mom, "I'd have never thought this of Jim. I guess we can never foretell how a person might change, if I ever knew him at all."

Tears started rolling down my cheeks. Silent tears I could not stop.

"Oh, Dear. I'm sorry," said Mom, touching my shoulder. "Do you need to pull over? I suppose, like any loss, we must pass through the grief." She handed me one of her embroidered hankies, and I wiped my eyes and my cheeks and kept driving. As the rain waned to nothing, the tears stopped.

Nothing else was said until we came to the outskirts of Dalhart, and Mom suggested we stop for that soft ice cream, and, sitting on a bench, we talked about Curtye Lee's upcoming wedding. I told Mom about the suit Curtye Lee had chosen and that Suzie Johnston was altering the skirt for her.

"Oh, that's nice. Does Suzie know it's for a Catholic wedding?"

"Mom, stop it. Love's all the same, but Curtye Lee and George are having a very small ceremony since it's a Catholic mass. They've planned a big reception so all their friends can join in. Even us Baptists. You're invited, and yes, it'll be at the parish."

"Oh dear. There'll be talk. But I'm coming. They'll probably have wine. I doubt Blanche Preston is invited, but if so, y'all have ta' lock up the liquor."

"Mom! Stop the gossip. Blanche is invited. Don't know if she'll come."

"Bless Jesus. I'll be there." I couldn't help but laugh. "Guess I'd better pull that good blue dress out of the back of my closet. See if I have shoes to match. And you wear something pretty, Shelby. There'll surely be some eligible men, and there ain't a better place to meet someone special than at a wedding."

"What am I going to do with you, Mom? The last thing I

need is another man. All I need is a good farmhand."

I dropped Mom at her house before driving over to the school to wait for the end of Billy's school day. Lorene got out later, so I'd leave her to take the bus home. I honked the horn when I saw Billy come out and walk toward the bus. He waved and came running.

"Mama!" he yelled as I stood next to the car. My heart took a leap in my chest at my son's eagerness to see me on the very day I needed such a greeting, and I hugged him when he reached me. We drove over to the place where Mom and I'd gotten our cones and ordered one for Billy.

"Aren't you getting one?" he asked.

"Nope. Your Nana and I got one earlier."

"'Cause you gotta divorce today?"

"Well, yes. That's not why we got ice cream. Or maybe it is. But you know we'll all be good, and you'll get to see your daddy when you want. He says he'll pick you up every other weekend, and the judge said you can spend a month with him each summer."

"And with that Dixie lady?"

"Probably. That's up to your daddy."

"Well, I like hanging out with Bruce when he comes over. I can work with him in the barn, can't I?"

"Yes, you can. Sometimes," I said as we drove toward the ranch, hoping we'd beat Lorene's bus. "You know, Bruce has a new baby, so I think spending time working together will be good for both of ya. What d'ya want for supper tonight?"

"Grilled cheese."

"I can do that, and I have some minestrone soup to go with it."

I had the table set before Lorene's bus arrived.

"A good day at school?" I asked when she walked in.

"Well, I've got a date for the homecoming. That's good."

"With who?"

"Chuck Miller. He sat down with me a lunch and asked me to go with him."

I could tell by the smile on her face and the skip in her step that she was excited. I knew the Millers. They went to our church and had a ranch just east of town, and their boy knew his way around cattle and a tractor. Helps his pa and was raised right, so I was hopeful this friendship would last.

"I've got homework," Lorene yelled as she ran upstairs.

"I'm glad to hear you're excited about doing it. Supper in twenty minutes," I yelled as I watched Billy riding his bicycle outside.

It was late September when Jane and I hosted a wedding shower for Curtye Lee at Jane's home. Jane had fresh flowers and punch, a green gelatin mold, and small sandwiches filled with creamed cheese and vegetables, some with peppers or bits of bacon. A big plate of cupcakes. It was a full house. My mom was there, as well as Blanche Preston and some ladies from our church.

Curtye Lee was gifted with advice and stories and some lovely scarves and perfumed creams. Jane gave her a fine suitcase, in blue that matched that little train case that Willie Bob had given her on her birthday. I'd sewn a lovely challis robe, a fabric good in both summer and winter, in an ivory and pink floral, but the biggest surprise was Blanche's present, beautifully wrapped.

Curtye Lee opened it to find a racy satin negligee in red. I think I gasped a bit when Curtye Lee held it up for all to see, and I can assure you there were a few hanging jaws and a short silence at the sight of it. With Blanche, one couldn't know if the gift was calling out Curtye Lee as a floozy or if it was a true kindness to start off her marriage with a man who wasn't her son. But Curtye Lee, the lady she is, graciously thanked Blanche and refolded the delicate piece before carefully placing it back in the box.

"And I'm sure George will appreciate it as well," said Curtye Lee, and an awkward laughter ran through the room.

After I helped put the gifts in Jane's guest room, where Curtye Lee pulled out the robe, negligee, and one of the scarves to pack for her honeymoon trip, we finished cleaning up at Jane's house, and then I said goodbye to my friends.

"I'll see you both at the church early on the wedding day," I called to them as I left.

On the drive home, dusk slipped in with angry clouds lit almost red in the west. Soon, the winds would stir to remind us that it was fall, and I prayed it would not be too windy on Curtye Lee's special day. I'd already readied my dress for the wedding, a special royal blue dress, my special occasion dress. I couldn't even remember the last time I'd worn it, and I still had to find a dress for Lorene's homecoming and decided I'd take her to town after school on Tuesday. Since the divorce, my contrary teenage daughter had turned more helpful, but I suspect the new boyfriend was at the root of it all.

The meetings at Crawford's poker room were in the rearview mirror, but I missed talking about the mysticism, the ghosts, the ceremonies, each of us opening up our souls in friendship. I missed chatting about any topic, even a bit of gossip. Jane had suggested I lead the ladies' mission group at the church. She said it would do me good. I said it does me good to weed my winter garden. I'd made a decision to take the kids to visit my sister, Linda, in Oakland for Christmas. I'd save up some salary, and we'd take the trains to California. I'd grown up through that Dust Bowl, and before 1935, my older sister and her new husband had left the plains for opportunity in the West, like so many others. She'd last visited Mom in 1947, but I'd never seen her since then though we wrote letters. There had to be life beyond these endless fields and struggles. And there was the ocean. The kids and I would finally see an ocean.

Chapter 37

"Good morning," said Henry to his congregation. "We finally got a little rain, and the season's slowly changing the colors over the plains. God has answered our prayers."

Jane and I sat in our usual place in the third row, but Blanche Preston no longer sat in front of us. She sat in our row, sometimes next to us and sometimes not. We'd heard that her son, Willie Bob, had come for a visit but had still not brought his new family to Dalhart to meet his mother.

"Before I begin the announcements for this week, I want to say that I've had a couple of calls about a misprint in our weekly bulletin. Thank you, Peggy, for pointing it out," said Henry as he looked through the congregation and did not find Peggy Brown. He bowed his head for a moment. "However ... it was not an error. Let me read it for those of you who may not have seen it. '*At 5:00 pm on Wednesday, the church will host a potluck supper of home cooking, hymns, and gracious hostility. Come one and all!*'"

He looked up, gazing through the expressions of the congregation.

"There will be a potluck this Wednesday at 5:00 pm. Please come. There'll be plenty of biscuits, chicken dumplings, and pies, likely a hymn or two. I'm hopeful there will be no hostility at the supper, and that's a hint for our sermon today. On a happy note, one of our former members is getting married this coming weekend. Curtye Lee Logan, our bright light from Colorado. She's marrying George Breville from over at the bank, and we all wish her well. Sadly, we'll likely lose her to George's church, but she's a cherished gift to Dalhart." He paused and looked over the congregation as if a warning. Gossip of the young woman had come and gone and come again since Curtye Lee had walked into church with Blanche Preston last month.

"I ask that we all send up some prayers for Millie Mae Johnson, who is currently in the hospital. She is permitted visitors." He looked over toward the piano. "Hadley, would you please lead us into the hymn."

"That was slick of Henry," I whispered to Jane, "slipping that wrong word into the bulletin."

"That's our Henry."

She grinned, and the church stood in unison to sing "The Old Rugged Cross."

Henry returned to the pulpit and opened his Bible to a bookmarked page.

"Let's start with some gratitude. For those following in your Bible, turn to Acts fourteen, verse seventeen. We still struggle with drought, but the Lord has blessed us with some recent rains. We are grateful, and in Acts, the apostles cried out to the crowd: *Nevertheless, he left not himself without witness, in that he did good, and gave us rain from heaven, and fruitful seasons, filling our hearts with food and gladness.*"

Jane watched her husband in his glory. She saw the changes that had come over the last year, how he'd softened. How he practiced what he preached and preached what he practiced. How he reached out more often for the goodness and not the brimstone. He was a man who gave more than he ever received, and he was good with that. Jane knew how lucky she was.

As Henry spoke the words of the gospel, I could hear the quiet of the vast room, the precious sound of listening. I saw the comfort of love held in my best friend's tilted gaze at her husband as he told a story of his childhood on a farm in Georgia. A story of a young mother, abandoned and homeless, and how a neighboring family took her and her young child in. A story of compassion where others had once judged her.

In spite of my broken marriage and all my whining, I felt

I sat right where I belonged. In this pew with friends, in this small town where we'd struggled and persevered. In spite of the loss, I held a new belief that doors would open and take me to new places, maybe next week or next year. Someday. I felt the warmth of my teenage daughter sitting next to me and knew she would soon be a woman and leave our nest, or what was left of it. I silently gave thanks just before Henry closed his sermon.

"And in all this, let's look forward to Wednesday's potluck supper with hospitality, not hostility, and *above all, keep loving one another earnestly since love covers a multitude of sins*," said Henry, looking up at his congregation. "First book of Peter, chapter four, verse eight. See y'all Wednesday evening for some good food."

Henry nodded toward Hadley, and piano music rang through the church with "It Is No Secret What God Can Do," the new song sung by Jim Reeves. Afterward, greetings filled the room as everyone inched to the front lobby in search of pastry and coffee. Jane had walked off toward Henry, but she was pulled into greeting friends along the way.

"Go get your brother," I said to Lorene. "We're fixin' to head home."

"Oh, Mom, I want to visit a bit with Chuck."

I looked at her, saw the pity face she used when she wanted something.

"Okay. Just a bit. Fifteen minutes, and then you go get Billy so we can leave."

"Thanks, Mom."

As I grabbed a coffee and said "hello" to friends, I saw Lorene and Chuck across the room, standing close to each other, sharing a muffin, and whispering words I could only wonder.

Thirty minutes later, we were on our way back to the ranch and the chores that called us home.

After the sermon, Henry cleaned off his desk in his office, grabbed his keys, and stood to leave when he heard a soft knock at his door. He looked up to see Hadley.

"Hey, Hadley. How's it going?"

Then he noticed how tired the man looked and his red eyes.

"Are you alright, Hadley?"

"No, sir. And I suppose you saw Mama wasn't at church today. She's hidin' 'cause she knows what happened, and the rumors are beginning to stir. Gina's left me."

"Sit down, Hadley." Henry walked over to shut his office door.

"What happened?" Henry sat in the chair next to Hadley.

"She was just up and gone Friday mornin'. Musta' left in the middle of the night. Took her stuff. Left her car."

Tears fell onto Hadley's white shirt, but not a sound came with them.

"And Ella? Your daughter?"

"Nope. Ella and I both woke up to her ma being gone. She left with that fella called Walter from over at Harry's Automotive Repair. She knew him from high school. When I woke, I had no idea where she'd gone, but I knew she and Walter were friends, and finally, at a loss, I went over to see Harry at his auto shop. See if he knew anything. Said Walter told him he was heading down to Florida. Harry told me he was pretty certain the two'd been seeing each other for a couple a years. Told me he was sorry."

Hadley pulled a handkerchief from his back pocket and wiped his face. Looked up at Henry.

"A couple of years. Gosh, Hadley."

"I'm sorry for all your time we've wasted. Just wanted to let ya know. Before someone else told ya. Don't mean to be all tearful. I just never saw that coming."

Henry sat quiet, dumbfounded.

"What are you going to do, Hadley?"

Hadley looked at Henry, his eyes wide and bewildered. "Do?"

"Are you staying here?"

"Sure I am. Ella's in school and has her friends. Got my shop here, and don't worry—I'll keep playing the piano for the church."

"Glad to hear that," said Henry, and he shook his head. "I'm shocked about Gina. She seemed so intent on keeping your marriage together when she came to see me. But, Hadley, I'm glad you're staying. You're like family here. This'll be hard on your daughter, and Jane will be upset to hear this. As am I."

"You know my mama. She'll be all off-kilter about this. Tell everyone how Gina brought shame on the family. I'll do what I can to quell her gossip," said Hadley. He paused, looking down as if he were uncomfortable. "Just between you and me, Henry, I think Gina came to you to ease her conscience. By shaming me. Looking back now, with what I've learned since Friday, I think she felt a need to justify her own actions. Had she not come to you, my secret would still be held within."

Hadley folded his handkerchief and put it in his pocket. "I just wish she'd told me. Been honest and upfront. She didn't even leave a letter, or if so, I haven't found it yet."

"I'm sorry, Hadley. Maybe she was struggling with her choices. We don't know what's in another's heart, do we? Is your shop doing okay?"

"Yep, and I'm grateful for it. But I'm feelin' a bit aimless. I'm supposin' that bond wasn't enough for Gina, but I don't want any badmouthin' of Gina around our girl. It's a hard thing to explain to a girl her age 'cause I can't even explain it to me. But Ella and I are tight. I might have her help me out some at the shop. Keep her close and out of trouble."

"Hadley, I must say I'm taken aback by this. Clearly, neither of us saw it coming. As for Gina and Walter, I'm baffled how anyone kept a secret like that in Dalhart. But be sure, we'll all keep an eye on Ella. Make sure she feels special to us while she tries to grasp what's happened. I do hope you both hear from Gina," said Henry.

"Thank you, Henry," and he stood to leave.

"I'm headed out too," Henry said as he picked up his car keys. "I can't tell you how sorry I am, and I'll count on you to tell me if you need anything. I mean it. I'll walk out with you."

They said goodbye in the parking lot, and as Hadley climbed into his pickup truck, he yelled back at Henry.

"I guess Gina planned her trip to the ocean without me." He chuckled after he said it. Laughing off buried pain. "I'll definitely be at Curtye Lee's wedding next Saturday. See ya there."

Henry's heart sank at the thought of his friend having to play at next week's wedding, but at least he'd be around people who loved him.

Chapter 38

My arms were folded in front of me to hold in the warmth as I stood outside St. Anthony's church, an old brick building once part of the Dalhart Army Airfield. The old military structure was all polished into a church, one more sign that things were never what they used to be.

Jane was picking up Curtye Lee at Sue's boarding house. I'd pulled on my wool topper against the cool morning temperatures, but the day was supposed to be in the seventies by the time friends arrived for the reception. George was not yet here, and I looked up to see Jane's car approach the curb. Everyone in Dalhart recognized the Connors' car, Henry's polished Packard such a contrast in this cowboy town.

The three of us girls settled into a small office the church had allowed us for bridal preparations. It looked to be the church library, edged in shelves of books with a long table surrounded by chairs, but perhaps it was their meeting room or both. George had arranged for flowers in the chapel, but I'd not yet seen them. As Curtye Lee sat in one of the chairs, Jane brushed, swirled, and pinned Curtye Lee's hair into a chignon just far enough down from the crown of her head so her hat would sit just right. I pulled the suit and blouse from the garment bag.

"Do you have a lipstick?" I asked.

"Yes," said Curtye Lee. "I brought my dusty rose. And I brought some hairspray, Jane, just in case the winds stir up today."

"Oh, let me put that on now. We can always count on a good breeze if we step outside."

"Where are you spending the night?" I asked. "Your train to Colorado leaves tomorrow, right?"

"Yes. I have my luggage at George's apartment. Where we're spending the big night." Curtye Lee winked at Jane and me.

"Doesn't sound fancy, but I guess that's where you'll be living," said Jane.

"No worry. Y'all know I'll put my touch on his place. Soon to be our place. And I've done meetings with a priest at the parish, helping me to recall the formalities of today's rituals. I really hope y'all won't be awkward with all the formality of it. Just follow the priest's lead." She stood, and we helped her with the suit that fit her so well, and then, she checked her hair in a mirror on the wall as Jane gave her a hand mirror to check the back. "No one here at the parish bites," said Curtye Lee. Our friend laughed with an ease that told me how happy she was. "George's best man has the rings. Did you make that pretty dress you're wearin', Jane?"

"Yes, I did. It's a damask weave. I thought it would go with Mother's pearls and look special for your wedding."

Curtye Lee smiled.

"Are you nervous?" I asked.

"Of course." She handed the hand mirror back to Jane and took my hand in hers as if we were best friends, which we were, and as if we were young, which were no longer, yet Curtye Lee always oozed youth. "I'm just so happy to have found George. Like it's my destiny." A contemplative look emerged. "We never did discuss that. Destiny and fate. In our little secret group, did we?"

"Secret no more," said Jane with a giggle. "No, we didn't, Curtye Lee. But I think we're all living it. Aren't we?" Curtye Lee smiled wide, and a knock at the door startled all three of us.

I opened it to find a young man, a white collar at his neck, clearly a priest.

"There's a gentleman here who wants to see Miss Logan," he said.

"It's not George, is it? The bridegroom?"

"No, ma'am," said the young priest. "It's an older gentleman. Said he's a relative without an invitation," and the young priest smiled.

Curtye Lee came up behind me.

"Who?"

A bearded gentleman in a navy suit stepped forward. He looked stately in the suit, his hair a bit gray at the temples and smiling eyes, but I could see a mountain man beneath his Sunday clothes, and before my mind realized who it was, Curtye Lee, dressed in her cotton robe, ran into the hall.

"Papa!" And with that one word, she jumped into his outstretched arms.

"Couldn't miss my only daughter's wedding," he said while still hugging her.

"I can't believe you're here, Papa." She pulled her father into the room, and the priest stepped back and asked if we needed anything.

"No, thank you," said Curtye Lee. "No, wait. Yes. When the best man, George Breville's best man, arrives, will you send him over here to get my papa?"

"I will." The priest nodded to them as he turned and walked away.

"You'll walk me down the aisle, right?" asked Curtye Lee with the pleading eyes of a little girl, likely a look familiar to the old man.

"I wouldn't miss it for all the mountains in Colorado," he said, and I saw a twinkle in his eye and knew right then where sweet Curtye Lee had gotten her spark.

"Papa, these are my best friends. Shelby." She grabbed my hand and pulled me closer. Then turned toward Jane. "This is Jane. She's the pastor's wife. Henry Connor from the Baptist church. They're dear friends, all lookin' out for me here in Texas."

The man shook my hand, which was swallowed into the grip of his large palm. Then Jane's. "I'm mighty glad for you lookin' out for my girl. And I'm only Catholic by the influence of my mama, bless her, but I haven't spoken to a priest for decades, till today. I guess it's only Curtye Lee who could get me back inside a parish. Growing up as she did, Curtye Lee can be a bit of a bulldozer disguised in a charmin' smile." His daughter laughed.

"Papa, we were going to come see ya. In Colorado."

"I know. I'll travel back with ya. Got connections at the railroad, ya know. We'll go visit Mabel. And your beau's family, if it's alright. If it's pleasin' I tag along with ya. I gotta meet this George guy. I don't believe he's asked permission to steal away my baby girl."

"He's a fine man," I said. "We gave him the once over early on."

"See, Papa. I told ya they were my angels."

A knock at the door proved to be George's best man, and after introductions, he led Mr. Logan away to meet George.

The private ceremony began at two, promptly, as Hadley played a piece unfamiliar to me but clearly, a hymn and Teddy Logan walked his daughter down the aisle, the priest leading the way and me behind them as George and his best man watched from the altar. Jane and Henry sat in the front pew with one of George's friends. As I took my place to the side of Curtye Lee, I smiled when I saw George's boutonniere was a cutting of a cotton blossom, white tinged in magenta. The ceremony was formal and longer than I was accustomed to, including a communion. Communion with actual wine and bread and prayers, and the couple knelt before the priest as he blessed their union, with me taking Curtye Lee's bouquet of white yarrow, cosmos, and purple aster. I don't recall ever seeing a couple who looked more in love than our Curtye Lee and George. A reverence for the sacredness of the ritual filled me as I watched my good friend's union and pushed away my fleeting thoughts of the failure of my own.

When Jane, Henry, and I entered the reception room, it was alive with conversation and friends we knew and new friends we'd not yet met. I walked over to the piano and put my hand on Hadley's shoulder, whispered "thank you" so as not to interrupt him, then turned to give his daughter the biggest hug and told her she could sit by me at the meal if she'd like. My heart broke for her, but she seemed in good spirits. I looked around the room and saw my mother sitting at a table with Blanche Preston. *Oh, dear, what could go wrong with that?*

Henry, accompanied by Jane, was already pressing hands with friends from the church and introducing himself to some of George's friends from the bank, a couple of whom were members at Victory Church. Teddy Logan was talking to George's best man, and I saw Jane pulling Henry over to meet Curtye Lee's father. Then there was some laughter, and the Colorado man's guffaw rose above the others just as the door opened and in walked the bride and groom to cheers.

I watched them amidst so much glee and could not help but think of how this sweet girl following a cad like Willie Bob cross country to Texas ended up like this. Clearly, God had a plan.

The meal of London broil, well-seasoned, and creamy scalloped potatoes was delicious. George and his friends had done a fine job with the dinner, the wedding cake, and the flowers. The punch wasn't spiked, which was good with all the Baptists in the room, but there was wine. I'm sure Mom was keeping an eye on Blanche Preston, but I imagined Mom might well indulge in a glass of white wine and encourage Blanche to join her. And there, next to my mother, sat Teddy Logan, laughing. Mom had a bit of a prankster in her, and I realized just how grateful I was for her presence near me all these years. Hadley's daughter did sit by me at dinner, as did Hadley for a brief time, and we talked about Ella's favorite subjects and working in her father's shop on weekends. Jane sat with me for a bit, and we talked about the old days when my brother Paul was still alive, school days, and my sister Linda, now in California. How they all had left, and I remained alone, without them, in the days Dalhart pulled itself out of despair and toward better times.

We all watched George and Curtye Lee have their first dance to "You Belong to Me," and when George handed her off to dance with her papa, I cried. When Hadley played "Unforgettable" by Nat King Cole, everyone joined in on the dance floor.

A young man walked up and asked me to dance. He was a tall young man dressed in brown slacks and a tan chambray shirt with a brown notched yoke. His dark brown boots were polished to a shine.

"I don't know how," I said, feeling awkward about doing something I hadn't tried for years.

"I'll show ya. We'll go slow," he said with a drawl, and I agreed.

As I placed my left hand on his back, he smelled of an earthy fragrance. We stepped in time 'round the floor, and I noticed he had an ease in leading me through the dance. Dancing was tricky for me as it was still frowned upon by many in our church, but the music and joy had coaxed us all to the dance floor.

As the young man and I turned and stepped in time with the music, I had an eerie feeling as if I'd known this young man.

"Do you work with George? At the bank?" I asked him when the music slowed.

"No. I'm from the ranch," he said, his voice bashful and soft. "From the dancin' winds of the high plains."

Had I met him before? What ranch? He smiled wide as we parted at the end of the song, and his familiar smile lingered.

"Thank ya, ma'am. It was like dancin' in the light," he said and disappeared into the crowd. For moments, I stood still on the floor. It was *déjà vu.* Like the moments of me and my brother Paul spinning in the pasture, long ago. I remembered Paul always saying he was *dancin' in the wind.*

Curtye Lee waved at me from across the room. I waved back and looked toward my mother still sitting with Blanche and Teddy at the table. Jane and Henry were deep in conversation at the end of another table. I decided to hold these moments close for as long as I could, and Jane's story of feeling her mother's presence one night hung in the air. *Had I danced with a ghost?* No, he'd been a charming young man. *Was there such a thing as reincarnation?* We'd decided, in our group, that God was beyond all we knew, all we could see, beyond the possibility of our befuddled understanding. *Where had the young man come from? Where had he gone?* One day, I might tell Mom I may have danced with my little brother at Curtye Lee's wedding, and then she'll tell me I'm crazy. Or maybe not.

Before dusk set in, we all said our goodbyes. I wished Curtye Lee and George Breville a safe trip.

"I'll see you both when you get back," I said. I gave Papa Logan a hug goodbye.

As I drove home, I thought about how it had not quite been a year since Curtye Lee Logan had arrived in town and how all our lives had changed. As I drove south, to my left, the skies were turning to night with a full moon. The moon. Like God smiling on us once each month and then turning away to see the rest of the universe. Suddenly, I felt the marrow in my bones no longer held the ache that had haunted me for so long. I remembered a boy who'd once chased rabbits and foxes at our farm and died too young. *Or had he been here, near me, all along?* I'd never felt so present in a moment as I did then.

After I stopped to unlock the gate, I saw the porch light on at the house and heard the lowing of cattle, like a melody. Jim had sold our herd, but a few cattle had gathered by my neighbor's road fence. Nosy neighbors, these cows, no different than life back in Dallam County. Thinking I was bringing them supper, these bulls and heifers called out to me. I told them all to hush and wished them goodnight. I told them the sun would rise tomorrow morning—for them and for me.

Epilogue — 1987

As I sat in my living room in front of my fireplace, waiting for my friends to arrive, I thought back on our years in Dalhart, all the years since then. Our destinies had been forged in our early years. For all the heartache I'd felt when my marriage ended, all the terrors of our years in the Dust Bowl, our losses, God's plans had been larger than all we could have imagined back then.

It's 1987, and both my children have married. Lorene married her high school sweetie, Chuck Miller, about a year after she graduated high school, and they now lived at the ranch, both of their children grown and off in the big world. It warms my heart that the ranch remains in the family. Over the years, I'd return to the Panhandle to visit, but now, as I've grown older, my daughter travels more often to New Mexico.

Let me share how I got here to Truchas, New Mexico. After Lorene married, I decided to move in with my older sister, Linda, in Oakland. Her husband had passed away suddenly. I found an administrative job at Berkeley University, and it was there that I met Jack. He was a Physics professor, and we hit it off right from the day he walked into my office to retrieve some records. *Can you believe the odds?* A Physics professor. We fell in love and married, and when he learned of our secret club back in old Crawford's store, he laughed and laughed. He had the cabin here in the mountains where we'd vacation, but after he died, I decided to move here. For all my connection to the high plains, I'd come to love the mountains and their serenity.

Little Billy came to California with me over Jim's half-hearted objections, but my son had thrived on the West Coast.

He developed a love of the sea and ended up teaching science at a high school in Petaluma, across San Pablo Bay, where he lives with his wife, Julie, who is also a teacher. Life's been good to me. Not so much for Jim. Dixie left him about two and a half years into their marriage, and I've heard gossip that he's a regular at Pete's Cut-Rate Liquor on Pine Street. Lorene, who sees him now and then, told me he works part-time at the Coca-Cola Bottling Company on Chicago Street and rents a room in Sue's old boarding house, though Sue is gone now.

When my mother's health failed, she moved back to the ranch with Lorene and her family. When Mom passed, we buried her between my father and my brother Paul, and I was heartened to see how my daughter and mother grew close in Mom's last years. *Me?* When the end of my time comes, I'll be buried in Taos, where Jack is buried. He loved the summer months and holidays we'd spent here in the mountains.

I stoked the fire and looked out the window. Curtye Lee was due to arrive any minute. She was driving over from Dalhart. Yes, she's still there in the Texas Panhandle, the mother of five children, four boys and a girl, all grown and left the nest but the youngest boy. It was heartbreaking when her second son, Phil, died in a pipeline explosion near Odessa in 1975, and both Jane and I traveled home to comfort our dear friend. George is vice president at the bank and is due to retire in the next year or two, according to Curtye Lee. And Jane. Dear Jane. She just arrived back in Santa Fe after losing her husband, Henry, last year to a heart attack. She's moving into the house her parents had and will be near me.

Near the time I moved to California, Jane and Henry left Victory Church to a new pastor sent from Virginia, the group who'd sponsored Henry in the 1940s. A professor of the Lutheran Seminary in Springfield, Missouri, had approached Henry about his sermons and outreach, offering him a contract to finish his education at the Seminary in Missouri, including pastoral and teaching duties. The Seminary enticed him away from Dalhart, and Henry ministered in Springfield ever since then until his recent death. Jane always suspected Hadley Brown had something to do with the Seminary's offer to Henry. The Lutheran visitor to Dalhart had talked to Hadley extensively about music, and Hadley had praised Henry's relentless encouragement to his congregation to support each other as well as the sermons. The professor had stayed to attend a couple of Sunday services.

Jane told me at Henry's funeral that he'd been encouraging the church in Springfield to start an outreach for families impacted by AIDS. Henry loved Springfield, but when Jane's father passed away, they kept the Santa Fe home and would vacation in New Mexico. Jack and I would visit with them when they were here.

My hope was to stay in Truchas as long as I could, though Lorene has always said I should come stay at the ranch. But I've found peace in Truchas where, every now and then, I'll pull out my easel and paint an amateur landscape, sometimes a remembered sunset in the Texas Plains.

The doorbell rang, and I answered the door to see Curtye Lee dressed in that big smile of hers. We hugged long since I hadn't seen her since I'd visited Lorene in April, and I told Curtye Lee which room to put her bag in.

"Jane should be here shortly," I said when Curtye Lee joined me in the kitchen, pouring herself a glass of water. "She called last night to say she'd arrived in Santa Fe two days ago. How's George?"

"Oh, he's fine. Gone quail hunting," said Curtye Lee. "With Jacob." Jacob was her youngest son, the only one still at home and in high school. He'd been a surprise when Curtye Lee was in her late forties when the couple thought their family had been complete with four. Her husband George planned on retiring once Jacob graduated from school, but the boy was itching to study at Texas Tech in Lubbock, so Curtye Lee worried the retirement might be delayed.

"I was so sad to hear of Henry's passing," said Curtye Lee. "He was always there for all of us, even when we disappointed him. From Jane's letters over the years, I could tell he was happy being part of the Missouri church. Teaching and preaching."

"Yes, he was," I said, and my mind wandered to our lives. To how Henry never got to enjoy his retirement. To how my friend Curtye Lee worried that her husband might follow the same path.

"When I come over to visit Lorene, I can bring Jane with me. Come to the kitchen, and I'll start a pan of hot chocolate before Jane gets here."

When the doorbell rang, we both dropped what we were doing and ran to the door. There stood Jane, her hair just as coifed as always. She'd changed little since our old days together and wore a green dress and black jacket to ward against the mountain chill. We hugged each other over and over.

"We're so sorry about Henry," said Curtye Lee.

Jane handed me her jacket. "Thank you, Curtye Lee. It's nice and cozy here, Shelby. I'm happy to be back in New Mexico, but it'll take me a bit to get the house set up."

"Y'all, come to the kitchen," I said. "I'm making hot chocolate, and we'll sit by the fire. There's a chicken in the oven for supper. You're staying the night, right, Jane?"

"Yes, I am. We'll get into more trouble if we all spend the night here. Together," and Jane chuckled. "Papa's old friend arranged for a young man to help me unload the car at the house, so that's done," said Jane as she sat at the table with Curtye Lee. "That old place feels like Mother and Papa are still there. How's your family, Curtye Lee?"

"Still got the one boy at home. And a couple new grand-kids since the last time I saw you." She reached for Jane's hand and squeezed it. "I'm just thankful to be here. I've missed y'all so much, though I see Shelby every year when she visits her daughter."

"Lorene told me Willie Bob's youngest son moved into the

old Preston house," I said.

"Yes, he did," said Curtye Lee, "with his wife and baby. That house sat empty quite a while after Blanche Preston died. Hard to imagine Willie Bob a grandpa, ain't it? But I think he found the girl he needed. One who was loving and kept him on the straight and narrow. I think she turned his life around." I heard a touch of sadness in my friend's voice as it faded into her thoughts. She and I had talked back in the day, and she knew more of that boy's struggles than any one of us did.

"Ya know," continued Curtye Lee, "I wasn't a big fan of the rodeo back in the day when I dated Willie Bob, but with three of my boys joining Future Farmers in school and then two of 'em ridin' rodeo, I've spent a lot of days in those dusty bleachers cringing and cheering. Life's funny like that, isn't it?"

"Yes, it is. Here, you each take a mug," I said. We stood in the kitchen as I topped off three mugs of hot chocolate with a bit of whipped cream. "We'll get comfortable in front of the fireplace."

We talked and laughed and talked through the afternoon, recounting the old days and meetings at Crawford's old store and continued our reminiscing through supper. After we'd cleaned the kitchen, we gathered for wine around the rekindled fire. And as we sat there, Jane pulled some paper from her purse.

"Did you all know that Hadley died?" she asked.

"Oh, no," I said. "I hadn't heard. Lorene would have told me, I think."

"I'd heard nothing," said Curtye Lee. "How sad. His daughter lives over in Canadian."

"Well, there are secrets here. Now that he's gone, I'll share that he was a gay man." She looked up at us, but we'd not been surprised at this revelation.

"Jane, I think we had an inkling," I offered. "How the kids teased him. I think we all reckoned he was in denial, what with his marriage, but the piercing eyes of Dalhart can be relentless. God forbid, I reckon his mother would have died on the spot at finding out such a thing. She died long ago with dementia, I've heard."

"Yes, she did," said Curtye Lee. "But I had no idea about Hadley. To me, he was always a kind man, gentle in his ways. He stayed at Victory, playing the piano, after y'all left. After his daughter married, he started traveling out west once or twice a year and then moved to San Francisco. That's what I heard."

"Yes, and Henry and I'd get a Christmas card each year. Back in the day, when Gina left him, he was devoted to his daughter, but when this letter came, he told us he'd met a man, an artist living in San Rafael across the Bay. They fell in love and lived together there, but his friend died." Jane's eyes watered.

"Oh my," I said. "All those years, he lived so near to us. Just across the Bay."

"Yes," said Jane as she looked at me. "This is a part of the letter Henry and I received the year before Henry died." She unfolded the paper and read. "*Now that I've relayed the path of my life, I want to say how often I think of you both. How kind you were to me when I felt so lost in Dalhart. You supported me as I tried to be both mom and dad for my daughter. You accepted me as I struggled to find me. The me I struggled to reveal. But now, I must confess that I have been afflicted with AIDS and lost my beloved Manuel, yet I cannot leave this Earth without telling you both how much you mean to me. Your kindnesses gave me strength and solace, and eventually, the courage to love myself and to acknowledge who I loved.*"

We were all crying. I stood and got a box of Kleenex and passed it around.

"Then, when we got this letter," said Jane, "then my beloved Henry packed a bag, bought a plane ticket, and went to San Rafael. He spent five days sitting with his friend, who was, by then, bedridden. He told Hadley the Lord loved him, that we all loved him. Stayed until Ella arrived. Henry was unafraid of the vile disease. Told me he couldn't catch it, though I still worried. And that is the big heart my Henry had, even more so than when we were in Dalhart."

"Oh, Jane," I said. "That is the Henry we knew. Generous. An example of what he preached. Did you ever tell Henry about the eerie visit of your mother after she died?"

"Yes, I did. And more. Such as that beautiful phrase written by Miss Underhill: *God comes to the soul in his working clothes and brings His tools with him.* He loved that, and that visit with Hadley gave Henry a great peace, and I must say, knowing that when he died so suddenly, comforted me."

"Wow," said Curtye Lee, still wiping her wet eyes. "I remember Henry telling us, at church, that we never truly know another's struggles or sorrows. Told us to be kind. We were never thankful enough for Hadley and his big-hearted giving of himself, were we?"

"Probably not," said Jane firmly. "But that's all the sadness we're allowed on this trip. I just wanted you to know. About Hadley and how deeply it impacted my dear Henry."

"Well, on a lighter note, in January, I'm getting a new knee over in Santa Fe," I said, and we all laughed at the turn of topic. "So, I reckon we can indulge in more mischief."

"Yes," said Curtye Lee. "And I'll make all the arrangements. Perhaps a bit slower than before, but y'all know I'm the master of tomfoolery."

"Yes, we do, Curtye Lee. And Shelby, you'll stay with me after your surgery," said Jane.

"That would probably be best," I said. "For all our adventures, I must say I miss those big skies of the plains. The bold colors of our sunsets, even the dark storms, were full of promise. God's hand reminded us who we are. In spite of all the judgment, we had a community. And doggedness."

A snug silence filled the room.

"You know, as much as I love it here, when I travel back to

the ranch, it feels like home. I loved sharing the land with the cunning foxes, antelope, pesky rattlers, and even the dogged jackrabbits who persevered in spite of man's short-sighted deeds. Sometimes, all I see are the plains with the rolling tall grass, now gone, and the embrace of God's big skies so full of dazzling grace."

We, each one of us, sat there, in my mountain cabin, knowing well the sorrows that had carried us forward toward hope and the joy we now lived in. We missed Henry but knew a fruitful life when we saw one. I gazed into the flames dwindling in front of us, still sparking and reminding me of our enduring friendship. We had, years before, bonded in this friendship with all those ghosts in the room. The space between them and us is growing narrow, yet it is a good place full of new dawns.

Acknowledgments

As many of my books are birthed from short stories, this one was as well—from a story I wrote years ago called "Sacred Cache," but there's too much in the high plains of Texas to fit into a short story. The tale of these three women came from a nugget shared by an acquaintance, Jean, who mentioned to me how, with some friends, she'd studied mysticism in the 1960s. In my fictional story, it's the pastor's wife, a ranch wife, and the engaging outlander from Grand Junction, Colorado—all three come together in the gritty town of Dalhart, Texas, where they decide to quell their curiosity about the mystical and spiritual in a back room of a small-town store.

Let me say, first of all, that I love the color of the horizons and plains of northwest Texas—a place dear to me. I was a military brat and somewhat rootless when I attended Palo Duro High School for two years, and I have cherished memories of riding horses with my dad and sister in the magnificent Palo Duro Canyon. I cherish my memories of my days as a Palo Duro Don and my friendships at school and at the Air Force base, now gone. The Panhandle is a generous community and holds an unearthly beauty in the canyons and plains of Texas that I've never forgotten. Therefore, this novel is dedicated to the history and to the people, those present and those long gone, of the Texas Panhandle—all still an inspiration to me.

When I read the book *The Last Hard Time* by Timothy Egan—the history of the heart of the Dust Bowl in the panhandles of Texas and Oklahoma became an integral part of this story and these characters. Those years are the very backstory of Dalhart, a small, resilient town in the 1950s. I am thankful to the many websites and articles I've meandered through in my research and to those books quoted in this novel that related to the women's conversations on mysticism.

I want to stress that this story is fictional, and as all fiction writers do, I've taken the license to create places and people who fit into the place, time, and heart of the story.

I thank all those who helped me get this book to completion. First, there are two writers whose comments to me carried this tale from that original short story to a novel. They are Wells Teague (author of *Calling Texas Home*) and Susan Mack. Thank you, Wells and Susan. Many thanks to my publisher, particularly Nick Courtright, poet and CEO of Atmosphere Press, who has been encouraging me since I found my purpose in retirement—writing—and I miss the days when he had time to edit my work. His staff, especially BE Allatt, my editor, and my cover designers Ronaldo Alves and Kevin Stone were instrumental in pulling everything together. I must give kudos to my proofreader, Chris Beale, because he was the absolute best proofreader I've had in years. Consistently pushing me onward to the culmination of this story were my beloved critique groups, the writing group at the senior center who listened chapter by chapter, and the readers of my books.

As always, I come to love my characters. The friendship of the three beloved women in this book is one that is dear to me and will resonate with me for years to come. Perhaps one or more of them will show up in a yet-to-be-written short story.

About Atmosphere Press

Founded in 2015, Atmosphere Press was built on the principles of Honesty, Transparency, Professionalism, Kindness, and Making Your Book Awesome. As an ethical and author-friendly hybrid press, we stay true to that founding mission today.

If you're a reader, enter our giveaway for a free book here:

SCAN TO ENTER
BOOK GIVEAWAY

If you're a writer, submit your manuscript for consideration here:

SCAN TO SUBMIT
MANUSCRIPT

And always feel free to visit Atmosphere Press and our authors online at atmospherepress.com. See you there soon!

About the Author

Sandra Fox Murphy is a published poet and the author of the novel *That Beautiful Season* and the *Fidelia McCord Series*, starting with *Let the Little Birds Sing* and culminating with *Mourning of the Dove*, a Civil War novel. Originally from Glasgow, Delaware, and growing up around the globe as a USAF brat, she retired from the U.S. Geological Survey and lives in central Texas, where she hunts down small-town history.